"Why do you do that?" Lena asked.

"Do what?"

"Every time you get real with me, let me see behind the smart-ass persona, you have to ruin it by being all annoying."

Matt shifted closer and ran a finger along her jawline. She jerked away. "Lena. Look at me."

She reluctantly turned to look. He was too close. Too everything. Those eyes. How could such icy blue be so hot?

"This," he said as he took her hand. "This feeling right here is why you put up with me."

He traced his fingers lightly across her palm. The sensation bypassed her brain, going straight to the very core of her.

She started to say he was crazy. She started to tell him to get out. But his lips were on hers and her hands were in his hair and oh dear God the man could kiss. He pulled her even closer, deepening the kiss. She kissed him back, ignoring the alarms from some distant rational part of herself.

Right now, she cared about nothing except for how good this felt.

Dear Reader,

Welcome back to beautiful Charleston, SC! I was very excited to have the opportunity to tell Lena's story. It was also fun to bring Lena and Sadie back together.

For Lena, family is everything. Even when they are driving her crazy. She's dedicated her life to lifting her family out of poverty, but now that the dream has been realized, she is left wondering, "What next?"

"What" did not include the impossibly annoying and sexy artist Charles Beaumont Matthews the Fifth. Or Matt, as he prefers.

For Matt, family is a touchy subject. A troubled youth led to estrangement and very hard feelings. While he is working to repair the damage, he struggles to accept that to fully live the life he wants, he may have to walk away from his family.

Family, by blood or by choice, is a central theme in my writing. The contrast between Lena's family, who had been poor in money but rich in love and support, and Matt's wealthy family, to whom obedience to family tradition is more important than personal fulfillment, is rather stark.

It is somewhere between those two extremes that Lena and Matt will find their HEA.

I hope you enjoy their journey.

Janet

JANET LEE NYE

Boss Meets Her Match

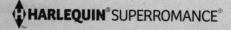
HARLEQUIN® SUPERROMANCE®

Recycling programs
for this product may
not exist in your area.

ISBN-13: 978-0-373-64022-5

Boss Meets Her Match

Copyright © 2017 by Janet Lee Nye

Printed in U.S.A.

Janet Lee Nye is a writer by day and a neonatal nurse by night. She loves a good pinot grigio and a well-placed "f-bomb." She wants to be Helen Mirren when she grows up. She lives in Charleston, SC, with her fella and her felines and spends too much time on Twitter and not enough doing adult things like making doctor's appointments and dusting.

Books by Janet Lee Nye

HARLEQUIN SUPERROMANCE

The Cleaning Crew

Spying on the Boss
Boss on Notice

Visit the Author Profile page on Harlequin.com.

My love, my strength, my wailing wall, the occasional boot in my rear, my partner in everything: Jason Zwiker. Love you, baby!

CHAPTER ONE

THAT IS THE ugliest thing I have ever seen. Lena leaned forward and squinted at the tiny white sticker in the corner of the painting. *Five thousand dollars? Tie a paintbrush to my cat's tail and she'd do a better job.* She shifted on the bench. The sounds of the party echoed loudly from the floor below. Sipping her wine, she wrinkled her nose. *Cheap chardonnay.*

She didn't want to be here, which was why she was hiding out on the second floor of the City Gallery. She wanted to go home. Take her shoes off and put pajamas on. Drink some wine that didn't taste like battery acid. She straightened with a sigh. Might as well get it over with. Dr. Eliot Rutledge, famed neurosurgeon, very old money Charleston—and her first of many clients—was waiting for her.

Footsteps on the hardwood floor caught her attention. A man ambled slowly around the corner, looking at the art exhibited on the walls. Lena cut a glance in his direction. He didn't fit with the suit-and-cocktail-dress crowd downstairs. His beige linen pants were slightly wrinkled—and that shabby white dress shirt. *No. Just no.* His dark blond hair was long and tied in a ponytail with a length of leather. A neat beard covered his face. He leaned down, looked at a price tag and whistled. Lena smiled.

"Pretty pricey, huh?" he asked, sliding down on the bench beside her.

She looked directly at him. *Damn. That is a fine-looking man.* The hair and beard couldn't hide his high cheekbones and eyes so blue they almost didn't look real. White teeth appeared as he grinned at her. Her stomach went quivery under that bad boy grin. She looked away and sipped more wine. She didn't do bad boys anymore.

He gestured at the painting in front of them. It was an abstract, not quite as dense as a Pollock but not as minimalist as Munch. Slashes of red and blue, smears of purple and yellow. "What do you think of this one?"

She shrugged. "Not my style, to be honest."

"Ah, man. I saw you sitting up here instead of being downstairs with all the mingling and small talk and I thought to myself, now, there's a woman who doesn't go for polite society bullshit. Thought you were up here seriously contemplating the meaning of art."

She tried her perfect one-eyebrow-arch-and-glare trick. "Did you, now?"

All that got her was another of those inappropriate thought-provoking grins. "Indeed I did."

"I think it's ugly," she said, taking another drink. "I think my friend's nine-year-old could do better."

His laugh echoed off the narrow corridor. "But one of those people downstairs will buy it."

"Probably." She stood. "Excuse me, but I have to find someone."

"Ah," Eliot Rutledge said, as he walked around the corner. "You've met. Wonderful."

Lena looked from Dr. Rutledge to the man smiling up at her from the bench. "No," she said, ice cubes practically dropping from the word. "We have not met."

"Lena, this is our artist."

A hot spark of anger flared in her chest and spread to her cheeks. The man stood, still smiling, and held out a hand. "Matt. It's a pleasure to meet you, Lena."

"Did you know who I was when you approached me?"

"Nope. Just a happy accident."

She stared at him until the smile melted from his face. A long string of profanities pushed against her pressed lips. *Breathe. Just breathe.*

"Matt asked for a recommendation. Told him I wouldn't have anyone else in the city watch after my portfolio."

"Thank you," she said automatically. She

turned back to Matt. Gave him her iciest smile. "I'd be happy to discuss this with you. In my office. During business hours. Call my secretary and make an appointment." She turned to Dr. Rutledge. "Eliot, it was good to see you."

As she rounded the corner to the stairs, she heard Dr. Rutledge's voice. "Did you make her angry? I'd recommend not doing that anymore."

Smiling as she pushed through the doors out into the perfection that was Charleston in October, she nodded. *That's right. Don't piss me off.* Her condominium was a short walk away along Waterfront Park. She ambled past tourists and college kids. There was still light in the sky and it was a perfect sixty-five degrees. Maybe she'd go for a run. Or maybe she'd collapse on the couch, order some Vietnamese and binge-watch something. Her phone vibrated in her purse. She fished it out. Sadie. Her best friend. The woman she called sister. Her finger hovered over the screen. Completely tired of talking to people for the day, she was sorely tempted to dismiss the call.

"What's up?" she asked.

"Your mother is what's up."

Lena smiled. At least she wasn't the only one being tortured by her mother. "What's she done now?"

"We went to look at dresses. I swear to God, Lena. I'm going to get married in jeans and a T-shirt just to spite her. You should have seen the dresses she begged me to try on 'just to see.' I looked like Scarlett O'Hara's cousin from the trailer park. A full veil. To the knees!"

"Sounds perfectly lovely. At least she's off your case about getting married in a church."

"For now," Sadie replied grumpily. "What are you doing this weekend? I need a rational human being for dress shopping."

Lena reached her condo door and leaned against it. She could hear her cat meowing indignantly from the other side. Supper was an hour late. "We can do that. But don't invite my mother. I'm trying to stay off her radar right now."

"Yeah, by throwing me at her."

"You're the blushing bride. Much more fun than the dried-up old maid."

"Is she still on that?"

"She's backed down a bit. I think my aunts are planning something. Every time I see one of them, I feel like I'm being interrogated. Look, I gotta go. I just got home and *la gata* has complaints."

"Okay, grumpy. Bye."

"KEEP YOUR FUR ON," she said as she entered her condo and kicked her shoes off. Sass, the cat, did not keep her fur on. Winding her way around and between Lena's ankles, she complained bitterly of the near-death experience of having supper one hour late.

An hour later, she'd been forgiven by Sass, her business suit had been replaced with pajamas and Bon Banh Mi had delivered dinner. Wallowing happily on the couch, she scooped salad into her face and resumed binge-watching *Supernatural.* Her phone buzzed and Sass smacked at it. "Sthop," she said around a chunk of lettuce. *Estrella Acosta. Shit. What now?*

"*Hola, Tia. Qué pasa?*"

"Are you coming to church on Sunday?"

Okay. Getting straight to the point. That's new. "I hadn't planned on it."

"*Contestame*, will you come to church on Sunday?"

Lena made a face at the phone. "I haven't been to confession."

"You don't have to go to confession to go to church, Miss Smarty Pants."

"Which mass?"

That was important because no way she was getting up at four in the morning on a Sunday to drive an hour for a sunrise mass.

"Ten." Lena grinned at the clipped tone in her aunt's voice. "You haven't been to church since Luis died. It would mean a lot to your mother."

That melted the smile off her face. She slumped into the couch. "Okay. Yes. I will come to the 10:00 a.m. mass this Sunday."

"And to the house for lunch too?"

"Yes."

Sass swatted at her hair hanging over the arm of the couch. "This is why I should have got a dog instead of you, Sass. I'd have to walk a dog. Take it out to pee and stuff. Perfect excuse to stay home. But no. I got a cat."

It wasn't that she didn't want to see her family. It was that ever since Sadie got engaged, everyone was starting to look at Lena like she was supposed to just pick out a man and start popping out babies. Her mother was calling Sadie's soon-to-be stepdaughter *nieta* and dropping grandbaby hints like it was her job. Problem was Lena had spectacularly rotten luck with men.

CHAPTER TWO

MATT PLANTED HIS hands on the balcony railing and looked down at the crowd below. He was bone tired and the voices below were echoing off the high ceiling, making his head hurt. The only thing keeping the smile on his face was the memory of Lena Reyes's departure. Her long black hair swinging side to side as she strode away. He smiled again. She didn't look like any financial expert he'd ever met. He hadn't missed the heat in those nearly black eyes either. When he'd sat beside her and she looked at him. There was nothing professional in her eyes at that moment.

A hand patted his shoulder. "Very good turnout, don't you think?" Dr. Rutledge asked.

"Great turnout. Thank you again for putting it together."

"I'm seeing a great many sold tags going up. You're going to be the next big thing."

"For now. Problem with being the next is there always someone behind you, ready to be the next next."

Dr. Rutledge laughed. "Very true, but what's that old cliché? Make hay while the sun shines?

Keep this going for as long as you can, give the money to Lena. I don't know how she does it, but she has the magic touch."

"If she'll even take me as a client now."

"Don't worry about it," Dr. Rutledge said. "She'll get over it. If you're lucky."

"I hope so. I really need her help."

"What you really need is to get back downstairs and charm wallets out of purses."

"If I must."

Dr. Rutledge's rich laughter echoed in the open area. "Just smile at the ladies and remember what this is all for."

"I never forget that. I will also never forget all your help."

"You're welcome, son. But I'm doing it for selfish reasons."

"I wouldn't call helping sick kids selfish."

"No. I'm doing it because of that look I saw in Clarissa's eyes when she was painting with you. That joy? All her pain forgotten? I want to see that for a very, very long time."

Matt followed the older man down the stairs and into the crowd. He hadn't known who the man was who'd come into the playroom at the Children's Hospital and interrupted his therapy session with several kids in for cancer treatment. The little redheaded girl's grandfather, he'd surmised by their greetings. He didn't know then that Eliot Rutledge was a world-famous neurosurgeon who felt helpless as his beloved grand-daughter battled leukemia. Matt didn't know then that his world was about to change. His dream was suddenly much closer.

But it was going to come with a price. He had to go back into that upper-crust society that he'd rejected when he left Maryland. He smiled and nodded and shook hands. It all came back so easily. Too easily. He gave his patented, panty-melting bad boy grin to the little old ladies and was perfectly polite to the single women. Firm handshakes and backslaps to the men. *God, get me out of here.* His thoughts drifted back to Lena Reyes. She'd stood out. She didn't even realize how radical an act sitting alone at a function like this was. It intrigued him.

"I'D LIKE TO know exactly what was wrong with my original plan to get married at the UPS store by a notary."

Lena stared openmouthed at Sadie, lowering the bridal gown she was holding. "What were those words that just came out of your face?"

Sadie pouted, flipping quickly through the gowns. "No. No. God, no. Not in a million years no."

"Slow down. You aren't even looking at them." Sadie didn't answer. "Sades? What's going on?"

"Nothing."

Replacing the gown on the rack, Lena grabbed

Sadie's hand and pulled her to sit on the bench by the dressing room door. *"Digame."*

"It's nothing. I just… I didn't want all this fuss."

"Then why are you doing it? Go to the UPS store then."

Sadie leaned forward, propping her elbows on her thighs, chin in hands and shook her head. "Because Jules wants to be a flower girl."

"Wait. You are having this lavish wedding just so Jules can throw some flower petals around?"

"It's not lavish. It's very small. And simple."

"Then what's the problem?"

"There's just so much stuff to do. I don't like to do stuff."

"See. That's where you made your fatal error. You let my mom help you because you were lazy. Next thing you know you're in a Scarlett O'Hara dress. You better pick out something today before she makes up her mind for you. Just sit here. I'll pick out some choices."

She returned to the rack. Part of her was a bit annoyed. She hadn't expected Sadie to turn into a Bridezilla by any means, but this pouting was unexpected. Taking a deep breath, she began to pull dresses. Three. That was Sadie's problem. Anything new was overwhelming. A store full of dresses was too much.

"Come on," she said. "Let's try these on."

It gave her a small amount of pleasure that it

was the first one. She'd known it was the one. Sadie came out of the dressing room looking stunned. The creamy ivory looked good against her fair skin and the cascade of black curls down her back was the only veil she'd need.

"It's perfect," Sadie whispered.

"Of course it is. I have excellent taste."

"Great! You can pick out your own maid of honor dress then."

"I was going to do that anyway."

That got a laugh out of Sadie and seemed to relax her. Lena put her hands on Sadie's shoulders. "You deserve this."

"I know. I want to marry Wyatt and maybe start a family. I just don't want to have to do all the wedding stuff. It seems like showing off."

Sadie turned to look in the mirror. "This is a beautiful dress though."

Lena grabbed Sadie's hand as she reached for the price tag. "Don't look. Just don't. I'll take care of it and you can reimburse me after the wedding."

A look of horror crossed Sadie's features. "Why? How much? Please don't pay more for a dress than I'd pay for a car."

"It's not that bad. Go change."

While Sadie was changing, Lena paid for the dress so she couldn't change her mind. Sadie needed this. She deserved this. After everything she'd been through in her life, Sadie needed to have something normal. And nothing was as normal as a nice fancy wedding.

"All done," she said as Sadie returned from the dressing room. "It's yours. We'll arrange for a fitting closer to the wedding date."

"How much was it?"

"That doesn't matter. It's your wedding day, Sadie. You don't have to go full formal, princess fairy-tale wedding, but you deserve the day to be special. Be the center of attention for once. Let the people who love you celebrate your happiness with you."

Sadie rolled her eyes. "Fine. We'll do it all. Flower toss, garter toss. Everything. Except cake smashing in the face. I despise that."

"Agreed. It's a perversion of the original intent."

"Fine then."

Lena laughed at Sadie's bulldog expression. "I'm going to make you love every minute of the wedding if it kills me."

"I'll enjoy the wedding. I refuse to enjoy the planning."

"Deal. But remember, if you leave it to my mother, it's going to be *quinceñera* and Catholic wedding meets *Designing Women*. You need to set limits with her. Come on, let's get out of here."

As they walked to Lena's car, Sadie hooked her arm in Lena's. "Thank you for the dress. But I can't be mean to your mom. She's so sweet."

Lena made a rude noise. "That's just a disguise to lure you into her plans."

The BMW beeped as Lena hit the unlock button and they climbed in. Sadie leaned back and closed her eyes. "It's just so exhausting. Having to make so many choices constantly."

"I know. It'll get better."

"How? The dress is the only thing we've done!"

"And the wedding is in two months? Sadie! Have you picked a place? A cake? Invites? Save the dates? Anything?"

"No."

Lena let loose a stream of Spanish.

"Hey!" Sadie said. "I understand some of that."

Lena cranked the engine. "I'm going to send you a list. I want you to do two things on the list every week."

"Fine."

"Fine!"

As she pulled out into traffic, Lena glanced over at Sadie. She was pretending to be grumpy but they'd been friends long enough that she knew it was better to give Sadie a single task to do rather than a giant mountain of them.

"Want to come for lunch on Sunday?" Sadie asked. "Jules wants to learn more Spanish."

"I wish I could. But I promised I'd go to mass and have lunch with the family."

"Oh?"

"Yeah. I think they're up to something."

"Like what?"

"I don't know, but it can't be good."

CHAPTER THREE

THE PLAYROOM AT the Children's Hospital was a bright, open room with a wall of windows and several skylights. Matt made his way to the art corner, high-fiving a couple of frequent fliers.

"What are we painting today, Mr. Matt?" a little girl called out from the book nook.

"Scary stuff for Halloween," he answered. As if these kids would be scared of Halloween fakery when they were battling real monsters like cancer and sickle-cell anemia and cystic fibrosis. But that was why he did this. Art allowed kids to express themselves in a way that didn't involve words. They might not be able to verbalize their fear but they could draw a picture of it.

He sat down at the long table and began to lay out supplies. Heavy white paper precut into mask shapes and elastic string. "Gather 'round, little ghosts and goblins," he called out. "We'll be making Halloween masks today."

Clarissa slid into the chair next to him. She smiled up at him shyly. Her dark red hair had all fallen out but she still had a spark in her amber-brown eyes. "Mr. Matt? Can I make a witch face?"

"You can make anything you'd like. Want to help me get set up?"

Ten minutes later, he was circling the table. Seven kids were all in varying stages of finishing their masks. He had a witch, a vampire, a zombie and assorted monsters. Today's exercise wasn't so much about revealing or relieving some inner emotion, but simply to have fun and do something normal. Once they'd finished, he attached the elastic string to hold the masks in place.

"Grandfather!" Clarissa called out.

Matt looked over as Dr. Rutledge approached the table. He stopped and put his hands on his hips. "Grandfather? My granddaughter is the most beautiful girl in the world. Not some witchy woman!"

Clarissa giggled and lifted the mask. "It's me, Grandfather!"

Matt smiled as Dr. Rutledge gathered Clarissa up in his arms. A familiar tug pulled at his heart. He'd been so terrified of his own grandfather that he called him "Mr. Matthews." Being with him had been like being in the principal's office for an offense he didn't commit. He turned away and finished cleaning up the detritus of the project.

"Matt."

He looked up at Dr. Rutledge. "Yes, sir?"

"Eliot. How many times do I have to ask you?"

"Sorry. Prep school indoctrination."

"I just wanted to thank you again for all you do here."

Matt stood. "No need for that. This…" He trailed off. How to explain it? That it was like a drug? That moment when a kid who is scared or angry or feeling overwhelmed lets go of it all and smiles and laughs? Acts like a kid? He lived for, craved those moments.

"This is your passion. I can see that. Anything I can help out with?"

Matt shrugged. "Your patronage has helped a lot. I'm funneling all the funds from the sale of my art into setting up a nonprofit so I can do this full-time and reach kids outside the hospital setting. There are a lot of kids in not-so-ideal situations that art therapy can help."

"Well, Lena Reyes can help with that."

"I hope so. The sooner the better. Thanks again for getting me in the door with her. I know she's very picky about what clients she takes on."

"You're welcome," Eliot said, but a slight frown creased his brow. "You know…"

Matt waited. "Yes, sir?"

Eliot shook his head. "Just chasing down an idea. For an outreach outside the hospital setting. Let me talk to a couple of people and I'll get back to you."

"Okay. Any tips on how to smooth things over with Lena?"

Eliot's rich laughter echoed in the cavernous playroom. "Grovel."

Grovel. Matt smiled, remembering the look in Lena's eyes when she realized he was the artist of the work she'd just called ugly. He hadn't meant to trick her. There was something about her. She hadn't hidden her anger behind a simpering smile. He'd embarrassed her and she'd been angry and let him know. He liked that. The honesty in her reaction. No games. No nonsense. He'd grovel to get her to handle his meager proceeds. He'd grovel to get her to do almost anything.

"Yo, dude! You ready?"

He looked up to see Dylan standing in the doorway, gym bag slung over a shoulder. Dylan was a respiratory therapist at the hospital and the first guy friend he'd made since moving to Charleston.

"Yep. Let me just finish cleaning up in here."

THE DRIVE FROM downtown Charleston to the rural church halfway to Beaufort took a solid forty-five minutes. Which meant she had to wake up, on purpose, before nine on a Sunday morning. Lena sighed as she wiggled into a suitable church dress. It wasn't that she didn't want to see her family. Well, that wasn't quite true. The unspoken question was always hanging in the air. *How had Sadie snagged a husband before her?*

Not that anyone would ever actually say it out loud. Except Estrella. She'd probably do it. Estrella had been a giant bag of disapproval since Lito, Lena's grandfather, died. For what, Lena wasn't sure but only the deeply ingrained respect for her elders kept her from pointing out to her aunt that it had been her hard work that lifted the family out of poverty. Estrella would still be in that trailer park if not for her. Not that she begrudged helping her family, but a little gratitude might be nice.

Pulling into the gravel parking lot beside the tidy, small white church relaxed something inside her. Maybe it was the way the ancient oak trees surrounded the church like sentinels. Or the quiet of the countryside. Perhaps she should go to confession. She'd been venial sinning up a storm lately. She checked her lipstick in the rearview mirror before climbing out of her BMW. A thin thread of suspicion wound around her peacefulness when she saw her mother and Aunt Estrella waiting on the porch steps.

"Mamacita," she said as she approached and kissed her mother on both cheeks, before pulling her into a hug.

"Lena," her mother said as she wrapped strong arms around her. "It's been too long."

"*Lo siento*. It's just work has been crazy busy."

Estrella snorted rudely. "You work too much."

Lena kept the fire out of her eyes and forced

her lips up in a small smile. "I'm the boss, Tia. If I don't do the work, it doesn't get done."

Ana hooked her arm through Lena's. "Enough of all that. Today is for family."

The familiar rituals of the service soothed away Lena's irritation. It was true she didn't go to church often, but she found comfort in the tradition of it. The litany and the responses that never changed. The rising and kneeling. Making the cross. She found herself relaxing for what felt like the first time in forever.

Until mass was over. As the crowd milled around in the aisles on the way out, Lena felt a strong hand grip her elbow. Estrella wasn't going to let go anytime soon. "Maria! It's so good to see you."

Estrella chirped out the greeting while dragging Lena with her toward the woman. And, aw crap. A guy. *It's a setup. This whole thing is a setup.* Every bit of relaxation she'd felt slipped away.

"Is this your son? *Qué guapo.*"

Only the fact that they were in a church kept Lena from rolling her eyes. She jerked her elbow away from the vise grip.

"And this must be your niece I hear so much about. Magdalena, it's a pleasure to meet you."

Smiling and nodding, she shook the woman's hand. "A pleasure to meet you also." She looked at the guy. He looked as blindsided as she felt.

Meddling aunties. Where would we be without them? She extended a hand to him. "Lena Reyes."

"Eduardo Jiminez."

Ana joined them and put an arm around Lena's waist. "Maria, please, you and Eddie must come to the house for dinner with us."

The fake smile melted from Lena's lips as she gave her mother some epic side-eye. Which Ana pretended she didn't see.

Maria put a hand on Estrella's shoulder. "That is so kind of you. As I recall, there isn't a chef in any fancy restaurant downtown who can cook as well as the three of you. Eduardo? We'd be delighted to join you, right?"

Lena didn't miss the slight change in tone of voice on the word *right.* She was definitely in on this. Eduardo's cheeks darkened and his shoulders slumped. "Of course, Mamacita."

DINNER WAS AN awkward hour of competitive bragging by Maria and Estrella. The only comfort she had was that Eduardo looked as horrifyingly embarrassed as she felt. Then, as if prearranged, everyone disappeared and left the two of them alone.

"So, I guess this is the part where we fall madly in love at first sight, get married tomorrow and start having grandbabies immediately?" Lena asked.

"I'm so sorry. I had no idea they'd planned this."

Lena dismissed his apology with a shrug and a wave. "I understand. I had no idea either. Don't worry about it."

"But, I'm kind of glad they did," he said.

Lena's stomach dropped. *No, no. Go back to being embarrassed so we can both run like hell.* She looked him over. Dark complexion. Black glasses that gave him a good-looking-nerd vibe to match his job as a software engineer. Thinner than she liked. "Oh?" she asked through numb lips.

"You're very pretty." His cheeks darkened with the words.

Blushing? You've got to be kidding me. Hoping the smile on her lips didn't look as fake as it felt, she rose. "Thank you. It was nice to meet you. I have to go now."

Before he could say anything more, she fled to the kitchen. She shot Estrella a look that should have burned the flesh from her bones. "Do. Not. Ever. Do. That. Again."

"Lena…" her mother began.

"*Lo siento*, Mamacita, but I can't take any more of this. Do you understand? No more." She left through the back door so she wouldn't have to face Eduardo again. Footsteps chased her across the porch.

"Magdalena Teresa Reyes!"

Wow. It'd been a long time since her mother three-named her. She turned. Still mad but wilting under her mother's glare. "I'm sorry, Momma. But that was embarrassing."

The look in Ana's eyes softened and she took Lena's hand. "Lena. We want you to be happy. You've worked so long and so hard and you've always put the family first but we're okay now. You're okay now. It's safe to slow down a little."

Tears stung at her eyes. Is that what it was? Is that what was wrong with her? Was she still that same little girl terrified of failure? Of letting her family down? "It's not that," she said.

"Then what is it?"

Lena looked away. Across the expanse of lawn to the forest behind the house. Fifty acres. There was a path through the woods that led to a creek where her parents caught fish and sank crab traps. She'd given them this. Built all this. All these things. This house. Her fancy car. The expensive condominium. The Jimmy Choos on her feet.

"I want the magic, Mamacita. I want the romance. The whirlwind. I don't want to be set up by my meddling aunt."

"No reason you can't have both. Give him a chance. He's a nice guy."

Lena smiled. She leaned in to hug her mother so she couldn't see her dubious expression. Nice guys weren't her type. No. She liked the bad boys but knew they weren't in it for the long haul. She needed a nice bad boy. Matt rose in her mind's eye. All long blond hair and that beard. Sort of

Viking-ish. Those blue eyes and rakish grin. *God, no. Overgrown frat boys were definitely not her type.*

"I understand that, Momma. But no more ambushes. It made me feel like a yard-sale item." She waved her hands in the air and adopted a carnival barker's voice. "Over here! Fifty percent off the old maid. Come check 'er out."

Ana crossed her arms and gave Lena a cool gaze. "Don't get dramatic. I'm still your mother and I can still take a switch to your backside. Estrella made it seem like she would ask them over in private. I didn't know she was going to make a production out of it."

Lena pushed her lower lip out.

"Stop pouting. You are almost thirty years old."

"I'll stop pouting when you all stop treating me like a child."

"Stop acting like one."

"I am not acting childish. I'm acting attacked and embarrassed and humiliated."

The two women stared at each other for a long minute. A heavy step on the porch stairs drew their attention.

"Papa," Lena said with a respectful nod.

Her father approached and put his hands on Ana's shoulders. "Ana, go on back inside. Let me talk to Magdalena."

Great. Here comes the final word from the man. The head of the household. Lena held her tongue and schooled her expression into some semblance of neutrality.

After Ana shut the door behind her, he turned and took Lena's hands. "*Carida.* Don't be angry with your mother."

"I'm not. I'm angry at Estrella."

He made a face. "I'm not her biggest fan either, but she's your mother's sister so we're stuck with her."

They walked back to the porch and sat on the bottom step. Lena leaned against her father as he put an arm around her shoulders. "I know I'm a huge disappointment to—"

"No." The word cut curtly across her words. "You are nothing but a blessing to this family. No one is disappointed in you."

"It's just that ever since Sadie…"

He shifted away to put a hand to her chin and turn her face to his. "Look at me. We are all happy for Sadie. After not having a family all her life, she's getting one. But you are not Sadie. You are my daughter. Yes, the women are all stirred up about this. It's normal. You start talking weddings and everyone wants to be a grandmother."

Lena nodded. Looping her arms around his middle, she snuggled her cheek against his shoulder. "Thank you, Papa. Will you tell them to stop it now?"

His rich laughter rumbled through his chest to her ear. "I value my peace and quiet. I don't tell the women in this family what to do."

CHAPTER FOUR

MONDAY FOUND HER back in her element. Her office on Broad Street was only a few blocks walk from her condominium. Tucked away in the back of a historic building, it was a small office, but she didn't need a lot of room. She loved the space with its two-hundred-year-old pinewood flooring and walls of exposed brick. Sleek, minimalist furniture decorated the reception room. Less was more, she'd learned.

"Good morning," Chloe, her receptionist, greeted her. "How was your weekend?"

"Annoying. How was yours?"

"So much fun! Some of my sorority sisters and I went up to the mountains and the leaves are all turning for fall. Met some cute guys."

Lena smiled. Chloe was virtually a cliché of a sorority girl. Pretty. Thin. Blonde. Obsessed with fashion. She'd almost dismissed her application out of hand, but during the interview, she'd found Chloe to be smart and disciplined. The fact that she'd grown up in the homes of the rich people who Lena hoped to make richer was a bonus. Chloe knew how to tease and charm the clients but more importantly, she was an amazing manager.

The door opened and Lena's second employee came in. If Chloe soothed the nerves of the upper crust about having an unknown Hispanic woman handle their money, Mose certainly challenged their faith. Mose, named Moseley Braun after the first female African American senator, was almost six feet tall with a strong, athletic build and dark skin that made her hazel eyes stand out. She wore her hair shorn close to her head and usually about two pounds of jewelry. She was also poised to be the first partner in Reyes Financial Management.

"Did you hear about Hong Kong?" Mose asked the second she crossed the threshold.

"Good or bad?"

"Good. I'll have a report on your desk in an hour."

Lena and Chloe watched as Mose continued through the reception to her tiny office in the back. "Well, okay," Chloe said. "Welcome to Monday."

"Any messages over the weekend?"

"Just one. A..." Chloe cleared her throat and continued in a dramatic tone. "Charles Beaumont Matthews *the Fifth* said he had been referred by Eliot Rutledge and would like to set up an appointment."

"The *fifth*? What is wrong with these people?"

Chloe shrugged. "Not a clue. Usually whoever is the third breaks with tradition and names
their child something new. But some of these old-
money dudes are awful attached to *the name*."
She made air quotes around the last two words.

Lena waved a hand. "Set it up. Earliest this
week."

She stopped at the coffeemaker before heading
to her office. Mondays were generally appointment
free. The stock market didn't stop for the weekend, and while she kept an eye on the happenings
over the weekend, unless something monumental
happened, she waited until Monday. It was a day
of review and planning. Taking what action was
necessary to either protect or improve her clients'
portfolios. She kicked her shoes off the moment
she sat at her desk. *Charles Beaumont Matthews
the Fifth.* She'd pegged him 100 percent. Spoiled
trust-fund baby. Playing with daddy's money. She
couldn't wait to tell him no, no matter what Eliot
thought of him. She flicked her eyes in the direction of Mose's office. Unless he really had a lot
of money. Maybe she'd kick him over to Mose as
her first client.

She plugged her phone in and opened her Pandora app to her classical music station and began
sorting through the weekend's financial changes.
Knowing what changes would affect which clients
and adjusting accordingly was the thing she loved
most about her job. It was a constant dance. She

had to keep the perfect balance between daring and caution. Most of all, she loved when that little tingle of intuition that she couldn't explain proved to be successful.

A flickering light caught her eye and she frowned at the phone. She'd been deep in the zone. Lowering the volume, she picked up the phone. "Yes, Chloe?"

"Sorry to bother you, but William Durant is on the phone. He says he needs to speak to you about his accounts."

"Put him through." She pulled up Bill's account. Not her biggest. Not her smallest. Nor her most challenging. A cautious investor, Bill Durant was. "Good morning, Bill. How can I help you?"

"Well, I have some good news and some bad news. Good news—I've taken a position with a medical ministry in Scotland."

"Wow. Okay. That sounds amazing. Tell me about it."

"Essentially, I will be coordinating medical missions for the School of Medicine in Glasgow. A dream job for me. And, of course, we'll be moving there. The kids are very excited."

"Well, where's the bad news, then?" She smiled as she said it, but she knew what was coming. He was taking his money with him.

"The thing is, my wife and I have talked about it and we don't think we're going to come back."

"So you're going to need to transfer your accounts to Scotland. That's reasonable."

"Yes. It won't be right away. I'm leaving in a month. Sandra and the kids will follow if the house hasn't sold by then. And I'll have to find someone as good as you in Scotland. Will you be able to do the transfers once I'm over there?"

"Yes. It won't be a problem. I'm sorry to lose you, but I'm excited for you. Sounds like an amazing opportunity for the whole family."

She carried on the chitchat for a while. "Well, shit," she said out loud after she ended the call. She kept her list small and exclusive so that she could give each client all the attention they deserved. It was a delicate balance that kept the agency's lights on.

She let out a low stream of Spanish expletives. Now she had to hope Mr. Charles Beaumont Matthews the Fifth had an account big enough to replace what she was going to lose.

MATT LOUNGED BACK in one of the two armchairs that made up his living room in the cramped apartment. The downtown location was perfect for his needs. He could walk to both his jobs, the grocery store and the waterfront was near enough to haul his painting supplies to. But damn, it was pricey. He bounced his phone in his hand. He did not want to make this call. Talking to his father never ended well. Playing briefly with the idea of calling his mother instead, he shook his head. No. She didn't know anything. How in this day and age a woman could defer every financial detail of her life to her husband, he couldn't comprehend.

"Ah, screw it," he muttered. *Do it for the kids, man.* He made the call before he could talk himself out of it.

"Hi, Millicent," he said to his father's executive assistant and suspected lover. "It's Matt. Is my father available to talk?"

"One moment, I'll check."

If she was surprised to hear from him, her voice didn't show it. She was smooth, almost coldly polite. With one quick click, classical music filled his ear. He waited. And waited. He hooked the other chair with his foot and pulled it around to prop his feet up on and let his head fall back to stare at the ceiling. Warm October sunshine flowed through the window. He noticed the fall of the light and the swirling dust motes. He should probably dust.

Finally, after whatever length of time his father deemed necessary to exert dominance, the line clicked again. "What is it, Charles? I'm very busy."

"Hey, Dad. How are you? How's Mother?"

"What do you want? And don't say money."

Narrowing his eyes at the dig, he pressed his lips together against the automatic response that wanted to fly out of his mouth. A fight wasn't why he'd called. He had never asked his father for a cent. *Keep calm. Don't get drawn in.*

"Actually I was calling to get some information about the trust fund Grandmother left me."

"You can't access it early if that is what you want."

He kept careful control over his temper. But his father could make him lose it faster than anyone on the planet. "That isn't what I was going to ask but it's heartwarming that you still have such a low opinion of me."

"Then what *do* you want?"

"I'm having some success with my art recently and I'm getting ready to hire a financial manager. I wanted to know if I can transfer the administration of the trust fund over to her, or does it have to stay with the executor of Grandmother's estate?"

The long moment of silence made him grin. *He hadn't expected that, now, had he?* If he heard a throat clearing, that would mean he'd scored a direct hit. But alas, his father's voice was steady and cold. "That's something you'd need to discuss with the executor."

"Can I have the contact information?"

"I'll send you back to Millicent for that."

"Thanks, Dad," he said as the call ended on his father's end. "Nice chat. We should do it again sometime."

After getting the information from Millicent, he tossed the phone on the couch beside him. *Nice to know nothing's changed. Still the black sheep, the wayward son.* Growing up under the weight of his family's expectations had been suffocating. They'd given him little choice: join the law firm or go away. So he'd gone away. Only his grandmother had believed in him and encouraged his art from a young age. Her death six years ago had driven the last wedge between him and his family. The bulk of her estate had gone to charity, but she'd left a sizable trust fund for him. His parents had been furious with their tokens and his father even tried to contest the will.

Trouble was he wouldn't get the money until he was thirty-five. Which was why he was scrambling between his part-time jobs as an art therapist and giving lessons to anyone who would hire him. This little windfall needed expert guidance. And Lena Reyes was the woman he wanted to do it.

He grabbed up the phone and dialed her number.

Ten minutes later, he was making his way to the Children's Hospital with a grin he couldn't quite keep off his face. He'd get to see the lovely Lena on Friday. The sun was shining. The sky was blue. The temperature was a perfect seventy degrees. Maybe he could take the kids outside to paint in the horseshoe area.

As IF THIS Monday wasn't sucky enough with losing a client and having to make an appointment with a bad-boy trust-fund brat, now her mother was calling. All Lena wanted was to sit on the couch, drink wine and eat pizza. "Hey, Mom, what's up?"

"Eduardo would like a date."

Lena dropped the slice of pizza back on the plate. Sass jumped up and stuck her face in it.

"No!"

"Excuse me?"

"Sorry. I was talking to the cat. Come on, Mom. Really? Y'all are setting me up on blind dates now?"

"It's not a blind date. You've met him. He liked you."

Lena frowned and picked at a piece of pepperoni. She'd have to go for a run tomorrow to make up for this. She tried to put a name to the emotion squirming within her at the idea of going on a date with Eduardo. *Don't want to. Yeah, that's it.*

"Magdalena."

"I don't want to."

"You sound like a whining six-year-old. He's a nice man. Educated. Has a good job. Not bad-looking. What? You got so many men falling at your feet that you can be picky?"

"Damn, Mom. You can lay one hell of a guilt trip."

"Don't curse. It isn't ladylike. And I'm Catholic—we've cornered the market on guilt. May I give him your phone number?"

Slouching down into the corner of the couch, Lena sighed. So, she'd go on a date. Give him a chance. Then maybe they'd leave her alone. She could say she tried. "Okay."

Hanging up, she looked up at the ceiling.

Sass jumped back up on the couch and stared at her. "What do you think, Sass? Eduardo?"

Sass responded by lifting her leg and licking her privates. Lena took a huge bite of pizza. "Now, that," she said with her mouth full, "is unladylike."

THE MELLOW MUSHROOM restaurant in Avondale seemed extra noisy. Lena frowned and scanned the restaurant for Sadie. Spotting a hand waving in the air, she headed in that direction.

"It's so loud in here tonight," she said.

Sadie gestured at the wineglass on the table. "That's for you."

"Thank you."

"What's going on?" Sadie asked, lifting her own glass.

"Not much. The usual."

"No. I mean—" Sadie waved a hand in Lena's face "—what's going on with this face?"

"What's wrong with my face?"

"You look like you'd like to kick a puppy."

Lena scowled. Sometimes having a best friend wasn't all it was cracked up to be. Especially when said best friend was all chirpy happy and sleeping with a gorgeous hunk of man every night. The scowl deepened when Sadie laughed. Loudly.

"Stop it." Sadie gasped. "Now you look like you want to stab a nun."

The waitress appeared and Lena gave her order without looking at the menu. Pizza twice in one week. She'd *definitely* have to do some running this weekend. She sipped wine and tried to relax her face while Sadie ordered.

"So, what's going on?"

Lena made another face. "My mother. That's what's going on. She made me agree to go on a date with some random dude my aunt Estrella dragged to the house last weekend."

"Pooh! A date. Tell me more."

She told Sadie about the date, that there was no spark.

"What else?" Sadie asked in a leading tone.

"I lost a client. He's moving overseas. Sort of bummed about it."

"Ah. I'm sorry. Do you have another client waiting?"

Lena looked down at her drink. Matt's smile and appraising blue eyes came to mind. She felt a little rush of heat. "Yeah. But I don't know. I may give him to Mose to be her first client."

"Whoa! Whoa! Stop the planet. What did you just say? You? OCD queen? Are going to turn over a new client?"

Lena shrugged and Sadie leaned in close to stare into her eyes. "Stop staring at me."

"What's up with Mr. New Client?"

"Nothing."

"Lena. You are practically blushing. Tell me. I'm your best friend. You are required by law to tell me the details of your life."

Their pizzas arrived and Lena took a few bites, ignoring Sadie as hard as she could. Sadie grinned at her from behind her wineglass. "Sass barfed up a hairball the size of my fist on the bathroom rug and I accidentally stepped in it."

"Gross. Lena, I'm trying to eat here."

"You said I had to tell you all the details of my life."

"Point. Revision—tell me all about this new client you don't want to take on."

"Trust-fund frat boy."

Sadie made a face. "Ugh. Yeah. Give him to Mose."

They ate in silence for a few minutes. Sadie's instant agreement helped. She was attracted to him simply based on his looks and that bad boy vibe he gave off. But she was over that. She was almost thirty years old and she didn't have time to play. Serious applicants only. She let out a long sigh. "Eduardo it is."

"Ha-ha. Mr. Dream Nerd."

"Knock it off, okay? It's bad enough I have to

go out with him. Ugh. My life sucks. And why are they so loud up there?"

"It's a restaurant, Lena, not a library."

The waitress stopped by to refill their water glasses.

Lena pointed at the upper level. "What's going on up there? They are so loud."

"A wedding party," the waitress replied with a smile.

"Aww," Sadie cooed. "A wedding party."

"Who has a wedding party at a pizza joint?"

"Indeed," Sadie said, looking up at the waitress. "Do you know the happy couple?"

The waitress nodded. "Kim and Ben."

Sadie pushed back her chair and, grabbing her glass of wine, stood. "Hey," she yelled. She lifted the glass toward the party above. "To Kim and Ben. May all your ever-afters be happy!"

"Seriously?" Lena asked as Sadie sat back down. "Am I going to get all chirpy and goo-gooey if I fall in love?"

"Yes. Yes, you are. And you'll stop being a grumpy muffin."

"Grumpy muffin? Oh geez. Next thing I know, you'll be cutting my food for me."

"Go out with Eduardo. Maybe you won't want to stab him in the face. Give him a chance. What's the worst that can happen?"

Lena shoved a bite of pizza into her mouth to stop the ready retort. She loved Sadie like a sister, but that woman had been on maybe two dates in her life. Wyatt fell out of the sky into her lap. *What's the worst that could happen?* "Chad."

Sadie coughed as she choked on a sip of wine. "Chad. The serial killer! I forgot about him."

"He wasn't really a serial killer," Lena said. "Just creepy."

"The one who wanted to take all those pictures of you."

"*Dios mío.* Remember all the messages he left me once I told him to shove off?"

Sadie leaned forward. "Lena," she said, imitating a deep male voice, "You're my soul mate. You and I were written in the stars. You can't deny fate."

A shudder ran through Lena's body. "Stop doing that. You sound just like him. What a pervert."

Sadie sat back. "Wonder what ever happened to him?" She pulled out her phone. "Want to look him up on the sex offenders list?"

"No!"

"Want to look up Eduardo?"

"No."

"You sure? I can have Wyatt check him out."

"And y'all wonder why I don't want you poking your noses in my love life."

"You have no love life, Lena. You do nothing but work, go home, order delivery and watch

Netflix. If you didn't meet me for dinner every Wednesday, you'd have no social life either."

Glancing around for their waitress, Lena held up her wineglass. That hit a little too close to home. Problem with having a best friend is they told you the ugly truth about yourself.

"I know. I'm in a rut."

"You're in the Grand Canyon, sister girl."

"No, I'm not."

"Tell me one thing you did this week that wasn't family or work related."

"I went for a run every other day."

"That doesn't count."

"What do you want me to do? Cook for myself? Get on one of those stupid ass dating sites? Volunteer at some charity? Build a house for Habitat for Humanity?"

Sadie's teasing smirk faded as she reached out and took Lena's hands in hers. "I'm not trying to be mean, Lena. I'm sorry. I have no room to talk here. Before Wyatt—"

"Fell into your lap."

"True. I was in that same rut. Work. Sleep. Work. It's just that I want you to be happy. And I don't know how to help you."

She tightened her fingers against Sadie's. "You help by being my friend. By kicking my butt when I get whiny."

"Or pull the princess routine."

"I'm going to be okay, Sadie. I think I'm at a

crossroad. I've achieved all the goals I set for my-self. Just need to set some new ones."

"Like telling me about this new client."

"Oh, you mean Charles Beaumont Matthews the Fifth? Old Virginia money. Trust fund from his grandmother. It's kind of obvious."

"Have you met him yet?"

Lena hesitated as their food was delivered. Sadie dived into her pizza like she'd not eaten in a month. She stared at hers, her appetite mostly gone. Pulling a bit of mushroom off, she popped it in her mouth. "Yes. He was obnoxious."

"Normal people limit of obnoxious or Lena Reyes's standards?"

"What are you saying?"

"I'm saying you have a history of judging people—and by people, I mean men—rather harshly."

"Do not."

"Do too."

"I'm not even talking to you anymore."

"Jules wants you to help her with a Spanish project for school."

Lena sighed and took a huge bite of pizza. Sadie knew she couldn't deny Jules anything. One pleading look from her dark eyes would melt the hardest of hearts.

"Fine. Whatever."

"Grouch."

"Meanie."

"I'll have Wyatt run Eduardo through a background check. We don't want you hooking up with another serial killer."

CHAPTER FIVE

MATT SLOWED HIS pace as he approached the building. Glancing in a store window, he ran a hand down his beard and checked his hair. He was actually a little nervous. He'd made a bad impression that he really wanted to change. *Deep breath. She's just a person. Apologize. Mean it and move on.* He grinned as he walked the few feet to the door of Reyes Financial Management. He had a suspicion that Lena Reyes was far more than *just* anything.

A pretty blonde sat at the receptionist's desk as he entered. She looked up and smiled. Her polite business expression didn't change, but her eyes moved over him and her smile widened. "Mr. Matthews?"

"That's me. You can call me Matt."

She stood and swept her hand in a graceful motion toward a leather sofa against the exposed brick wall. "Please, have a seat. I'll let Ms. Reyes know you're here." She stepped through the doorway to the back of the office and paused. "May I bring you anything? Coffee, water?"

"No, I'm good."

He sat and looked around. Broad Street was a pricey location. The reception area was small but tastefully decorated. His experienced eye noted the antique reception desk. The leather sofa was butter soft. Dark wood end tables held an array of local magazines. The floors were the original pine, probably two hundred years old and the brick wall behind him looked to be made of hand-kilned brick.

The blonde was back. "Ms. Reyes is ready for you."

"Okay." Question was, he thought as he followed the blonde, was he ready for her?

Lena stood as he entered her office. It was a bit more spacious than the reception area, but just as richly decorated. "Thank you, Chloe," she said. "Sit down."

He sat in the chair across from her and smiled. "I really want to apologize for the other night. Really. I had no idea."

Her cheeks flushed but the expression on her face remained cool. "I've asked my assistant to sit in with us." She picked up the phone. "Mose, we're ready."

He sat back. *Okay. Definitely not forgiven. Let it go. Get this money stuff over with.* He reached into his messenger bag and pulled out a file, setting it on the desk. "I had the accountant who is handling this for me send the information." He put the file on the desk.

"Good. You're here. Let's get started," Lena said when a striking African American woman walked in and took the chair next to him. She smiled. "I'm Mose. It's nice to meet you."

"Matt," he said, shaking her offered hand.

Lena pulled the file to her and opened it. Matt watched her face as she flipped through the papers. He was sure she was unaware of how readable her face was. Little nods, quick quirks of the lips, fleeting frowns. It was her eyes that held his attention though. Nearly black, keenly focused and simply gorgeous. He wanted to paint those eyes.

"Good," she said, looking up. She handed the file to Mose, who took it and began riffling through the pages. "Mr. Matthews, what is your financial goal?"

Mr. Matthews. Inwardly, he groaned. He dropped his voice a few octaves and put on a snooty country club voice. "Well, Ms. Reyes, the thing is, you make me feel like my father when you call me Mr. Matthews and I'd really prefer not to feel like my father."

Mose snickered but Lena's face did not change. "Your goals then, *Matt*?"

He leaned forward. *Give it up, man. Stick to business.* "Okay. You can see my grandmother left me a sizable trust fund. I won't have access to that for another four years, but I'd really like to put it somewhere and let it grow. My immediate

goal is to take the money I'm making now selling art and grow that now. Quickly but safely. I
want to open a nonprofit to provide art therapy
for kids who need it but can't afford it."

*Wait. What was that? A flicker of warmth in
those black eyes?*

"Art therapy," Mose said. "What is that?"

He turned to her. "Basically what it says. It's
a form of therapy using art instead of talking or
what have you. Works really great for kids who
may not have the vocabulary to say how they feel
about things, but they can draw pictures and talk
about the things in the pictures."

"Is that what you do now?"

"Yes. I do it part-time at the Children's Hospital. And teach private art lessons also. But I really
want to take advantage of my sudden popularity
as an artist before it goes away to get some capital and connections to help make my nonprofit
a reality."

He looked back at Lena. There was a definite
thaw in her expression. "Sorry," he said with a
sheepish grin. "Get me talking about it and I'll
go on all day."

A smile curved Lena's lips and now he really
wanted to paint her. *Gorgeous and complex and
shut up, man, she's handling your money.* "I can
see you are very passionate about it."

As she began listing options for him, he felt his

eyes glaze over. He held up a hand. "Listen. I'll be honest. I'm an artist. I don't know anything about money or markets. I trust you. Do your magic."

The ice was back. "I don't like to do business like that, Mr. Matthews. I want my clients to know exactly what I am doing and why."

"That's fine. Keep me in the loop. But just do what you think is best."

"OH. MY. GOD."

Lena looked up as Chloe appeared in her doorway after seeing Matt out. "What?"

"What?" Chloe and Mose asked in shocked unison.

Fanning her face with her hand, Chloe leaned against the doorjamb. "Seriously, Lena. That was about the hottest chunk of man I have ever seen in real life with my own two eyes."

Mose made a sound. "For a white boy, he's all right."

Lena closed Matt's file and handed it to Mose. "Wipe the drool off your chins and get to work, ladies."

"Don't even start with me, Ms. Frosty Cakes. I know you. You were checking him out. Hell, I'm gay and I was checking him out."

"Get out of my office. Both of you. Degenerates. We don't drool on our clients."

Chloe shoulder-bumped Mose as she reached

the door. "Because our clients are all ninety-year-old farts."

Lena smiled as they left. She'd tried to hide it but those blue eyes had about undone her. The long dark blond hair, the slightly too-long beard, neatly trimmed over his cheeks and longer at the chin was a look she was sure only he could make look so sexy. And when those luscious lips parted in that grin of his, she'd about lost her ability to count to ten much less evaluate his portfolio.

"Basta."

She logged on to her computer and began going through her emails. *Frat boy. Trust-fund brat. Probably a man whore. Bad boy.* She repeated the litany over and over in her mind. In English. In Spanish. Still, the memory of those eyes looking directly into hers would not go away. Nor the feeling of breathless heat she'd experienced. The look on his face when he talked about helping kids. Melt.

Yeah, well, get over it. Ain't gonna happen. Serious men only need apply. Like Eduardo. Serious. With a job. Ready for a commitment. A cold jab of fear in the gut made her press her lips together. *What about you? Are you ready for a commitment?*

Shaking the thought from her head, she turned back to the computer. Numbers. Numbers made sense. The give and take of the market place made sense. It was all just a shell game. Moving money here. Buying stock here. Selling it there. No messy emotion. No baffling personalities. Just numbers.

SATURDAY MORNING, SHE rolled out of bed with a groan and, not bothering with a shower, put on her running clothes and shoes. Sweeping her hair up into a high ponytail, she stepped out the rear entrance of her condominium. Perfect day for a run. Sixty-five and sunny. She stretched for a few minutes, and then headed out on her normal three-mile route. Along Waterfront Park to Adgers Wharf, East Bay to the Battery, Murray to South Battery back to East Bay, where she reversed her course. She started out and made it all the way to the High Battery before she needed to start her mental narrative of "Pizza and wine, pizza and wine, pizza and wine." She'd inherited her mother's and aunt's tendency for a big butt and running was the only thing that kept it in check.

Mentally adding another two hundred calories burned from dodging tourists, she reached the stairs to the Low Battery and pressed on. The throngs of tourists thinned out dramatically once she'd passed White Point Garden and left her obligated only to lift a hand or grunt out a greeting to fellow runners as she passed. And she had a date. With Eduardo. Tonight. *Just do it. Suck it up. One night. Then maybe* la familia *will leave you alone.* The thought made her kick up her pace. Was there anything more excruciating than dating at her age?

The food. Just think of the food. She turned down South Battery with the menu of Halls Chophouse on her mind. *An hour or so of awkward small talk is a fair price to pay for some of the best food in Charleston, right? You can do this.* She huffed out a sigh. Flipped a middle finger at a dude who called out *"Qué pasa, chica"* as she ran past him. *What to wear? You're gonna have to shave if you want to wear a dress.*

The "to shave or not to shave" debate got her back to Waterfront Park. She slowed to a walk as she approached the pineapple-shaped water fountain at the center of the park, cooling down and getting her breath back. Nope. If she was going to be forced on a date, she was going to pull out all her weapons. And her legs were killer.

"Hello, Ms. Reyes."

She turned at the sound of the voice. And froze. *Great. Here you are dripping sweat and probably smelling like a dead goat in the sun and there is Mr. Hot-Frat-Boy.* She stopped and put her hands on her hips. *Dear, sweet baby Jesus in the manger.* He was splayed out on a blanket in the grass, propped up on his elbows. The paint-smeared T-shirt he wore rode up just enough for her to get a glimpse of hard abs and a little dark blond fuzz. There was an honest-to-God palette on the blanket beside him and an easel holding a canvas. Bad-boy grin was on full power.

She took a few steps in his direction. "*Mr.* Matthews."

He pulled himself up to sit cross-legged on the blanket. "Matt, please. I beg of you. Mr. Matthews makes me feel like I should get a haircut and put on a suit or something. Beautiful day, don't you think?"

She stopped at the edge of the blanket. She didn't get him. Everything about him screamed entitled, rich white boy but he didn't show it. At all. "Yes," she said, sarcasm dripping from each word. "It is quite a lovely day, Mr. Matthews."

He grinned and her stomach went quivery. A frown creased her face. *Do that again, gut, and no dessert for you tonight.*

"Come on, I'm sorry for the other night. Really, I am. Why won't you accept my apology? I'd like to be friends."

She looked at the painting. Unlike the large, minimalist paintings she'd seen at the Gallery, this was much more to her taste. A softer Jonathan Green–style of the fountain and the trees with their trails of Spanish moss swaying in the breeze.

"Whatcha think?" he asked.

"I like this better than the other stuff."

"Why won't you accept my apology?"

She looked back at him and crossed her arms. "Because you don't get it."

He held his hands out, palms up. "Then tell me what I don't get."

She pressed her lips together for a moment. *Think, Magdalena, think. He is a client.* "What you did was wrong. Not because I turned out to be who I am but because it's wrong to pull that on anyone. Any woman would have been embarrassed. You are apologizing to me because you need me to handle your money. You need to be looking at why you wanted to embarrass a woman like that."

She waited as he stared up at her. *Here it comes. It was just a joke. I didn't mean it like that. You're overreacting.* He got to his feet with one graceful motion.

"Crap. I never saw it like that. You're right." He ran a hand down his beard. "Now I feel like shit."

She managed to hide how stunned she was. *He was taking responsibility? He was being enlightened? Wow. Okay. Don't gloat. Be nice.* "Now," she said, holding out a hand, "I'll accept your apology, Matt."

He took her hand and held it between both his. "Thank you for telling me that. I do try not to be an asshole most of the time."

She slipped her hand away from his before she couldn't hide the rush of heat she was feeling.

"We're all just humans, doing the best we can in the moment."

"Now, if you'll excuse me," she said with a vague gesture at her sweaty self. "I need to finish my cooldown."

MATT WATCHED LENA walk away. The grin came back. He could think of a couple of things he'd like to do with her *in the moment*. He liked that she'd made him work for his apology. Liked that she'd surprised him with her blunt assessment of his behavior. Fawning sorority girls had never been his type. He'd always preferred brains over beauty. But Magdalena Reyes seemed to possess ample amounts of both. The bits of fire and steel he saw in her only intrigued him further.

He carefully cleaned his brush and bent to pick up his palette. He normally didn't paint in public, preferring to paint from photographs when doing landscapes, but the day was so perfect. Much different from Chevy Chase where October meant winter was on the way. Charleston was near perfection in October.

As he put a few finishing touches on the painting, he kept glancing up, watching Lena's progress along the path. Two buildings past the fountain and the City Gallery, she turned into one of the many condominiums that lined the park. *Expensive real estate. Must be true what Dr. Rutledge said. She spun money out of straw.*

"Pack it up," he muttered under his breath. "She's about ten miles outta your league, man."

He broke down the easel and cleaned off the palette. Sitting back down on the blanket, he cleaned the brushes. Those things were not cheap and he needed them to last as long as possible. After packing everything away for the long walk back home, he lay back down on the blanket to enjoy a bit more of the day and to let the canvas dry. His phone rang and he fished it out of his back pocket.

His mother. This couldn't be good.

"Hey, Mom, what's up?" he answered. Knowing she hated *Mom* and preferred *Mother.* Capital *M.*

The brief moment of silence was to chasten him for his word choice. "Nothing," her frosty voice finally replied, "is 'up,' Charles. I am phoning to let you know that your father and I will be visiting Charleston in a few weeks. Your father has a business meeting. We will see you for dinner."

He let his own silence play out. She knew he hated being called Charles. He also hated the way she *told* him he'd have dinner with them rather than asking. Nothing new, but he'd hoped that since he was over thirty years old now, she'd treat him somewhat like an adult. He sighed. Such was the life of the black sheep. If only he'd become a lawyer. Interned for some powerful senator who

owed his father a favor, then moved on to a lu-
crative lobbying position, scamming people for
the sake of a billionaire or two, then his parents
might not treat him like a dirty secret.

"Sure, that'd be great. Just let me know the
night so I can clear any plans I might have."

"Your sister is having another baby."

*Ah. Moving right on to major disappointment
number two. His two sisters were popping out the
grandbabies left and right, but he, the only son,
the only carrier of the Matthews family name,
had thus far failed to produce a Charles Beaumont Matthews the Sixth.*

"Awesome. Which one?"

"Susannah. She's due in April."

"Tell her and Biff I sent my congratulations."

"His name is Bill."

"Is Biff Charlotte's husband? I get them mixed
up."

"You are being unpleasant. Goodbye."

"Bye, Mom," he said as she ended the call.

It wasn't that he didn't love his family. He just
didn't *like* them very much. Boring. Predictable.
And so many damned rules.

He stood to gather his things when the phone
rang again. He almost didn't look, sure it was
his father calling to yell at him for upsetting his
mother. And his mother merely annoyed him. His
father could push buttons that made him want to

punch walls. But it was Eliot Rutledge. *This was random.*

"Dr. Rutledge, how are you?"

"Eliot, please, son. How many times do I have to ask?"

"Enough to overcome the ruthless teachings of several deportment for proper gentlemen classes, sir."

Eliot laughed. "Yes. I have a daughter who was politely asked to leave several of those."

"How may I help you?"

"I have an idea. Now, I understand you have a lot going on with your job at the hospital and your art career beginning to take off, so tell me no if you need to."

"Okay. Go ahead."

Like he was going to tell his benefactor no. He just hoped it wouldn't be too onerous.

"I do some volunteer work at the St. Toribio Mission out on John's Island. Are you familiar with it?"

"Vaguely. They work with the migrant workers?"

"Yes. Primarily, but the doors are open to anyone needing help. I was thinking about creating an art-therapy program for the children. I see them there while their parents are getting medical or legal help and they have nothing to do but sit and wait. I thought an art room with supplies would be helpful."

Matt nodded. "Actually, sir, that sounds like an amazing idea. I'm sure it would help them quite a bit. What are you thinking? Weekly sessions or just get it set up?"

"For now, getting it set up. We have plenty of volunteers who could watch the kids and keep the room and supplies in order."

"Okay. I'm in. Just let me know when and where."

"Very good. Thank you. I'll be back in touch."

Matt ended the call with a smile on his face. At least someone appreciated his art and his desire to use it to help others.

CHAPTER SIX

LENA STOOD IN the doorway of her walk-in closet. Sass wound her way around her ankles, getting cat hair on her still-damp and freshly shaved legs. "What do you think, Sass? Standard black? Or should we pull out all the stops and go with the red?"

As she moved into the closet, Sass dashed under the row of neatly hanging dresses, her tail trailing along the hems as she walked. Lena sighed. "I might as well just buy everything in Sass orange. It'd be cheaper than all the lint rollers."

She'd always wanted a pet. It was nice to have someone to talk to, even if it was a cat. Sass seemed interested in what she had to say, so that was all that mattered. Lena leaned down to scratch behind Sass's ear. Lifting a dress from the rod, she turned to the mirror. "I'm going with the red. I shaved my legs for this." She hooked a pair of shoes out of the shoe rack. Black stilettos with four-inch heels. "Let's see what poor old Eduardo thinks about this."

She slipped the dress on, careful not to smudge

her makeup, and wiggled the zipper up. *Oh, hell yes*. She smoothed down the front. The dark red set off her hair and eyes and it clung to her curves like nothing else. Bonus, it actually came down to just above her knees so she didn't have to worry about accidently flashing anyone.

Trying to ignore the butterflies in her stomach, she fluffed her hair and grabbed the shoes. "All right, Sass. It's showtime."

THE UBER DRIVER pulled up to the curb directly outside Hall's Chophouse. Lena frowned. Eduardo was there, waiting. In rumpled khaki pants and a short-sleeved, blue plaid shirt. And was he wearing sneakers? *For this, I shaved above the knee*. She slipped her shoes back on and stepped out of the car.

He didn't even notice. Just stood there, hands shoved in his pockets, staring the wrong way down the street. "Idiot," she muttered under her breath. Shaking her head, she approached him. The clack of her heels on the sidewalk must have caught his attention because he turned in her direction.

"Oh, hi," he said.

She stopped in front of him. "Hello."

He pressed his lips together and looked down at his shoes. "You know, I know our families sort of pushed this on us and I was just trying to go along with it, but, so if you don't want to do this, we don't have to."

Her mouth, she managed to keep shut. Her eyes, however, fixed on him in a stare so hot he should have burst into flames. He glanced at her and a shadow of fear crossed his features. The door to the restaurant opened and an older man dressed properly in a suit walked out. He smiled at Lena.

"Excuse me, sir," Lena said to him. She motioned at Eduardo. "This gentleman doesn't want to go on the date he asked me out on. What do you think about that?"

The man stopped and, with a slow up-and-down look, smiled. "I think he's a damned fool."

"Hey. I didn't say I didn't want to. I said if you didn't want to," Eduardo protested.

Lena lifted a finger. "Dude. We are going on this date. I shaved my legs and put on a bra. We will each pay our own way. We can talk or not. Then we can each go tell our families that, oh well, didn't work out. Okay?"

The frightened look returned. "Okay," he said.

Lena smiled. "Okay."

As they were seated, Lena asked for a chardonnay. She tried to hide her irritation because Eduardo was staring at her like she was going to gut her. She didn't mean to be a bitch. She simply could not stand a wishy-washy man. Made her teeth itch.

"So, you're a software engineer?" *See, I'm being nice.*

"Yes."

Silence. *For the love of God.*

"What sort of software do you engineer?" *Come on, man. Give me something here.*

"Mostly design-and-build commercial websites."

Lena nodded. She had no idea what that even meant. "I understand Charleston has a thriving technology community."

He fiddled with his napkin. "Yeah."

Lena eyed the steak knife. This was going to be a long night.

"So," Eduardo said. "How many kids do you want to have?"

Lena froze. Stared. Gave him a long, slow blink. "Um. I don't know?"

"Oh. Because I come from a large family. Very traditional."

Lena raised her eyebrow in a perfect arch. *Traditional. Didn't teach you any machismo, that's for sure.* "Honestly, Ed, I think I'd like to shelve the topic of children until after my wine arrives at least."

"I think it's important. At your age, you can't afford to wait, you know. Your aunt said you wanted to settle down and start a family. Me too."

The waiter appeared with her wine and she practically snatched the glass from his hand.

"Thank you. Go ahead and bring me another one, please."

She took several steadying sips. Let out a long breath and looked back up at Eduardo. "So, you think we should just go ahead and get married? Twenty-four-hour wait on the marriage license. We could go get it Monday and be married by Tuesday. Maybe I could be pregnant by this time next week. Unless my withering eggs are too old and feeble to crawl out of my ovaries."

His face went dark. "No wonder you have to have your family out hunting men for you. You're mean."

"And you're insulting."

"Actually, I'm leaving."

Lena shrugged and took another sip of wine. "Bye."

The waiter came over as Eduardo left. "Everything all right here, ma'am?"

She gave him her brightest smile and was rewarded by the pure male appreciation in his eyes. "Everything is perfect. I'm ready to order. I'll have a cup of She Crab soup to begin. The petit filet mignon, medium well, with the parmesan truffle fries, thank you."

She discreetly kicked her heels off and took her phone out of her purse. She was going to have her favorite meal and finish the book she'd started last weekend. Eduardo could scamper back home and tell his mommy how mean she was.

"So, how'd the date go last night?"

Lena groaned and rolled over in bed. "It's not even nine o'clock yet, Sadie. Ugh." Sass hopped on the bed and stomped across Lena's stomach to stand on her chest, singing the song of her people. The song of long suffering, slow starvation and the horror of a half-empty bowl of dry food.

"Are you murdering your cat?" Sadie asked.

"Not yet," Lena muttered, pushing Sass aside and rolling out of bed. "I haven't even had coffee yet."

"So, how was the date?"

"He got up and walked out on me."

"Ha! Wyatt! You owe me twenty dollars."

"Are you betting on my dates? You bet against me? Bitch."

"I know you. You are mean."

"I'm not mean. I just don't take bullshit."

"What'd he do?"

"Literally, Sadie, the second question out of his mouth was how many kids did I want? Then he said I'd better hurry up before I got too old."

"Tell me you only verbally emasculated him."

"Yes. He called me a meanie and ran away."

"Lena. You have to know that you can be a bit…ah…intimidating when you get angry."

"Weeds out the weak."

"Well maybe just give them a chance to see the nice you before you unleash your inner Latina *guerrera* once in a while."

"Next time. Right now, I want coffee. Good-bye and don't call me on a weekend before noon again unless it's an emergency. *Bruja*."

Ending the call, she tossed the phone on the counter. "Don't even try tripping me this morning, feline."

Ten minutes later, Sass loved her again and she was stretched out on the couch with a large, steaming cup of coffee warming her hands. Maybe Sadie was right. Maybe she was mean. Maybe she could have handled that whole situation more graciously. "You know what, Sass? Maybe he should have not asked that. Maybe he shouldn't have brought up my age. Maybe I'm not mean but he's a rude dork. Do they ever think that?"

No, they didn't. It was always her fault. She eyed the clock. At some point she was going to get a phone call from her mother. The way Estrella and Eduardo's mother had planned this, there was no doubt a full report would be made. The only question was: before or after mass? Probably after.

By one that afternoon, she started to think that maybe she'd gotten away with it. Maybe Eduardo hadn't ratted her out to his mother. But that hope was dashed shortly after two. Darth Vader's "Imperial March" pierced the quiet, sending Sass scurrying for the bedroom.

"*Bueno*, Mamacita," Lena answered.

"So. I understand things went poorly?"

Lena rolled her eyes and made a face. "Yeah, that wasn't a good matchup. Eduardo and I aren't on the same page. In fact, we weren't even on the same date."

"There was no reason for you to be rude."

"He was rude first."

"Now you sound like a child."

"I'm not the one who ran tattling to my mommy." A flood of rapid, long-suffering Spanish filled her ear. When it died down, she continued. "No more fix-ups. Promise."

"I promise."

"Thank you." A frown creased her forehead. That was way too easy. "Promise, Momma."

"I promise I won't try to fix you up again. And I did have another reason to call. Don't forget that Louisa's daughter is having that operation tomorrow to fix her leg."

"Ah, yes. Thanks. I did forget about that. I have a present for her. I'll bring it to the hospital when I get off work."

She ended the call feeling lucky to have gotten off that easily. She got Ava's present and set it on the entryway table next to her purse so she wouldn't forget it in the morning. Glancing at the time, she sat back down with a sigh. She and Sadie would usually do something on Sunday afternoons. Now Sadie was busy with

Wyatt and Jules. She fired up her laptop. Might as well get some work done.

A FEW HOURS LATER, both her stomach and Sass were grumbling. She closed down her work files. Grabbing her phone, she scrolled through her delivery restaurant contacts. *Mmm. Brown Dog Deli.* Setting the phone down, she thought about what Sadie had said about being in a rut. Maybe she should change out of her pajamas, put on real clothes and go outside. Do something that involved people.

"I don't want to people," she moaned, flopping back on the couch. She picked up the phone and did a search for "Charleston events." A moment later, she was sitting straight up. "Sass! It's the Color of Music Festival!" Checking the time, she got to her feet. She could still make it to the Ebony and Ivory Piano Recital.

After calling to make sure there were still tickets available, she showered and changed clothes. The church hosting the recital was only a short walk away. As she reached the street, she called Sadie but the call went to voice mail. "I'm outside and peopling, for your information."

Smiling as she strolled down the sidewalk, she realized she did feel much better. The sun was shining. The sky was blue. Everyone in her family was safe and happy. There was a line already queued up at the church. As she walked to the end of the line after buying her ticket, she heard someone calling her name.

"Hello, Dr. Rutledge," she said, shaking hands with him. "Mrs. Rutledge. Nice to see you both."

"I was going to call you tomorrow, Lena," Eliot said. "I'm putting together a group to do a little charity work for the St. Toribio Center. We'll be setting up an activity room for the children to use while their parents are being seen. We could use your Spanish skills."

St. Toribio, the patron saint of Mexican immigrants, was more than familiar to Lena. She'd given money and attended benefits for the charity that offered not only medical and legal assistance, but English classes and adult continuing education. She'd never been actively involved in a project before.

"Wow. Yes. I'd love to help out. What do you need? A translator?"

"Thank you. Yes. Definitely translation. Also, we might need some printed materials made. Would you be able to help with that?"

"Ah," Lena said. "I grew up speaking Spanish with my older relatives. While I'm verbally fluent, my reading and writing skills are very rudimentary. But one of my cousins has a degree in Hispanic Literature. I'm sure she'd help out."

"Great. Well, the first planning meeting is going to be next Saturday. Right now, we've got it slated for ten in the morning, at my house. Is that good?"

"Got it. Thanks for asking me."

After saying goodbye and walking to the end of the line, she realized she was grinning ear to ear. *Uh. Okay. Maybe you should try this actual volunteering stuff more often. Feels pretty good.*

CHAPTER SEVEN

LATE MONDAY AFTERNOON, Lena wandered the labyrinth that was the Children's Hospital. Ava, her cousin's little girl, had broken her leg in a trampoline accident the previous summer. It hadn't healed correctly over a growth plate and now required an operation.

Finally, she found the correct unit. She paused outside the open door to Ava's room. She could hear voices. Ava and a man. Not a relative. She stepped into the doorway.

Ava was in the bed, her leg up in something that looked like a torture device. In a chair beside her was a man. She recognized that flow of dark blond hair, tied back with a length of leather. Recognized those shoulders. That voice. In a moment, she'd be seen and he would turn and those impossibly icy blue eyes would look into hers and those lips would curve into a smile and…

"Auntie Lena!" Ava squealed.

Matt turned with a surprised expression, but she had Ava to distract her. She circled the bed to the opposite side and leaned in to give Ava a hug and kiss on the forehead. *"Ava. Mi probo prima! Como te sientes? Tienes dolar?"*

"No, it doesn't hurt and it's rude to speak Spanish in front of people who don't," Ava said prissily. She held up a sketchbook. "Mr. Matt is drawing pictures with me because I can't go to the playroom."

"Ms. Reyes," Matt said, his tone dripping with pleasured surprise and more than a little teasing. "How delightful to see you. I didn't know Ava was your niece."

"Technically, she's my second cousin. But since I'm an only child, it's agreed I get to be aunt to all my cousins' children."

"Did you get me a present?" Ava asked.

"You know I did."

Lena handed Ava the gift bag she'd brought with her. Ava took out the small teddy bear. The present wasn't really the bear though; it was the envelope dangling from its arm by a ribbon. Ava tore it open eagerly.

"Oh my gosh! Five hundred! Thank you, Auntie Lena! Am I there yet?"

Lena sat on the edge of the bed. "Not quite. But you have time."

Ava turned to Matt. "Auntie Lena is paying for all of us to go to college."

"Mr. Matthews doesn't want to know about all that, Ava. And I've interrupted your time with him. Where are your parents?"

"They went downstairs to get Granddaddy."

Matt lounged back in his chair, arms across his chest. His mouth was twisted in a smirk, but his eyes were warm and full of questions. "You didn't interrupt. We were almost done."

Lena stood and smoothed down her skirt. "Well then." Her voice sounded prissy even to her own ear. Matt's grin widened to a smile. "I'll leave you to wrap it up. I'll be back with your parents, my sweet."

She tried to make a graceful, dignified exit. One that didn't make it seem like she was running away. But she was fooling no one. Matt's loaded "Goodbye, Ms. Reyes," followed her out of the room. *Saco de huevos. So infuriating.* She'd like to wipe that smirk off his face.

She'd just rounded the corner when she heard her name. Turning, she saw her parents with her aunt Paula and her husband and Ava's mother, Louisa. "There you are! I just peeked in on Ava."

"Is the art therapist still with her?" Louisa asked.

The question took Lena aback for a moment. She'd been looking at Matt as the smirking, snotty frat boy who pissed her off by just breathing, not as a therapist doing his job. "Yes," she stammered out. "I think they are finishing up soon though."

"Good. Good," her uncle Tomas said, looking over his shoulder.

Lena frowned and looked down the hallway. A

man was walking toward them. A man in a white coat. A Hispanic-looking man. *No. Just no.* She shot a murderous look at her mother, who shook her head slightly and lifted her hands palms up.

"Ah, Vincente," her aunt Paula said. As if she was surprised. *Yeah, right.*

Lena narrowed her eyes and felt her jaw clench. Louisa hid her smile behind her hand. "I'm going to kill your parents," Lena muttered under her breath at her cousin.

"Hey! I'm going to go check on Ava," Louisa said brightly before making a run for it.

"I think we'll go too," Lena's mother said, grabbing her husband by the arm and following Louisa.

"Vincente, this is my niece Lena Reyes. Lena, Vincente goes to church with us. He's a doctor."

Lena smiled lukewarmly at the man. Okay. He wasn't bad. Tall. Rather handsome. Nice smile. "Hello," she said, reaching out to shake his offered hand.

"Lena. It's a pleasure to meet you. Your aunt speaks very highly of you."

He had just the tiniest scrap of an accent. He held on to her hand a bit too long, forcing her to pull away. "Nice to meet you," she said automatically.

"Doctor Perez is single also, Lena," Paula said.

Lena turned a furious, incredulous face to

her aunt. "Aunt Paula!" she hissed out between her teeth.

Vincente chuckled. "Come now, Mrs. Hernandez, you'll make me blush."

He looked over at Lena. His expression was both embarrassed and amused. *Okay, so maybe he wasn't in on this setup. Still. What next? Were they going to offer him a dowry to take her dried-up, old spinster self?*

"And," he continued, "I think you've embarrassed your beautiful niece."

Infuriated. That's the word you're looking for Mister Doctor Man. Infuriated. Before she could form a coherent sentence, Paula nudged her.

"Give Dr. Perez one of your cards, Magdalena."

A motion in the hall caught her eye. *Oh, this just makes it perfect.* Matt breezed past. Close enough to make sure that she saw him seeing her trapped in this moment. He turned a few feet beyond them, walking backward and grinning at her. *Pendajo.* As she fumbled out a card, an idea popped into her brain. A way out of this.

She held the card out and let her gaze drift over the doctor's shoulder. She looked back at him and smiled. "It certainly was a pleasure to meet you, Dr. Perez. Now, if you all will excuse me, I'd like to speak to Ava's art therapist."

She ran for it this time. Didn't even look back to see her aunt's face. She reached an intersecting hall and glanced in both directions. There he was. "Matt," she called out.

He stopped and looked back, surprise clear on his face. "You need a place to hide?"

"Shut up," she said as she approached him.

He leaned a shoulder against the wall and grinned at her. "That looked like an ambush to me."

"That was an ambush. But I wanted to ask about Ava."

The smirk grin faded a bit. "Ask," he said.

"Is she okay? Did you learn anything from working with her that will help us help her?"

He straightened. His smile was different this time. Warm and sincere. "Yes. I asked her to draw the hospital room. Having kids draw their environment is a good way to get a glimpse into their feelings."

"And what did Ava show you?"

"Well. She drew the bed very small and the windows very large. Which can mean she feels overwhelmed by being here and she wants to escape. But she also drew herself smiling and surrounded by her parents and family. Which means that she feels safe and loved. I think she's going to be just fine."

Lena nodded. "Did you talk to her mother about this?"

"Yep. You've got a nice family, Ms. Reyes. I'm glad I got to help them out."

"Thank you."

She smiled up at him. *A moment. This was a real moment.* Then his smile twisted back to that little sideways grin and the glint came back into his eyes. "If only I could have helped you out with that scene in the hall. If you'd drawn that for me, my assessment would be that you were being set up."

And moment over. She gave him her most vicious glare and arched an eyebrow. "Why? Were you jealous?" Venom still dripping from the words, she turned and stomped down the hallway, putting a little extra swish in it just to give him a show.

His laughter followed her. "You are surely something, Ms. Reyes."

Humph. Just how much of something, you'll never know. She turned the corner and flipped her hand dismissively in his general direction.

MATT WATCHED HER sashay down the hall. Because she wanted him to watch. Still smiling, he shook his head and entered the playroom. She was something. Hot. Cold. Smart. Sexy. *Let it go, dude. A woman like that isn't to be trifled with.* And he had too much on his plate right now to take on the likes of Ms. Reyes.

As he set up the table where he'd lead a session with several of his regular kids, his mind drifted back. Not to Lena, but the entire family.

They'd shown up in force. Ava was never alone for a moment. When he was five, his nanny had taken him to the hospital when he'd had his tonsils out. When he developed a complication and had to stay overnight, she left at 6:00 p.m. The maid was supposed to stay with him, but never showed up. His parents were in London. He'd been terrified. And after that, he'd spent several scary nights alone in the hospital with asthma attacks.

Shake it off, man. But he wondered. What would it be like to come from such a family, full of loud laughter and love? And how did that family forge someone as guarded as Lena?

"Mr. Matt! Mr. Matt!"

He turned toward the voice with a smile. Clarissa. Dr. Rutledge's granddaughter. With her was a tall woman, whose red hair matched the wisps of hair still clinging to Clarissa's little head. She was being dragged by the hand across the playroom.

"Hey there, pretty girl. You seem mighty perky today. And you're the first to arrive, which means you get to be my assistant."

He shifted his attention to the woman beside Clarissa. He held out a hand. "Matt. Are you Clarissa's mother?"

The woman laughed. "No. Although you aren't the first to make that guess."

"This is my aunt Logan, Matt. She's visit-

ing me and I wanted to show her the playroom."
Clarissa looked up at Logan. "I told you he was
cute!"

Logan blushed and Matt felt a little heat on
his own face. Here he'd been teasing Lena about
an ambush setup and now he was the victim of
one. "Logan," he said. "Might you be the daughter who was asked to leave several deportment
classes?"

Her laugh echoed through the playroom. "Indeed I am. How did that conversation ever come
up?"

"I think it was my confession to having been
in a similar situation."

Clarissa grabbed his hand. "What are we doing
today, Mr. Matt?"

"We're going to make Halloween decorations.
So we are going to need construction paper,
glue and scissors. Do you know where they are
stored?"

"I do," Clarissa said seriously. She turned to
her aunt. "Promise me you won't leave."

"I promise." They watched Clarissa open the
supply cabinet. "I'm sorry about this. She just
said she wanted to show me the playroom."

"It's okay. She's a good kid. Has a lot of fight
in her."

"That she gets from me."

There was something in her stance. The slight

nuance of her voice. Matt grinned. "Baa, baa," he said.

"Black sheep," Logan returned with her own grin.

They did a fist bump. "May we ever run free," he said. "Hang out awhile. No need for you to miss out on time with Clarissa while she's doing this."

She glanced at her watch. "I really need to go. Clarissa, come give me a hug and kiss. I have to go back to work."

Clarissa wrapped her arms around Logan's abdomen. "Will you bring me a dessert?"

"Tomorrow, Mini-Me," Logan said as she kissed the top of Clarissa's head.

Clarissa looked up at Matt. "Aunt Logan is a pastry chef. She makes the best desserts ever in the whole world."

"Is that so?"

"Yes. You two should go on a date."

"Clarissa! That's not very polite," Logan said.

"Why? You're my favorite aunt. He's my favorite hospital person."

Matt held back laughter. He looked thoughtfully at the little girl. "Would it make you happy if we went on a date?"

"Yes."

Matt pulled over a chair and sat down to be at eye level. "What if we go on the date and we just want to be friends instead of boyfriend and girlfriend?"

Clarissa shrugged. "I don't care. I just think you should go on a date."

"Okay then," he said. "Go finish getting the supplies ready."

As she skipped away, he turned to Logan. "So we'll go on a date." He made air quotes.

Logan smiled and held out a hand. "Deal. But just so you know, this really isn't a date."

"I understand. But I'm new in town. A little short on friends. We'll talk about the lives of black sheep and Clarissa will feel like she did something good for us."

Logan looked back to where Clarissa was rummaging through the supply cabinet. Her eyes filled with sadness. "I just want her to have a date of her own someday."

"She will. She's a fighter. Like her favorite aunt."

Logan laughed. "I'm her only aunt. Give me your number and we'll arrange a time for this date."

CHAPTER EIGHT

"A LITTLE FARTHER off our beaten path," Lena said as she slid into the booth at The Glass Onion. She and Sadie usually met in the Avondale area for their weekly Wednesday-night dinners.

"I was craving shrimp and grits."

"They serve wine here?"

"Yes. So, you seem to be in a better mood than last week. Did your family let you off the hook after the what-was-his-name fiasco?"

"No. I have another date on Saturday. This time with a doctor that my aunt Paula set me up with." She smiled. A pretty, vacuous smile. "I'm just going to spend the entire night making this face."

They gave the waitress their order. Two shrimp and grits and a bottle of chardonnay. Sadie leaned back in the booth and looked at her.

"What?"

"I just feel like this is my fault."

Lena shook her head. "No, it isn't."

"But it is, Lena." Sadie leaned forward, her arms crossed on the table. "Do I need to get some shots and make you sister swear?"

Lena looked down at the table and spun her napkin wrapped silverware in a circle. Thing was, Sadie was right. But she wasn't going to be the one to rain on her wedding. Sadie's hand covered hers.

"Lena."

"Okay. Yes. No. It's complicated."

Sadie laughed, drawing the eyes of a couple of men sitting nearby. "I'd expect no less from you than complicated. Look. I've got some conflicted feelings about this too. You were always the one who wanted to find the guy and get married. Have kids and all that junk. Not me."

"Yet, here you are, deliriously happy. Wedding planning. Instant family."

"Yes. And I feel guilty about it sometimes."

Lena frowned and leaned forward to take both Sadie's hands in hers. "Look at me, Sades." When Sadie's dark blue eyes met hers, she squeezed her hands. "Don't do that. Never. I am beyond happy for you. You are more than my best friend. You're my sister."

A weak smile trembled on Sadie's lips. "But still. I just fell into this and now your family is driving you crazy."

"And that's my problem. Not yours. Your problem is that my mother is trying to hijack your wedding plans."

Sadie sat back with a groan. "That's the truth. Have you seen her Pinterest board? It's like Catholic tradition met upscale elegance and had a country-kitsch baby. It's a horror show."

"Can you imagine how she's going to be if I get married?"

"*When* you get married. Tell me about this date."

Their wine arrived and Lena poured a healthy glassful. "I don't know. He's a doctor. Cuban by the accent, I think. Sort of cute. Seemed embarrassed that Paula ambushed us both."

"Are you going to be nice? Not rip his throat out in the first five minutes like you did with poor what's-his-name?"

Taking a long sip of wine, Lena arched an eyebrow. "Maybe," she said.

But Sadie didn't laugh. A small frown crossed her features. "Come on. Sister, truth—you can be very intimidating. And sometimes you use it like a weapon. Especially with men."

"Men piss me off more than anyone else."

She meant it to come out snarky, but even she couldn't deny the undercurrent of anger in her words. She didn't know why it was true. But it was. If it wasn't some white dude trying to satisfy a Latina fetish, it was some jerk trying to assert dominance.

"Because you let them do that, Lena. You jump on anything. One misspoken word. One perceived insult and you come out swinging."

"Now you're being irritating."

"I don't care," Sadie said, pouring more wine into her glass. "You told me a lot of things I didn't want to hear. Your turn."

"So what do you want me to do? Be nice when some guy asks me if it's true that Latina women are hot in bed?"

"No. That guy you can eviscerate. But yeah, be nice. Give a guy a chance to prove himself."

Lena looked up gratefully as the waitress brought their food. "Thank you," she said. Unrolling her silverware, she concentrated on the shrimp and grits. *Okay. Mean. Not the first time I've heard that. I'm not mean. I just don't play games.* She sighed and dropped her spoon to the plate. "I'm mean."

"No. You can be. But you aren't mean. Not the real you. It's just a wall you put up. See who's brave enough to scale it."

"I'm a bitch."

"A strong, independent woman who has overcome obstacles that would have crippled most men. Successful. Beautiful. Savvy."

"I'm a mean bitch."

"Lena. Stop it. Listen to me. You are not a mean bitch. You just play one on dates."

That made her smile. It hurt to look at it, but it was true. She had left a long trail of bleeding men behind her. She ate a few more bites of shrimp. Thinking back, most of them hadn't been bad guys but she always managed to find something wrong with them. *Maybe it is me. Maybe I make up reasons to push them away. More like send them running away.*

"I think there's something wrong with me."

"There's nothing wrong with you," Sadie said. "Just like there was nothing wrong with me. You just haven't met your guy yet."

Lena shook her head. "No. That's not it. I don't think I can do the serious relationship thing. I'm too much of a control freak. I have to be in charge. But then I don't like a man who lets me be in charge. And then I get furious when a man tries to be in charge. See?"

"That's because being in charge isn't part of a healthy relationship, Lena. Being equal partners is."

Snagging her wineglass and leaning back in her seat, Lena mulled over those words. *Equal partners.* "I don't know," she said slowly. "I think I have a trust problem."

"Trust as in 'depend on'?" Sadie asked.

"No. Trust in myself."

She leaned forward, resting her forearms along the table. The moment was so alive in her memory that she could still feel the sting of his palm across her cheek. The shame was still so great that she'd never told anyone except her mother. Not even Sadie.

Sadie leaned in closer. "Tell me."

"I was in love. Head over heels, down the rabbit

hole, don't care about anything anyone says, this is my soulmate in love. Until he slapped me. Because I wasn't ready to sleep with him."

The slap had been completely unexpected. So out of character. It had taken her breath away. That moment and the rapid shift from shock to disbelief to heartbreak may have only lasted a few seconds in real time. But its legacy lived on in her behavior.

"That's what it is?" Sadie asked softly. "That's your trigger?"

She looked up into Sadie's eyes. "I think so. I know that was the moment when I realized I couldn't truly count on anyone except myself. When I got serious about school and college and getting myself and my family out of the constant fear and uncertainty of poverty."

"And now that you've accomplished that goal, that incident has changed from being an incentive to being a hindrance?"

Lena brought her hands up and pressed her fingers against her lips. *That was it.* That single-minded drive that allowed her to ignore naysayers and overcome every obstacle had nothing to do now that she'd reached her goal and was in a place of safety. *Sadie's completely right.*

"How do I change it though?"

"First step is realizing it," Sadie replied. "I'm no expert, but I think the next step is recognizing when your feelings are coming from that trigger."

"Oh. Easy." Lena snapped her fingers. "Okay. Done. Next."

Sadie took a sip of wine and raised her eyebrows. "See? That? That was the trigger. You realized you have emotional work to do so you went straight to sarcasm and being flippant."

She wanted to be angry. It was right there, brimming at the back of her throat but she pushed it down. *How did Sadie do it? She was right. Again.* She picked up her fork and began pushing grits around on the plate. "I'm tired of this, Sadie. I don't even know where to begin."

"You've already begun. You're tired because you've just realized the weight of this trigger you've been carrying for all these years."

"But what's next?"

Sadie shrugged. "For me, it was like I saw a truth about myself, and then I couldn't unsee it. Does that make sense?"

"No."

Sadie pressed her lips together and stared at the ceiling for a moment before looking back at Lena. "Like when I went to Asheville with Wyatt to meet his sister's friend, the one who was willing to take Jules if Wyatt couldn't. She and her family are like a second family to Jules. I was feeling scared and threatened. Before I faced my abandonment issue, I would have done or said something to alienate her, to push her away before she could reject me. Now I know that it was normal and okay to feel nervous about meeting someone new and that they might actually like me."

Lena nodded. "I understand that. But I don't know. Maybe I should cancel my date with the doctor. He might be a nice guy. Maybe I shouldn't date until I figure all this out."

"I think you should keep the date. Like a test run for when you meet a guy you really like."

"Test run. How romantic. I don't know. Just thinking about being set up like this makes me mad."

"Raise your right hand," Sadie ordered.

"What? No. We are in public."

"Levanta tu mano derecho."

"Jesucristo, your Spanish sucks. How can you be so bad at it after all these years?"

"Your hand's still on the table."

She lifted her hand. "Okay. Fine. My hand is in the air."

"Repeat after me—I will not be mean on my date with the doctor."

"I will not be mean on my date with the doctor."

"See? Easy."

"Unless he deserves it."

SATURDAY MORNING, MATT cruised the bike along Rutledge Avenue, Colonial Lake providing a small breeze across its concrete hemmed water. He stood on the bike pedals, powering across

Broad Street to the quiet and shady streets of the
promised land of Charleston real estate: South of
Broad. Taking a long, lazy left, he slowed as he
made his way up Tradd Street, not exactly sure
which of the multimillion-dollar, perfectly restored antebellum mansions belonged to Dr. Rutledge. That he'd just pedaled up a street named
for the doctor's family reminded him that while
Eliot's patronage was welcome if only to help the
nonprofit become a reality sooner, it placed him
squarely in the middle of that upper-class society
that he'd run away from before.

The flash of a white BMW door and a swing
of black hair ahead caught his eye. His heart
jumped a few more notches and a shiver of pleasure danced along his nerves, twisting his lips
into a smile. *Well, well, well. Ms. Magdalena
Reyes.* Had Eliot gotten her involved in the project? He sat up, coasting past the last few lawns,
watching her as she smoothed down the brick
red skirt she wore. A casual print T-shirt topped
the skirt. A thick black belt at her waist accen-
tuated her curves. She leaned in, checking her
reflection in the window. A small smile crossed
her lips. Why not? She was drop-dead gorgeous
and she knew it.

He made a quick turn up the sidewalk at the
neighbor's driveway and braked on the sidewalk
by her car. Pulling off his sunglasses, he smiled
at her. "Ms. Reyes. Imagine meeting you here."

He laughed as a scowl replaced her self-satisfied little smile.

"Is this your doing?" she demanded.

"No, ma'am. I had no idea Dr. Rutledge invited you."

"I take it this is your project?" She walked around the car to stand in front of him as he straddled his bike.

He unclipped the helmet and hung it from the handle bars. "No. Actually, it's Dr. Rutledge's. He approached me about it. How'd you get on board?"

"I'm the translator."

He swung a leg over the bike and pushed it, following her up the sidewalk. "So what do you know about the kids out there?"

Instead of the businesslike reply he expected, she gave him a long, speculative look. He held her gaze, trying to read her. She was evaluating him. On what, he wasn't sure, so he just kept his mouth shut and waited.

She turned away with a flounce of heavy dark hair. "Poor. Usually the kids of Mexican migrant workers. Usually more fluent than their parents."

He left the bike parked beside a row of azalea bushes. "So they don't get to be kids very often?"

She stopped on the porch step. The appraising look was back. "Exactly." She took a breath and her lips parted as if she was going to continue, but all he got was her back again.

He followed up the steps to the large front porch, replete with rocking chairs and hanging baskets. An honest-to-God maid wearing a white dress met them at the door and led them to a leather-furniture-filled and book-lined library.

Dr. Rutledge rose from the long couch and walked to them, hands out. "Lena," he said, clasping her hands and kissing her cheeks European-style. One, two, three. "So happy you agreed to help us out." He turned and held a hand out to Matt. "Matt. Thanks for helping us get this going."

"Happy to be here, sir," he replied. How easily the old manners fell back in place. He smiled and shook hands and flirted properly with the two society matrons, Camille Caulet and Alice Dufay. French Huguenot. That he knew that horrified him a little. He was less formal with the woman from St. Toribio, Sister Agatha.

Dr. Rutledge waved a hand at a small love seat. Lena sat first, shooting him an annoyed glance as he sat. He raised his eyebrows at her. *What?*

"Okay. Now that we're all here," Dr. Rutledge said as he sat back down. "First, thank you all for volunteering for this. As you know, I'm one of many physicians who volunteer at St. Toribio. In the last few months, my granddaughter was diagnosed with leukemia and this brought to my attention amazing people like Matt here."

Matt felt a flush cross his cheeks as all eyes

turned to him. Sister Agatha pierced him with an appraising look that made Lena's look like child's play. The gushy, Junior League, sugar-sweet smiles of the society ladies made him want to run, screaming, from the room. The fakeness of them. It was everything he'd rejected of the life his parents had wanted him to live. A quick glance in Lena's direction stopped those thoughts in their tracks. She was smiling at him. A real smile. The flush on his cheeks moved further south.

"It was Matt's work with Clarissa that sparked this idea. You see, he's an art therapist. He works with the kids, having them draw or paint and it gives him insight into how the kids are coping. Then he can let the treatment team know and everyone works together to help kids not only get better, but cope emotionally with what they are going through."

He paused for the society ladies. Matt had already forgotten which one was which. They murmured proper and polite oohs and aahs and blessed his heart for a moment. Sister Agatha looked slightly less suspicious. He tried his bad-boy grin on her and was rewarded with an un-ladylike snort laugh and eye roll from the nun. *Ow!* He rubbed the spot on his thigh where Lena had just popped him with a finger. Popped him hard. He glared at her. She looked at him, her eyes furious. She leaned in.

"Don't flirt with the nun. You'll go to hell for that, Mr. Matthews," she whispered in his ear.

He was going to go to hell for what her hot breath on his neck did to him. He treated her to the same grin. She made a face and shook her head. *Damn.* She was completely immune.

"Anyway," Dr. Rutledge said in a tone that clearly let them know he'd seen their shenanigans. "I'll let Matt talk about that."

Crap. Talk about what? He'd completely lost track of the conversation. "Well... Thanks, Eliot," he stuttered out. He turned to the three women. "I've been in touch with some other art therapists. What we've talked about is doing some education with the volunteers on what red flags to look for in the kids' drawings. Then they can bring concerns to the pediatric team. We'll set up an on-call list where the doctor or nurse-practitioners can call one of us for guidance or help interpreting."

Sister Agatha nodded. "I think this will work. First, we want the playroom to be fun. Fun is in short supply for many of these children. But we do want to be able to spot problems and get the proper help."

Matt leaned forward, forgetting the society ladies, forgetting Lena beside him. "Exactly. Nothing is gained by telling a kid to draw a picture of what is bothering him or her. Stifles the creativity that is necessary for the subconscious to express itself. Making art, for kids, should be fun and without boundaries."

"My women's group from St. Phillips is very eager to contribute to this," Society Lady Number One said. "We can either donate with supplies or money, whichever you would think more appropriate."

Matt looked to Dr. Rutledge. He wasn't going to get involved in the money part of it.

"I think money would be the most appropriate," Dr. Rutledge said. "Perhaps Matt and his fellow artists can come up with a specific list of supplies. That way the kids will have everything they need."

Matt sat back. "I can get that. And, in addition to us sitting down and educating the volunteers, I'm putting together a sort of a manual of things to look for, what certain images might mean. A guidebook to back up the verbal teachings."

"In English? Or will Spanish be available?" Sister Agatha asked. "Our volunteers are, for the most part, bilingual. But some don't read Spanish and some don't read English."

Lena raised her hand. "I guess this is where I come in. I'll be translating the text into Spanish. Actually, my cousin will help with that."

"Excellent," Dr. Rutledge said. "We'll meet again here next week. Matt, you'll have a list of supplies and the names of people who'll do the on-call rotation. Camille and Alice, can you have some figures for the initial setup and perhaps a pledge for a monthly stipend to keep the playroom stocked? And Lena, you can have the manual translated?"

Everyone agreed. Matt got to his feet with not a small amount of gratitude. The quicker he could get out of here, the better. The atmosphere of old money and high society was suffocating. He wanted nothing more than to be out in the fresh air, riding his bike. Free. Lena beat him to Dr. Rutledge. With a quick kiss to the cheek, she escaped. He was about to follow when Society Lady Number Two touched his elbow.

"Are you kin to the Matthews family in Chevy Chase?"

His heart sunk but he kept the polite expression on his face. No sense in lying about it. It'd be found out anyway. "Yes, ma'am," he said.

"Oh. I think my husband had business with your father when we were living in Washington, DC."

He nodded. "DC?" Polite society laugh. "Probably. My father's firm practices almost exclusively in the district."

"Well, you tell your mother Alice Dufay said hello. I'm sure she'll remember. We were in the Junior League together there."

"Yes, ma'am. I will."

He felt a steady gaze on him and turned to see Sister Agatha. Her face was perfectly neutral but her eyes were like lasers burning into him. Were all nuns like this? She stepped to his side and Society Lady moved on to a higher purpose: sucking up to Dr. Rutledge.

"Sister," he said, tipping his head politely.

"I had my doubts about you," she said. "Until you spoke about the children. Your light shone bright at that moment. You are going to do a good thing here."

Warmth filled his heart. "Thank you," he said, and meant it. That's all he was trying to do. Something good in this world. If he was going to leave his mark on this world, he wanted it to be something good. Something of his very own.

When he finally escaped, he was surprised to see Lena's white BMW still parked at the curb. The engine was running and she was in the driver's seat. Talking on her phone. He straddled his bike and adjusted the helmet. Wheeling slowly down the driveway, he turned and pulled to a stop outside her car window. After a moment, the window powered down.

"What?"

He grinned at her. "Have lunch with me."

"No. I have an appointment."

"Ditch it."

He was beginning to like the venomous scowls she threw at him. "No. Don't tell me what to do."

"Aren't you starving? I'm starving. What's more important than food? I'll even pay."

A river of Spanish flowed from the car. He was pretty sure it wasn't complimentary. When it ended, he leaned in closer. "Was that a yes?"

"How do you keep that bike balanced on two wheels with the weight of that ego?"

"I manage."

"Get away from my car or I'll run over you."

"Why are you running away from me?"

"I. Am. Not. Running. I have an appointment. Go paint something."

She slipped on a pair of expensive-looking sunglasses and powered up the window. He grinned as the car pulled smoothly away. *Paint something.* He'd like to paint her. She was a constantly spinning top of a woman. Hard. Soft. Cold. Warm. *Hot.*

His phone buzzed and he fished it out of his shirt pocket. A text from Logan Rutledge. Dinner? Stars? For Clarissa.

Time? he texted back.

Six thirty. I can take an hour or so between dinner crowds.

See you then.

He stashed the phone and began to pedal down Tradd Street. He'd start getting the manual together this afternoon. By evening, he'd be ready for dinner under the stars with a new friend.

CHAPTER NINE

HE SENT A CAR. Lena wasn't sure how she felt about this. The sleek black Mercedes stopped at the curb and a well-dressed young man leaped from the driver's seat to open the rear door for her. She hesitated for a moment before slipping into the backseat. She fished her phone out of her purse. "I'm in a black Mercedes. If I don't text again in ten minutes, call the police," she texted to Sadie.

She sat back, running a hand over the rich leather of the seat. It just seemed sort of controlling. She was perfectly capable of getting to the restaurant by herself. Or he could have picked her up. But sending a car? Her phone dinged.

Be NICE! You promised.

She sent back a middle finger emoji. She was going to be nice if it killed her. *Okay. So let's reframe this. Sending a car. Courtly? Refined. Old-world manners.* She sighed. Wasn't working. He was trying too hard.

The car pulled to a stop outside the restaurant.

Vincente was waiting on the curb. She tried to open the door and get out but he beat her to it. She had no choice but to take his offered hand and let him help her out. Irritation prickled again but she hid it behind a smile.

"Lena," Vincente said, kissing her cheeks. One. Two. Three times. *"Qué hermosa eres."*

Okay. The European cheek thing twice in one day was too much. She widened her smile. "Thank you."

Vincente put his arm around her waist as they turned to the restaurant. "I thought we'd start with a drink on the rooftop bar. The sun should be setting soon and it's a beautiful view."

"Sounds lovely," she said. Her face was going to crack in half with this smile.

And it was lovely. The view from Star's Rooftop Bar was unparalleled in the city. The weather was perfect. The service was perfect. The wine was even better. She needed it once she was face-to-face with Vincente across the table. He was cute, she'd give him that. Much better than the last one. But she had no idea what to say. Small talk was not her forte.

"How is your weekend so far?" he asked.

She shrugged, sipping more wine. "Busy. Having lunch with the family tomorrow so hoping to get some downtime. How about you?"

"Much better now."

She felt her cheeks warm. She looked down

at her hands. Vincente reached over and covered her hand with his.

"Now I've embarrassed you."

They were interrupted by a waiter. "Dr. Perez, your table downstairs is ready. I'll get your drinks down to you."

Grateful for the reprieve, Lena rose and followed the two men down to the restaurant. She sent Sadie a quick "all clear" text. This wasn't going to work. She couldn't do this let's-pretend-we're-not-on-a-blind-date stuff. She sat in the chair he held out for her. *Got to give him points for manners.*

"You didn't embarrass me," she said. "I'm just not very good at small talk."

"I see. I'm not either. Let's try not to engage in it. Let's be honest. We were set up."

"Ambushed."

"Yes."

He held up his wineglass and Lena tapped hers against it. *Okay. Maybe he wasn't so bad.* They paused to listen to the specials.

"Have you been here before?" Lena asked as she scanned the menu. It all looked good. And fattening.

"Yes. The steaks cut like butter. The lobster pasta is divine. I'd highly recommend it. Steak, you can get anywhere."

"Sold," she said, putting the menu down.

The waiter magically appeared at the table. As

Vincente gave their orders, adding an appetizer of deviled eggs, a movement across the room caught her eye. A woman with long, curly, dark red hair turned and scanned the room until her gaze landed on Lena. The woman smiled and gave a half wave.

She seemed familiar. Lena squinted. *Ah. Dr. Rutledge's daughter. What was her name? Laura? Lauren? Something like... Uh-oh.* Sitting across the table from what's-her-name was Matt. Waving at her and grinning like a fool. She looked away, gritting her teeth and wishing with every fiber in her being that she could show him her middle finger. *Freaking frat boy. What a massive, egotistical trust-fund brat.*

"Is there a problem?" Vincente asked.

She shook her head. "No. Sorry. I was thinking about something I need to do tomorrow."

An uncomfortable silence fell. Lena struggled to find something to ask. Something not stupid. "So, what kind of doctoring do you do?"

So much for not stupid. She couldn't concentrate with Matt over there, laughing at her. She peeked. He was saying something to... Logan! That was her name. As if he felt her glance, he looked over at her. That earned her an evil little grin. She looked away again.

"Urology" Vincente answered her question. He shrugged. "Not the sexiest specialty, but profitable. And the schedule is predictable. No hours and hours on call. My father was a surgeon. He was gone so much. I decided when I went into medicine that I would choose a specialty that wouldn't make my wife a medical widow. That I'd be there for my children."

"Oh," she said. *Nice, Lena. Brilliant.* "And you have children?"

"Not yet." He smiled at her. "I believe this is why we are here."

"Oh?" There was that brilliance again.

"Your aunt said you were looking to settle down. Start a family."

She did, did she? Paula was dead. Dead. "Eventually," she managed to stammer out. What was going on with her family? They expected her to just choose someone to marry based solely on his readiness to settle down and start impregnating someone?

"I know this seems strange," he said, closing his hand around her fingers. She fought the urge to pull away. She'd promised Sadie. "But this is how things are done."

"Done?"

"Families arranging a potential match. I'm ready to settle down. You are also. We get to know each other. If we are each pleasing to the other, we can take the next step."

She stared at him. Speechless. *Oh, Aunt Paula*

*was more than dead. She'd kill her, bring her
back to life and kill her again.*

"I'm sure your family didn't put it as bluntly,
but that's what this is. They are picking suitable
husbands for you."

"Lena?"

She looked up with equal parts relief and horror. It was Logan Rutledge with Matt grinning
at her like some evil imp from the whitest corner
of hell. "Yes?"

"I just wanted to say hello. You may not remember…"

"Logan. You're Dr. Rutledge's daughter. I remember."

"Sorry to interrupt. I just wanted to thank you
for your help with getting me set to open my own
shop."

"You're more than welcome. Just another day
in the salt mines."

Logan motioned at Matt. "Do you know…"

"Yes, I have met Mr. Matthews," she said, putting as much ice and fire in her tone as she could.
She was not in the mood for any of his crap tonight. Not when she was being offered up like
a brood cow to strange men by her own family.

"Always a pleasure to see you, Ms. Reyes,"
Matt said. He put his hands on Logan's shoul-
ders. "We should leave these two alone, Logan.
We are intruding. Enjoy your evening."

"Friends of yours?" Vincente asked as they walked away.

Lena finished off her wine. "Business acquaintances."

"Ah. Yes. You have an accounting business?"

Okay. This was too much. She should be recording this for Sadie. Prove that she wasn't mean. "No. I own a financial management company. I make people rich for a living. And I'm very good at it."

"That's admirable," he said. Dismissively. Lena felt her temper pulling hard on its leash. "I'll be honest. I chose a medical profession that would allow me time with my family. And I don't intend to have my children raised by a nanny. I'm looking for someone who will put family and children before business."

She twisted the napkin in her lap between her fisted hands. *Be nice. Be nice. Be nice. Oh, to hell with it.* "And what does that mean? You'd like me to sell my business? Be a stay-at-home mother?"

"If that's what it takes."

"Why don't you quit practicing medicine? Stay home with the kids? I probably make more money than you."

He looked shocked. "That's just not the way things work."

She carefully placed the napkin on the table. "Maybe they don't work that way in your world,

Dr. Perez, but that's how things are going to have to work in mine. I'm sorry I've wasted your time."

She took a deep, satisfied breath as she walked slowly out of the restaurant. She hadn't been mean. She didn't yell. She didn't curse. She'd calmly expressed herself and left before she stabbed his condescending face with a butter knife. That's progress. *But dang, I wanted that lobster pasta.*

She hit the Uber app on her phone and was relieved one was just around the corner. She sent the request and began walking to meet it. She was sure Vincente would come stomping out of the restaurant, outraged Latino machismo on full display. As she climbed into the car, she realized she was exhausted. Tired of all the games. Everything. It was all forced and contrived and she felt like she couldn't let her guard down with anyone.

I wasn't mean, she texted to Sadie.

Why is your date over already? the return text read.

I won't sell my business and stay at home popping out babies.

She got a thumbs-down emoji in response. Whether it was meant for her walking out or for Vincente's old-fashioned idea, she didn't know. All she knew was she wanted to be home with this damn bra off, in her pajamas, ordering Vietnamese food and watching *Supernatural* with her cat. Maybe she'd get a couple more cats. Embrace her spinsterly cat-lady future.

Once on her couch, face scrubbed free of makeup, her hair in a haphazard bun, shoving red-curry beef salad into her mouth with chopsticks, she felt more like herself. She clicked on Netflix and scratched Sass behind the ears. "This is more like it, huh, Sass? You and me. Dean and Sam."

Sass sniffed at the salad and returned to her corner of the couch. Lena's phone vibrated. She glanced down, expecting a Sadie guilt trip. No. *Seriously?* A text from Matt? *That sanctimonious prick. Texting her when she was on a date?* She put the phone on Silence and turned it over so she couldn't see any more messages. She turned the sound up on the TV. Sam and Dean and an endless stream of delivery food. That was all she needed.

CHAPTER TEN

THE NEXT MORNING, she laced up her running shoes. Time to pay for the caloric sins of the previous night. Picking up her phone, she saw the message Matt had sent her last night. I have the materials together for translation. Brunch tomorrow?

She frowned at the phone. Can't, she texted back. Lunch with my family today. She tucked the phone into an armband. It lit up as she did.

Can I come too? Smiley face.

The arrogance of this man. No.

Can I drop them off? Today is best for me.

She hesitated. Hannah, the cousin who had agreed to do the translation, would be at lunch this afternoon. It would solve a lot of juggling to bring it to her today. Ugh. I'm heading out for a run. Text you in about an hour?

That got her a thumbs-up emoji. "I'm heading out, Sass," she called out. Sass, snoozing in a sunbeam, ignored her. "I should have got a dog."

Sass slowly laid one ear back. The feline equivalent to a middle finger.

The morning air held a bit of a nip, reminding her that the perfection of October wasn't going to last much longer. November would usher in the four months of hot again/cold again weather that passed for winter in the South. She walked across the expanse of lawn that was the center of Waterfront Park to the path directly along the harbor. As she stretched her hamstrings, she watched a pod of dolphins working their way out to the ocean. She lifted her face into the strong breeze and smiled. She was a long way from the trailer park.

Best thing about an early run on Sunday was that the tourists were either still in bed or jostling for a spot at brunch at any one of a dozen restaurants. She had the High Battery almost to herself. Once she rounded the curve to the Low Battery, she began to pass other runners. She was going to have to have a talk with her mother and her aunts today. This crazy setting up stuff was going to have to stop.

Tradd Street became problematic as she dodged the cars of the faithful, heading out to Sunday school and church. She felt the familiar tug of Catholic guilt. She'd have to make an appearance in church soon. Give her confession. Take communion. Keep the aunties, and the saints, happy.

She slowed her pace as she finished her loop and reentered the park. Halfway to the Pineapple Fountain, she slowed to a walk, concentrating on getting her breath back and her heart rate down.

"Ms. Reyes, you look lovely this morning."

The hell? She looked up. Matt sat on the low wall just across from the entry to her condominium building. Grinning. She scowled. "I said I would text you when I got home."

"I know. How was your date with the doctor last night? Since you are up so early, I'm guessing he didn't sweep you away for a night of dancing until dawn?"

Lena pressed her lips together against the extremely foul language that wanted to come out. It was bad enough that he'd witnessed the ambush at the hospital, but running into him when he was on a date had been humiliating enough. She wiped sweat off her brow with a forearm. "I could ask the same about your date with Little Miss Debutante."

That grin appeared again. The one that made his blue eyes sparkle with all sorts of delicious mischievousness. She scowled harder, ignoring the stirrings it caused.

"Logan's not a debutante. She ran away from home at seventeen."

"Oh, my mistake. A rebel trust-fund baby."

"Don't be mean. She's a nice person."

"So, y'all gonna throw your trust funds together? Make more little trustafarians?"

He laughed at that barb. "Your slang is so '90s."

"Whatever." She held out a hand. "Give me the papers."

He pulled an envelope from the backpack at his feet. "I thought I'd go over it with you. In case you had questions."

She snatched it from his hand. "I'll give Hannah your number. If *she* has any questions."

"Maybe I should go with you. I could talk to Hannah myself."

"Go. Away."

Lena turned away and stomped down the alley to the building's entrance to the soundtrack of his laughter. *Ay, Dios mío. Ese hombre. Por lo exasperante.* One. What an arrogant prick, inviting himself along. Two. She'd smack a nun before she brought a white boy to the house in the midst of all this Hispanic Bachelor audition crap. Three. *Why are you letting him irritate you?*

BY THE TIME she'd showered, changed and made the almost-one-hour drive to her parents' house, Lena had refocused her irritation where it belonged: her mother and aunts. She was early, which was good. Not too many relatives around to witness the scene she was about to cause. The men were lounging in rockers on the front porch. She greeted them properly, then went inside. All the women were in the kitchen, preparing the meal.

Aunt Paula turned as Lena entered the kitchen. She made a face and turned her back. Apparently, Doctor Man was a crybaby too. What was it with men and their egos? Time to end this insanity.

"Good," she said, putting her purse down. "You're all here. I've something to say."

"Magdalena," her mother began.

The two aunts turned, hands on hips. Fire in their eyes. Lena rustled up some courage. *You are a grown woman. They can't boss you around.* Except they still scared her. She straightened as tall as she could in her three-inch heels. *Should have worn the four-inchers.*

"*Lo siento*, Mamacita," she began. "But enough is enough. No more setups. No more ambushes. No more."

"You embarrassed the family," Paula said, barely waiting for Lena to finish speaking. "Dr. Perez is a highly respected man and you just walked out on him? For shame."

She felt the heat of the flush on her cheeks, but held her head high and made eye contact. "Dr. Perez insulted me. I don't think anyone in this family would tolerate me being treated as nothing more than a potential broodmare."

Ana sighed and wiped her hands on the apron tied around her waist. "Lena," she said in that infuriatingly calm voice. "Listen."

"No," Lena said, feeling like she was six years old again but pressing on. "I don't know why you three decided to start with this foolishness, but stop it. I will find my own man, thank you very much."

Estrella let out a rude snort. "Haven't done so well with that so far."

Clamping her mouth shut, Lena forced herself to count to ten. In the silence, her mother came to her and took her hands. Lena felt her anger crumple with her mother's touch.

"Lena. Listen to me. We didn't mean to upset you. It's just that you've committed yourself to your job and we feel responsible."

"It's not a job, Mother. It's my company. I built it. I'm not apologizing for being proud of that. And I'm not throwing it away to pop out babies for some man who has no respect."

Ana held up a hand. "No. You shouldn't. What I'm trying to say is that we pushed you. From when you were a little girl, we pushed you. To succeed. To be the first to graduate from college. To do better than we did. It's what every family wants for their child."

"I never felt pushed, Momma. I felt supported."

"Good. But now you can relax some. Look what you've done. You've not only lifted yourself from poverty, but you've brought the entire family with you."

"Well, that was the point of it all."

Ana leaned in close, capturing Lena's gaze and holding it. "We're fine now, Lena. We are safe. We have a roof. We have security. We are happy. You don't have to keep pushing yourself. Take a breath. When was the last time you went on vacation?"

Tears stung at Lena's eyes but a swirl of fear stirred her gut. If not for work, what would she have? A fancy car and a cat. She pushed the thought aside. She loved her work. "That's beside the point, Momma. I'm talking about you guys setting me up with all these men. It's humiliating. And if you're going to continue, try to find someone who has his ideas about women in this century and not 1950, okay?"

The three women exchanged guilty glances and Lena felt the irritation rise. They had something planned for today. She held up a hand.

"I don't even want to know. Whatever it is, cancel it. I'm not going to play at this today."

"It's too late for that," Paula said. "And you will show respect under your mother's roof."

Lena glared at her aunt. That she'd paid for said roof meant nothing and she wasn't going to stoop so low as to point that out. The tense silence held.

"Lita," a voice called out as the front door opened.

Jules. Lena swallowed down the fact that Sadie's stepdaughter-to-be was the first to call Ana grandmother.

Jules skidded into the kitchen, her dark eyes lit up to match the huge smile on her face. Sadie followed closely behind.

"Guess what, Lita?"

Lena looked over at Sadie, who was scanning the faces in the room. Sadie reached out and stopped Jules midstep. "Hey, Jules, hold up a minute. I think I saw cousin Sam pulling in behind us. Let's go talk to him and I'll make him tell you about the time he proposed to me when he was fifteen."

"But," Jules protested, "I wanted to show my wedding dress!"

"Later," Sadie said firmly, guiding the girl out of the room.

Great. Just freaking great. Now you're the mean aunt who ruins everything. Jules's crestfallen and bewildered face. The guilt in Sadie's eyes as she backed out of the room was enough. "I can't even deal with this anymore," Lena said. She kicked off her heels and stormed out the back door. Slipping into the yard shoes Ana left on the porch, Lena hurried down the steps and across the lawn.

"Lena. Wait a minute."

She stopped at the sound of her mother's voice, but didn't turn around. A moment later, Ana put her arm around Lena's waist.

"*Hija*, we didn't mean to upset you. But all you do is work and go home. Come here a couple of times a month. We want you to be happy."

"That's not all I do," she said defiantly. "I have dinner with Sadie once a week. I'm working on a project for St. Toribio's. I have a life, Mom."

Ana uttered a swift prayer in Spanish under her breath. "You sound like you are fifteen years old again."

"Treat me like a child, I'm going to act like one. Look. I know what's going on. Sadie's getting married. All my cousins are getting married. I want to meet a guy. I want to get married. I want to have three kids. But I also want the rush, the thrill of falling in love. This fixing-up stuff feels so clinical and cold."

"Only because you make it that way. If you were open to meeting men, you might actually fall in love with one. But you judge every one of them before you even get to know them."

Lena bit back a sarcastic comment. *Trigger.* Her conversation with Sadie had left this subject more than a little sore. Feel vulnerable? Go to attack mode. She drew in a breath. Counted to ten.

"I'm working on this. I know I have trust issues, not with men, but trusting myself. I'm working on it. And y'all throwing strangers at me is not helping at all. Sorry I made the Aunties angry, but I really just need to go cool down."

Ana pulled Lena close for a hug. "Go cool down. We'll talk later."

The narrow path at the back corner of the lawn led through the thick woods. She normally didn't like to come back here because of snakes. And bugs. But none of that bothered her as she marched along the path, trying to sort out her feelings. Anger. Envy. Shame. She should be back there. She shouldn't be feeling like this. But it was nothing but the truth. Her family saw her as a failure in the one thing that was important to them: continuation of the family. Sadie had beat her out in expanding the family. As Paula's and Estrella's sons and daughters were providing them with grandchildren, Ana was waiting patiently for Lena.

The path widened to a clear patch at the edge of a tidal creek. There were camp chairs in a half circle where the men would gather with fishing poles and beer. She checked one over for bugs and sat down, leaning forward with her head in her hands. After all these years, now she was going to encounter sibling rivalry? Sadie was a sister to her. Lena sat up, crossing her arms against her chest. She heard a noise along the path and closed her eyes. She didn't want to talk to anyone.

She cut her eyes to the side as Wyatt slid into a chair beside her without saying anything. The shame of her thoughts burned hotter in his presence. He was a good guy. The kind of guy Sadie deserved. She was truly happy for them.

"You didn't even look," she said. "You could have sat on a snake or something."

"You wouldn't be here if there was a snake. You'd still be running away, screaming."

She felt a smile tug at her lips. If Sadie was the sister of her heart, Wyatt was the big brother she'd always wanted. "True."

They sat in silence for a bit. The marsh grass whispered in the wind. Birds chirped. Squirrels chittered. All the nature stuff that Lena hated. A loud splash from the creek made her jump. Wyatt laughed.

"Probably just a mullet," he said, leaning back and putting his hands behind his head.

"Sounded like an alligator."

Wyatt shrugged. "Could be," he said with a smile.

"I'm so mean."

A long silence. "You can be."

"Gee. Thanks. Pretend to argue with me, huh?" She leaned forward again, elbows propped on her knees and chin in hands. She knew she was pouting. When had Sadie become the golden child and she the screwup? The thought hurt her. Was she that petty?

"It's okay," Wyatt said.

His gentle understanding undid her. Tears

streamed down her cheeks. "I don't want to be like this," she stammered out.

His hand came down on her back. "You aren't like this. You're just feeling like this right now."

"Everything is backward. My family is driving me insane. I just want to go away and eat ice cream until I'm fat."

Wyatt's eyes shifted to the bottom of the chair. "I've been meaning to talk to you about that."

She smacked him on the arm, laughing as she did so. "Shut up. Like I can't see that pudge hanging over your belt there, mister."

Wyatt put a hand over his flat stomach. "Fat and blind is no way to go through life, Lena."

"Dad!"

Wyatt turned to the path. "We're back here, Jules."

"I really am happy for you guys. I am."

"I know. We know. Sadie feels guilty about your family ganging up on you."

"She shouldn't. It's not her fault. I'm being a bad sister right now."

"Nope. You're being a real sister. It's not always sunshine and happiness. Sometimes it's open warfare and jealousy."

"I hope it doesn't come to that."

"But it's okay, Lena. It's a complicated situation. It's normal for you to have complicated feelings about it."

Feelings. Yeah. Added to the disastrous fix-ups, she was about done with feelings. She let her head fall back and looked up at the blue sky. Took in a deep breath, filling her lungs with the acrid tang of pluff mud. "Thanks. I'll be okay. It'll all work out."

"Good. Because Sam brought a buddy home with him. I think he's your date."

"What?" Lena said, drawing the word out into at least six syllables. "This is like torture."

Jules hurried out of the woods with her hands clutched to her chest. "Dad, look what I found!" She held out her hands.

"Wow. That's a big one," Wyatt said.

A creepy-crawly feeling washed over Lena. "What in God's name is that?"

Jules turned to her and held out her loosely clasped hands. Something brown and fat and gross stared out from between the girl's fingers. "It's a toad! Biggest one I've ever seen."

Lena lurched back as the toad was thrust into her face. Wyatt laughed. "What's that saying, Lena? You gotta kiss a lot of toads?"

She bit back the profanity that flickered on the tip of her tongue. "Okay, Jules, just take it…"

The rest was lost. The toad leaped from Jules's hands, straight for her face. An echoing scream bounced back from the creek as Lena ungracefully fell out of the low chair and to the mucky ground. She rose to Jules's and Wyatt's laughter.

"It won't hurt you, Aunt Lena," Jules said.

Lena lifted a hand to scrub at the spot on her forehead where the disgusting thing had actually touched her flesh. "I don't care," she said. "Those things are full of diseases."

"No, they aren't. I learned about them in science class."

Lena twisted and groaned at the sight of her skirt smeared with the dark black mud. "Fine, whatever. I'm going to go burn this skirt now."

She stomped away down the path to the sound of Wyatt telling Jules it was okay. She felt bad if she'd upset Jules—again—but she shuddered. That thing had touched her. And Wyatt was just letting her carry it around? Ugh.

"Aunt Lena!"

She ignored the call from the path. She needed to calm down and get cleaned up. She'd apologize later. And…oh *Jesucristo*. What fresh hell is this? Her cousin Sam stood in the yard, just outside the porch. With him was a man. She slowed her steps. Another fix-up. *At least this one is hot.* The two men watched her approach. Tall. Dark. Drop-dead gorgeous with a body to match. "Aunt Lena!"

She stopped and looked back. Facing Jules was the lesser of two evils at the moment. "It's okay, Jules. I'm sorry I screamed. It just startled me."

As she spoke the words, she noticed with horror that the child had that…that…thing back in her hands.

"I didn't think he'd jump. I'm sorry. I thought I was holding on good enough. He's not slimy and he doesn't have diseases though."

"Okay. I believe you."

Jules held her hands up. "Touch him. You'll see. He's not slimy."

Lena looked down into the little girl's earnest face. She'd rather touch Sass's vomit with her bare hands. But she screwed up her courage and reached out to give the toad a quick tap on the head. Jules smiled up at her.

"See? Told you."

"Okay. You're right. I'm wrong. It's not slimy."

Wyatt walked up behind Jules and put his hands on her shoulders. "Okay, little bit, you've had your fun. Go put Mr. Toad back where you found him and go wash your hands."

Lena turned to find Sam and his hot buddy had walked up behind her. "Lena," he said, motioning with the red Solo cup he held. "This is my buddy Jake. He's a Marine too."

"Hi, buddy Jake. I'd shake hands but I'm covered in toad germs right now." She held her index finger up. Keeping it away from the other fingers.

This was great. Someone in her family drags out a man she might actually be interested in and she's covered in mud and toad slime.

Sam lifted the cup again. "Your mom made sangria."

She looked at the cup. Stuck her contaminated

finger in it. Stirred. "Thanks. That should kill off the toad diseases."

Sam shrugged. "Toads don't have diseases." He lifted the cup and drank.

"Oh my God, you are so disgusting. Excuse me."

As she made her way to the porch, she heard buddy Jake. "Not exactly how you described her, dude."

SHE STOMPED UPSTAIRS to her old bedroom where she kept some clothes for weekend visits. After scouring her hands and forehead with antibacterial soap, she found a pair of jeans and changed out of her muddy skirt. Flopping down on the bed, she wondered how long she could stay up here and ignore Hispanic Bachelor Number Three. Not long, her stomach answered as the smell of tomatoes and cheese drifted up to her. Whatever her faults, Aunt Paula did make a to-die-for lasagna.

Of course, they'd seated her next to Mr. Marine Buddy. Jake. What kind of name was that for a nice Mexican boy? Fine. She'd make an effort.

"So, Jake," she said as she passed him the garlic bread. "What do you do in the Marines?"

"I'm a member of the Marine Expeditionary Unit, ma'am."

She waited. Nothing. "And what does that entail?"

"Lots of training, ma'am."

Sam leaned forward. "The MEU's are the first wave of the force. They go in by sea. A pretty elite group."

Lena nodded. *Okay. No more questions. He can just sit there and be hot.* She locked eyes with Sadie for a moment before having to look away. Problem was they could read each other all too well. *All bod, no brains.* But her family was watching as if the fate of the world depended on the outcome.

She looked around. Glared at her mother. What did they expect? Bring some random stranger home and throw him at her in front of everyone. She looked down the table. "Jules," she called out, "did I hear you found your wedding dress?"

Ha. That did it. The focus shifted from her shameful spinster status to the wedding of the century. And the bride was currently not blushing but promising a painful death with her eyes. Hot Marine dude was Sam's guest. Sam could entertain him. Jules appropriated Wyatt's phone and brought up the pictures of the dress she was going to wear for the wedding.

That carried her for a few minutes. She kept her eyes studiously on the pictures on the phone, avoiding the entire conversation that was occurring between the women of the family. A conversation held entirely with glances, frowns, eyebrow raising and slight shakes of the head.

Every woman in the room knew exactly what was being said and not a man noticed.

After she'd strung out the dress conversation as long as possible, she looked over at Wyatt. Who was in full big-brother mode. He flicked his eyes in Jake's direction, then waggled his eyebrows at Lena. She gave him her most lethal eyebrow raise and glare. He laughed. Until Sadie elbowed him in the side the same moment Lena kicked his shin.

"Ow!" he exclaimed, rubbing his side.

"Behave," Sadie hissed at him.

"You two are the ones beating up on an innocent man."

"Do you three need a children's table?"

Jake leaned closer to her. "Sorry about this. Sam didn't say anything to me. I thought I was just coming for lunch," he whispered.

Maybe he wasn't so bad. Except that he was a good five years younger than she was. And lived in a different city. And was in the military and probably one day from being shipped out to some distant land. She forked a mouthful of lasagna and sighed as she chewed.

She escaped the table when she heard a car pulling into the driveway. That would be Hannah. Going over the package from Matt took up enough time to keep them out on the porch until Estrella opened the door and informed them that Hannah was late for lunch and Lena was being rude. "What'd you do?" Hannah asked as the door shut noisily.

"I've insisted on finding my own husband."

Hannah laughed. "They did the same thing with me. The Parade of Suitably Brown Husbands. Ugh. I'm sorry. It was humiliating."

"If their taste wasn't so horrible, it wouldn't be quite as bad. I've been calling it the Hispanic Bachelor Auditions. How'd you get them to stop?"

"Brought Rick home and told them to stop it."

Lena sat back in the rocker. Hannah's husband was biracial. Half-Hispanic, half–African American. "How'd they take it?"

"Dad was…unhappy. But Mom just said, 'at least he's not white.' And that was that."

"What do they have against white guys?"

Hannah shrugged as she tucked the file in her purse. "My dad. You know how he is. Can't let anything go. And Mom is just as bad. Her default setting for white people is 'shields up.' Come on, I'm starving. Her taste in men is awful, but Aunt Paula's lasagna is to die for."

Lena followed her back inside. She'd known Estrella didn't like white people. She'd been the first to object to her friendship with Sadie so long ago. But her parents weren't like that. She'd never heard either of them say a bad word about anyone really. She ignored Paula's glare and went to the kitchen for a glass of sangria. So, it's something her family did. *Scours the woods for... What did*

Hannah say... The Parade of Suitably Brown Husbands. But they'd accepted Rick. So maybe... Shaking her head, she rejoined the family at the dining room table. *Whatever you are thinking, just stop it right now.*

CHAPTER ELEVEN

MATT UNLOCKED HIS bike from the rack in the hospital's horseshoe driveway and walked it to Ashley Avenue. Straddling the bike, he strapped on his helmet and headed out into traffic. It was early afternoon and traffic wasn't too bad. Some days, he felt like he was tempting the fates riding the bike around downtown. He followed Ashley to the end, looping around Hampton Park and gliding through backstreets to Moe's Crosstown Tavern.

It was a popular, noisy spot most of the time, but this early on a Monday, they had the place almost to themselves. He'd skipped lunch, so he ordered a burger while he waited on the rest of the artists he'd called to show up.

Once they were settled, he quickly outlined the plan for the art room at St. Toribio's. "What I'm thinking is an on-call list, so if someone has a question about some of the art a child creates, they can call us. Even send a picture of it, so we can advise."

"How often is on-call going to be?"

Matt shrugged. "Depends. There are six of us

here now. The clinic is open six days a week. Everyone can claim a day. The more people we get on board, the less calls there'll be."

"Good luck getting the private therapists in on this," one of his fellow hospital therapists joked.

"I've put out calls. We'll see."

He had hoped to get more interest. Everyone at the table worked in a nonprofit of some sort. They were all struggling artists like him, piecing together part-time gigs. Art therapy was the ugly redheaded stepchild of therapy. Not even recognized by insurance, kids who needed it either had parents who couldn't pay for it or ended up in the hospital, where it was part of the treatment team. It was one of the goals he had in starting his own nonprofit. Open to everyone, regardless of income.

"I'll be meeting with the planning committee on Saturday. I'll be updating them on how we'll put together the call days and turning in the list of supplies. You've seen the list. Anything I'm leaving out?"

"Natural elements," one of his Children's Hospital coworkers, Megan, said. "Leaves. Twigs. Things like that."

"Can you get us some for the start-up?"

"When do you need them?"

"I'm assuming that shortly after this meeting, we'll be going out to set up the room. So, a week from Saturday?"

"Not a problem."

Over the next half hour, they refined the supply list and divided up the days for call. Matt had each of them promise to reach out to two other artists with therapy backgrounds. After everyone left, Matt ordered a beer to go with the remains of his burger. His phone vibrated on the table and he glanced down.

Reyes Financial Management. He scooped it up with a smile. "Ms. Reyes. What a pleasure."

"Do you try that cheesy white-boy act on all women? Does it work?"

He laughed. "Hey, Mose. Nope. Just Lena because it annoys her."

"Interesting hobby. Much like waving picnic baskets in front of grizzly bears."

"Grizzly bears are less dangerous, I think."

"Probably."

"What's up?"

"We've got your financial plan together. Can we schedule a time this week for you to come in and look it over? Sign some papers?"

"I would be delighted."

Mose laughed again. "Honey boo-boo. Whatever is running through your little Y-chromosome brain regarding Ms. Reyes ain't gonna happen."

He set a time and ended the call with a smile. Oh, he had all sorts of Y-chromosome thoughts running through his mind. Magdalena Reyes.

Who was she when she was alone in her fancy condo? Stilettos off, hair in a messy ponytail?

He glanced at his watch and signaled the waitress he was done. He had an art class to teach. One of those drink-wine-and-paint things. Not his favorite gig, but the money was good and essentially all he had to do was set up supplies, open wine bottles and make sure no one drove home drunk.

He shot the bike across Rutledge Avenue and cruised along the backstreets to the small, trendy studio on Upper King Street. The area was in the middle stages of gentrification, and the studio, squeezed in between a Turkish restaurant and a pawnshop, was painted a bright, sunny yellow. Something he was sure would never be allowed farther down the peninsula, where the Board of Architectural Review micromanaged even the colors of the house paint.

Just get through this class, he told himself. *Tomorrow you get to hang out with the kids. And Wednesday, you get to see the delightfully maddening Ms. Reyes.*

THURSDAY WAS GOING just fine. No financial crises. No hysterical clients. Quiet. Just Lena, her Bach violin concerto and the orderly progression of numbers. Exactly how she liked it. She treated Chloe and Mose to lunch delivered from her favorite deli. They ate in her office, shoes off, feet up as Lena described the fiasco of the Doctor date. Their laughter and eye rolling at the worst parts made her feel better about the whole thing. Maybe she wasn't insane.

After lunch, she settled into her afternoon routine without the little knot of guilt that had been lodged in her gut since the weekend. The private phone ringtone sounded and she muted the Pandora station. Hannah.

"Hola, chica. Qué pasa?"

"Hey. Just wanted to give you a heads-up. I emailed you the translated documents a little while ago. Some of the technical terms were a little hard so maybe have someone there go over it with whoever wrote it."

"Wow. That was fast. Thank you."

"No problem. I was happy to help. I remember those days of sitting out at St. T's waiting on Poppa to get all the paperwork done for his citizenship. So boring."

"Yeah," Lena said slowly, leaning back in her chair. "It was pretty bleak."

She ended the call but remained slumped back in the chair. She'd done her share of time out at the mission. She had a pediatrician but her mother had worked for that awful Marcus Canard and he kept everyone just under full time so he didn't have to provide health insurance. And they certainly couldn't afford private insurance. And in the years before her father became a citizen, her parents were so paranoid about doing anything to attract the attention of the government they wouldn't apply for Medicaid for her mother.

She'd spent many a day in the waiting room while her parents received health care and while the volunteers helped her father jump through the hoops of citizenship. It was an invaluable aid to the community, but it ran on a lean budget. The television may or may not have been picking up cable. The waiting room might have had a few threadbare magazines that made their way from the elementary schools. And honestly, most of them disappeared into the pockets of the parents who were struggling to learn English.

Maybe she should do more. She sat forward and opened the email to send it to the printer. Shaking her head, she chided herself. *No maybe about it, Lena. You need to do more for the mission.* She could talk to Matt about that. Find out how much he would need per month to keep the room fully stocked. The church ladies could move on to another project on a whim. The money from them wouldn't be forever. She could make forever happen.

Gathering the papers from the printer, she sorted through them, realizing she'd printed both the original and the translation. Fascinated, she began reading the English version. It was a glimpse into the mind of a child. Symbols that crossed all barriers, social, racial, cultural. The size of windows. The size of the child in relation to other people. Cars, trees, flowers, sun, clouds. They all had meaning. She picked up the phone and dialed Matt's number.

And it went straight to voice mail. "Hey, Matt. It's Lena Reyes. I just got the translations from my cousin. Didn't know if you wanted me to email them to you or if you want me to bring a copy of them to Eliot's house on Saturday. Let me know."

She felt a pang of disappointment as she ended the call. Irritation prickled along her nerves and she frowned at herself. *What? Were you looking forward to dealing with a snotty frat boy?* She pushed the thought away and powered up her laptop. She had to wade through all the legalese for transferring Will's accounts to Scotland. The initial forms looked like a nightmare and she'd been tempted to dump it on Mose, who loved details the way Lena loved shoes. But she knew she would be too OCD about it and would end up hanging over Mose's head, annoying her.

After a few hours of figuring out the transfer, she was happy for the interruption of her ringing phone. Glancing down, she saw Matt's name on the screen.

"Hey. Thanks for calling back."

"Anything to hear your lovely voice, Ms. Reyes. I'll save that voice message forever."

"Are you required to be a smart-ass at all times?"

"I can't help it. I was so overwhelmed with joy hearing your dulcet tones."

"Oh. So overwhelmed it took you three hours to call me back?"

"I was working at the hospital. Trust me, the joy I felt at seeing your name was such that I almost left those poor children alone with their paints."

"You are so full of shit."

"But you are smiling and trying not to laugh. I can hear it in your voice."

Lena lifted a hand to her lips. Damn it. She was smiling. She cleared her throat and scowled. "When do you want these papers?"

"Ah, there's the Lena I know. Chewing nails and spitting tacks."

"I don't even know what that means. Is there a big book of frat-boy clichés I know nothing about?"

She found herself smiling again at his laughter. She forced her lips to behave. Trust-fund brat was starting to grow on her. Like a fungus.

"If you've already printed copies, I'll be there tomorrow to sign papers. Mose set it up. I can get it then. That way, Sister Agatha and I can go over the translation on Saturday."

"Oh. Okay."

He laughed again. "You sound so disappointed. I can shoot over there now if you'd like. I don't have to go pour wine for the poor dudes dragged to the drink-and-paint class for another couple of hours."

"How many jobs do you have?" She was taken off guard by his remark.

"Three. Four if you count the freelancing."

"Wow."

"Is that a tone of real admiration I hear in your voice, Ms. Reyes?"

As much as it pained her to say it, she had to. "I respect hustle."

"I'm full of hustle."

"Don't make it dirty."

"Isn't that what spoiled frat boys do?"

"Are you coming today or tomorrow?"

"I can come today."

"Hold on. Let me check with Mose."

She walked to Mose's office. "Hey. Are the papers on the Matthews account ready?"

"Yeah, he's coming in tomorrow. You need to wear your red dress. The one with the V-neck. And a nice bra."

Lena pressed her phone against her stomach and glared at Mose. She gestured at the phone. Mose slapped both hands over her mouth. Not out of regret or horror. But to hold in the laughter.

She went back to her office, slamming the door behind her. Completely horrified, she lifted the phone to her ear. "Yes, the papers are ready."

"I can wait until tomorrow. If you need some wardrobe time. I prefer a pretty lace bra."

"Mention this again and I will fire Mose. Do you want that on your conscience?"

"I suppose not. She could probably take me. But do tell me, Ms. Reyes, why would such a suggestion even occur to the lovely Mose? Dare I hope?"

"No. You do not dare hope. When can you be here?"

"Um. Thirty minutes. Unless I get run over."

After ending the call, she stomped to Mose's office and dropped the manual pages on her desk. "Give these to Frat Boy when he shows up."

Mose rocked back in her chair, not showing even the slightest bit of shame. "You going to hide in your office then?"

Lena crossed her arms against her chest and gave her best boss glare. "No. I will be in my office tending to business. You will explain to our client why you behaved in such an inappropriate manner."

"Trying to get you a man, *boss*. Way you're stomping around here, you could use one."

"That's right. I need a man. Not an overgrown kid coasting along until Granny's money bag opens up."

The teasing grin left Mose's face. She shook her head. "I think you got him pegged all wrong, Lena."

"I don't want him pegged at all. Client. Make him money. That's what we do."

She turned and almost ran into Chloe.

"If you don't want him," Chloe asked, as she freshened her lipstick in the hallway mirror, "can I make a play?"

"No," Lena said. "You treat him the same way you treat Mr. Brightly."

Chloe made a face and Mose groaned from behind her desk. "The only way I treat that old goat is to stay out of hand's reach."

"Exactly," Lena said as she moved to her office doorway. "Keep yourself out of Mr. Matthews's way."

She shut the door and turned up her music.

MATT WAS DISAPPOINTED as he coasted the bike up Dr. Rutledge's driveway Saturday morning. No white BMW at the curb. No lovely Lena. He'd missed seeing her yesterday more than he'd thought. He hoped her retreat to her office was embarrassment over Mose's teasing, not because she really couldn't stand him. It was one of the many things that intrigued him. He couldn't read her. He parked the bike and pulled off the helmet. Running his fingers through his hair to smooth it down, he heard a snort of laughter. A smile jumped to his lips as he turned.

"Getting all pretty for Sister Agatha?" Lena asked.

"The Society Sisters," he shot back. "They've got the deep pockets."

She rolled her eyes. *Damn.* She was perfection on two legs. Her black hair fell thick and straight around her shoulders. The dark yellow dress she wore hinted at her luscious curves. But it was her eyes that captivated him. The darkest brown he'd ever seen and the most expressive. She could turn it off—he'd seen that in her office—but in unguarded moments her expression was in constant flux. Shifting, it seemed, with every thought. Like now. From smart-ass teasing to a dismissive flick of her eyebrows.

"You'd know all about that," she said.

He waited as she walked up the driveway to join him. "Where's the Beamer today?"

"In its parking spot, I hope. You trimmed your beard."

He stroked his chin, secretly thrilled she'd noticed. "Yeah. Was getting a little biblical."

That earned him a smile. "Made me think of Vikings."

He stepped closer. "Do you think of me often, Ms. Reyes?"

She turned away, shaking her head. "You are beyond vain."

Grabbing his backpack, he followed her up the sidewalk. Today was the last meeting before they went out to St. Toribio's to set up the art room. He wondered how he'd get his Lena fixes once this was done.

Everyone was waiting for them. Lena went

straight to a chair and turned stormy eyes in his direction. He suppressed a grin and turned to charm the Society Sisters.

"What do you think, Matt?" Dr. Rutledge asked. "Are we ready to go?"

"Almost," he said as he took a seat and opened the backpack. "Sister, these are the manuals in both English and Spanish. Thank you for that, Lena."

She lifted a hand. "My cousin did it. I scanned through it, but as I said, I'm essentially just verbally fluent."

"I'll read through it," Sister Agatha said.

"Ladies." Matt turned his super bad boy grin on the Society Sisters. He handed them a folder. "Your shopping list."

"Great. Thanks, Matt, for getting all this together," Dr. Rutledge said. "And the call list?"

Matt handed another folder to the doctor. "This is for the next two months. Still working on expanding this list."

"Good. Good. So, are we all going to be ready by next Saturday to meet down at the mission and make this a reality?"

Everyone agreed. One of the Society Sisters raised a hand. "Matt, we had questions about some of the things on the list."

He kept his eye on Lena as he went over the list with the two ladies. She was deep in conversation with Sister Agatha. A quiet conversation.

Lena looked hesitant and a little sad. An expression he would not have expected from her. She always seemed so self-confident. The nun said something that made Lena smile. Realizing that Lena was leaving, he hurriedly said his goodbyes.

"Hey," he called out as he hurried down the porch steps. "Lena. Hold up a minute."

She stopped on the sidewalk and waited for him to catch up. "I can't believe he made us come out for this. All this could have been done with a couple of emails."

"I know. But the old ladies need a reason to leave their houses. Come have lunch with me."

She blinked at him. He found that his heart was beating just a tad faster. He hadn't meant to ask her to lunch. He'd meant to ask her for a ride to the mission next week. But now that the words were out, he hoped she'd say yes.

"You want to go to lunch?" she asked. Her tone was so completely neutral, he had no clue as to whether she was angry, amused, interested.

He shrugged. "I'm hungry. It's almost noon. Seems a fairly reasonable thing to do."

"Why do you want me to go with you?"

"Honestly? You fascinate me."

One perfect black eyebrow arched. "I *fascinate* you? How do I fascinate you, *Biff*?"

He pressed a hand against his heart. "Ow. Biff? That's what I call my brother-in-law."

"Sorry, *Brad*."

"That's what I call my other brother-in-law."

Her dark eyes were steady. *Oh man.* He'd stepped in something. "Okay," he said, holding his hands up. "Poor word choice. I'd just like to get to know you better."

Some of the threat of bodily harm left her eyes. "And why is that?"

"Because you are one of the very few people I've met here so far who doesn't seem to have come out of the debutante cookie cutter, that's why."

That earned him a smile. A wry, twist-of-the-lips smile, but a smile nonetheless. "Brown Dog Deli?"

"Sounds perfect. Want to ride on my handlebars?"

"Sure."

He felt his jaw drop. "Really?"

A rich, warm laugh bubbled out of her. "No. Not really."

She walked back with him as he retrieved his bike. "Come on. It'd be fun. When's the last time you rode on handlebars?"

"Never. And I'm not starting today."

ONCE SETTLED IN the booth at the Brown Dog, Lena's phone rang out with the opening bars of "The Imperial March." Dismissing the call with a quick swipe, she looked up at Matt, who was fishing his phone out of his pocket.

"My mother. Not in the mood for her right now," she said.

His laughter rang out in the small restaurant, drawing the attention of everyone there. "That's my father's ringtone."

"Doubt I'm in the mood for him either."

"Oh? And what are you in the mood for? Right now?"

"Lunch."

That earned her a grin. "What's good here?"

"Everything."

"Hey, Ms. Reyes," the waitress said as she approached the booth. "Weird seeing you in here on a weekend. The usual?"

"Yes, Sally. Thanks."

Sally turned to Matt and the slow up-and-down look she gave him left no doubt as to her intention. "And for you, sir?"

"I'll have what she's having."

"It's a salad in case you're really hungry."

"In that case, I'll have the burger."

"So, why did you really invite me to lunch?" Lena asked once the waitress moved away.

"I told you. You interest me."

"How?"

"Well, let's begin with how you are acting like it's an insult when I say that. Most women would take it as an invitation to tell me their entire life story."

"I'm not most women."

"This is exactly what interests me."

Lena rolled her eyes and took a sip of water. She couldn't figure him out either. Usually by now the Latina-fetish guys had tipped their hand. "Tell me about your family. Where did you move here from?"

"Chevy Chase, Maryland. Land of old money and older people."

"Your family is quite rich, I take it."

"Yes. They are. But I wanted to know about you."

"Nothing to tell. Grew up here. Went to school here. Started my business. And here we are."

"I think there's more to it than that. Where is your family?"

"At home, I guess."

Matt leaned back in the booth. "Oh my God, you are so infuriatingly vague."

"I don't owe you my life story, Mr. Matthews. Just the best of my abilities as your financial manager."

"Is that all this is? Financial management?"

"Of course. Why would you think any differently?"

He leaned forward on his forearms. "I wouldn't use the word *think*. Maybe *hope*?"

She narrowed her eyes. This guy was just too much. "Listen up, frat boy…"

"Okay. Stop. You're going to have to pick another insulting nickname for me, because, believe it or not, Ms. Reyes, I was never in a fraternity."

The little bit of heat in his tone piqued her interest. She'd never heard it before. "Really? Isn't that like required or something?"

"It would have been if I'd just gone along with my parents' plan for my life. But I had my own plans."

"I don't get it."

"I was supposed to go to Harvard, Yale, one of the big-name schools. Become a lawyer. Go work for my father's law firm and end up with a soulless lobbyist job protecting other rich men from having to pay taxes or take responsibility for the damage they do."

"That sounds perfectly charming. I can't imagine why you wouldn't have jumped at the chance."

"When you were in school and college, did you have your family's approval?"

She huffed out a laugh. "Approval? It was an expectation."

Sally arrived with their meals and Lena murmured a thank-you.

Matt nodded as he took a bite of the burger and swallowed. "So it's not too far off base to assume you had your parents' full support."

"You could say that."

Her parents, her grandparents, all the aunts and uncles. She never really had a choice.

"Did they care what you majored in?"

"No. Honestly, college was so outside their experience, I'm not sure at that time they even knew about majors or how it worked."

"My parents cut me off when I said I wanted to study art and art therapy. That's why it took me six years to get my degree."

Lena stared at him. Truly stunned. That a family wouldn't help a child was unfathomable. She couldn't even wrap her mind around it.

"That's…" she said slowly. "That's just not right."

"Tell me about it. Try to get scholarships or grant money when your parents are filthy rich. I've had to pay my way. Got student loans up to my eyeballs."

"But you have money now. With the art sales. Your work is going for some pretty steep prices. I'll have that doubled for you in a year. Maybe less."

He shook his head. "Nope. All that money is for the nonprofit. I'll hold on until I get access to the trust fund. That should pay off my debt."

"Plus some," Lena said.

"That's why I wanted you to take me as a client. People say you work magic."

Shrugging, Lena hid the smile that his words brought. People asked her how she did it but in truth, she didn't know. Instinct. Gut feelings.

Magic. Didn't matter what label she put on it, the results were the same.

"Tell me more about your goals with the non-profit."

"My dream goals or my realistic goals?"

"Your dream."

He wiped his mouth with a napkin. "My dream would be to have art classes restored to every public school. With an art therapy trained teacher. The work at the hospital is amazingly helpful for kids, but there are a lot of kids who need help."

"Such as?"

"When I was doing my training at a public school in Virginia, we discovered one child was being physically abused and another was a victim of sexual abuse. We spotted the signs in the artwork and were able to get the kids out of the environment and get them help."

"Wow. Okay. That sounds amazing. What's your realistic goal?"

"At least getting into schools with at-risk populations. Community centers like we're doing at St. Toribio's."

Lena ate her salad in silence. An idea was beginning to come to her. "What are you doing Wednesday?"

The bad-boy smirk came back and his eyes went from ice blue to smoldering. Reaching out, he touched his fingertips to hers. "Why, Ms. Reyes. Are you asking me out?"

"No, you conceited trustafarian. I have an idea. Can you have dinner with me and a friend of mine?"

"I'll have to check my schedule. Are you sure it's not a date? I'd clear my schedule for that."

"No. You are a client. We will never have a date. We will never have anything more than a polite professional relationship."

Matt's fingers closed lightly around her wrist and turned her hand palm up. Calloused fingertips traced up her inner arm to the elbow and back down. "You say that," he murmured. "But your eyes are saying something much different."

She jerked her arm away, furious at her body's reaction to his touch. "Last guy who tried that was extremely sorry."

"But I'm not that guy." Before she could answer, he looked at his watch. "I've got to go. I'm due at the Children's Hospital in a few minutes."

He pulled his wallet out but Lena waved a hand at him. "We talked business. I can deduct this."

"Thank you. Looking forward to seeing you on Wednesday."

"Go away now, rich boy. You annoy me."

As she finished her salad, she thought about the idea that was forming. This art-therapy stuff would be right up Sadie's alley. She'd love it. And she needed a new charity to put some money in.

The Columbia branch of Sadie's company, the Cleaning Crew, was up and running at full speed way sooner than expected. They were raking in the money.

CHAPTER TWELVE

FINALLY, LENA HAD convinced Sadie to come downtown for their dinner. She loved the little spots in Avondale, but the downtown Charleston food scene was exploding. She settled at a table in one of the new hot spots, The Cabin, and looked around. Nicely blended rustic country and the uptown funky chic Upper King Street was developing. And it had easy parking. Sadie hated parking in town.

The waitress approached her. "Anything while you're waiting for the rest of your party?"

"A bottle of chardonnay."

Scrolling through her messages while she was waiting, her mood darkened. Sadie time was usually the highlight of her week. Sister time. But Sadie was caught up in wedding planning and she'd be a lot happier about helping out with it if her family would just leave well enough alone. All subtlety had been abandoned. Now she was getting pictures and biographies to which she was supposed to respond with yes, no or maybe. Her mother's version of not setting up, but "offering choices." She was working her way through the photos, responding with all nos just out of spite.

"Oh, dear, sweet granny pants in the morning, is that still going on?"

She looked over her shoulder at Sadie. "I'm sorry. What did you just say?"

Sadie slid into a chair, her long hair swinging loose and nearly taking out a wineglass. "I'm trying to quit cussing so much." Sadie snatched Lena's phone and began scrolling through the pictures. "*Dios mío*, Lena, this one. He's hot. Why'd you say no?"

"Because." She took her phone back and placed it facedown on the table. She took a healthy swig of wine.

"Because. You need to stomp a foot and pout with that face you got going on there."

"I have something to talk to you about."

"Good, me too. We're postponing the wedding."

Lena's stomach dropped to her feet. All her irritation at her family disappeared. "What? Why? Is everything okay?"

Sadie smiled and reached out to take Lena's hands. "Yes. Everything is perfect. We just decided December was putting too much pressure on everyone. Especially Jules. She's had so many upheavals in her life over the last year that even though this is a good change, she needs a little breathing room."

Pressing a hand to her chest, Lena let out an audible sigh. "Okay. Makes sense. But don't scare me like that again. Have you told my mother?"

The face Sadie made gave her that answer. "No. I'm too afraid to do it alone. I'm going to have to go to a family lunch with you for backup."

"That's a risky proposition. All the family will be there. You sure you don't just want it to be you and my mom? She's way more understanding than *Las Tias Brujahs*."

"The aunt whats?"

"Witch aunts. I have to find some way to get them off my back before I start saying things I regret."

The waitress returned and took their orders. Sadie sipped on her wine and eyed Lena thoughtfully. "They aren't ungrateful, you know."

"I know," Lena said, slumping down in her chair. "It's just…"

Sadie sat forward. "I know what you think it is. And I know what they think it is."

"So explain it to me please because my brain is so twisted up about this I can't be rational."

"You think it's because I'm getting married." Sadie held up a finger to stop the protestations that Lena was forming. "You think they are thinking 'how did Sadie the hot mess end up with a man before Lena the wonderful princess?' And it's okay, Lena. It's true. I was a screwup. You are the complete package."

Her gut churned at the words. "You're making me sound like a terrible, conceited person."

"You aren't a terrible, conceited person. You are my sister, Lena. I love you. I know you. You know me. We don't tiptoe around each other. It's just the simple truth. You made it perfectly clear you wanted the whole deal. Marriage, kids, happily-ever-after. I never expected to find it but it dropped into my lap. I know that you are happy for me. I know that you already love Wyatt as a brother. I know that you are and always will be the coolest aunt Jules will ever have. It's okay if you aren't one hundred percent rainbows and sunshine about it."

Tears stung at her eyes as she blindly groped for Sadie's hand. The strong squeeze reassured her. Sadie was right. They were more than friends. They were sisters. And they told the truth, even when it was not so pretty and hurt like hell.

"That's you. Now your family. All this 'find Lena a husband' stuff is their way of trying to thank you. To help you out the way you helped the family out. They respect and appreciate all the work you've done for them. Helping you find love and happiness after all your dedication is just their way of trying to pay it back."

"Argh," Lena groaned, dropping her head down into her hands. "I am a terrible, horrible person. That's what my mother said too, but I didn't believe her. I was so mad at them at the time I didn't try to understand."

"Suck it up, buttercup. That's why you keep me around. You are a person in need of a good strong kick in the ass on a frequent basis."

"You've got room to talk, Miss I-don't-need-anything-from-anyone."

Sadie lifted her glass. "To sister truth."

"Sister truth."

They clinked and drank. "Wonder if they have fireball shots here?"

Sadie groaned. "No. I've never been so hungover in my life."

As Lena laughed, Sadie's gaze moved to the door. The cool, professional appraisal Lena saw in her eyes made her glance over her shoulder. Matt was here.

"Holy Viking Raiding Party," Sadie murmured.

"That's Matt. He's joining us."

Lena hadn't planned to hold back that information just to see the look on Sadie's face, but she was now happy that she did. Sadie's gaze swiveled back to Lena. A million questions swirled in her eyes. Lena turned and waved at Matt.

"Are you dating him?" Sadie whispered as he approached.

Lena made a face. *"Un gringo? Con mi familia?"*

Sadie pushed out a chair with her foot as Matt

reached the table. "Matt. Have a seat. I'm Sadie. Would you like a job?"

Matt held out a hand and as Sadie put hers in his, he lifted it for a courtly kiss. "I'm always interested in a job."

"For Pete's sake, sit down and stop being weird," Lena told Matt.

He sat in the chair and pinned her with the twinkle in those blue eyes. "It's called being a gentleman, Ms. Reyes."

Sadie shifted her gaze between the two of them and grinned. Lena gave her a murderous glare that made Sadie cover her mouth.

"He couldn't work for you anyway, Sadie," Lena said prissily. "He'd fail all the testing. He's a hound dog."

Matt put a hand to his chest. "Only for you, my elusive Ms. Reyes."

Sadie did laugh out loud at the outrageous foppery. Lena scowled. "See. He's an unrepentant hound dog."

"And you want to love it but you refuse on general principle," Matt said with a grin. He turned his attention to Sadie. "What sort of job are we talking about?"

"I run a cleaning company."

"All her maids are good-looking guys," Lena explained.

"Okay. I'm flattered. Tell me more."

"She's not giving you a job. I wanted you to tell her about your nonprofit."

Matt looked back at Sadie. "As an interested investor?"

Sadie sipped her wine. "Benefactor is more my style. Lena does my investing for me."

"It's for kids, Sadie. Underprivileged. Poorly served communities. Art therapy."

Sadie held up a finger. "Okay. She had me at kids. Tell me more about how art therapy works."

Lena sat back and watched. It was truly remarkable. As Matt began talking, all pretense fell away. He wasn't the trust-fund kid. He wasn't the smart-ass flirt. He had a real passion for helping kids. Watching Sadie's reaction made her smile. She'd spent her entire life being shipped from foster home to foster home before ending up alone on the street at eighteen. Anything that would help a kid avoid or deal with the emotional scars of a traumatic or chaotic childhood, she would be fully on board.

"Stop," Sadie said after listening for about five minutes. She looked at Lena. "Match whatever he has now. Set up a monthly contribution."

"Seriously?" Matt said. "You're serious?"

"I never joke about children, Matt. Happy to help."

He looked at Lena, his mouth still hanging open. She reached out and pushed up on his bristly chin with a finger. "Yes. She's serious. How much, Sades?"

Sadie shrugged. "Pick a number. That's what I pay you for."

Their food arrived. "Order something," Sadie said. "I'm buying."

"I'd love to, but I've got to go to the wine-and-paint thing. Thank you again, so much for your support, Sadie. It's beyond generous."

Sadie stood as Matt did, ignoring his outstretched hand and giving him a hug. Lena stared at the spectacle. When had Sadie become a hugger?

"Not generous at all," Sadie said. "Just doing what I can, where I can."

After Matt left, Sadie sat down and pinned Lena with a hard stare. She tried to ignore it but when Sadie threw a French fry at her, she put her fork down. "What?"

"What? You dragged a Norse god in here that would make Wyatt look like the backside of a baboon and he's flirting his ass off with you. Clearly very interested, and you ask me 'what?'" She fanned herself with a napkin. "Those eyes! That smirky little grin. I would have clients throwing money at me for him to clean their houses."

Lena shook her head. "All the time you were lusting over Wyatt, all I heard was 'he's an employee, wah wah wah, I don't mess with employees.' Same deal. He's a client. The end. The only reason I asked him here was to meet you because I knew you'd jump at the chance to donate to his nonprofit and you need more tax shelters. This was all business."

"Oh. All business. Uh-huh. You might have the rest of the world fooled, Magdalena Teresa Reyes, but you don't fool me one bit. No, ma'am. You get this look in your eyes when you are contemplating all the dirty, dirty things you'd like to do to a man. And it was right there, clear as if you'd started stripping at the table."

Lena felt her face go hot. Sadie was right. She took a sip of wine and shrugged. "Doesn't matter. Yes, he's hot as homemade sin but that doesn't change the fact that he is a client. I don't sleep with my money. That's a potential disaster. Besides, can you imagine me bringing a white man home in the middle of this Hispanic Bachelor audition crap?"

"Yeah, what's up with that? I didn't think your parents really cared. Several of your cousins have interracial marriages, right?"

"Well. Sort of. Hannah's husband is half-black, half–Puerto Rican. And Tomas's wife is Japanese. No one has married a white person. It's my parents' generation. It's how they think."

"You know what I think? I think if you brought home a great guy who loves you, they won't even care what color he is."

"If you say so, but that guy is the Charles

Beaumont Matthews the freaking Fifth we talked about."

"Shut the front door!" Sadie put down her wineglass and stared, openmouthed, at Lena. "That's him?"

"Trust fund from Granny and everything."

"Huh. I would never have guessed that was him. Didn't pick up a hint of money."

"Yeah, he hides it. Pretends he's turned his back on his family and is making his own way in the world."

Sadie tilted her head and pursed her lips. "Maybe he's not pretending."

"No. Even if he is one hundred percent living by his own means, it's always there. His safety net is wide and soft. He can give up poverty whenever he chooses. It's not the same."

"I don't get it. Safety net?"

"He's playing poor. When we were poor, we *were* poor. There was no relief. There was no way out except hard work. But he has money waiting on him. He knows that once he hits thirty-five, he's rich. Boom. So all this he's doing is play. He doesn't really understand being poor."

"Maybe," Sadie drawled, and sipped her wine. "But the way he's chosen to play poor is quite telling."

"Meaning?"

"He's not just working some job, marking time until his trust fund kicks in. He's actively working to create something that will benefit kids who need help. You have to give him a little credit for that. His heart seems to be in the right place."

Lena snorted. "His heart is in his pants."

"Talk about working hard. You're working so hard to not like him I can see the sweat popping out on your forehead."

"Client."

"Sure. Okay. Keep him around for the eye-candy factor."

CHAPTER THIRTEEN

ST. TORIBIO COMMUNITY CENTER was much the way Lena remembered from her childhood visits. Tucked back off a busy highway on John's Island just south of Charleston, it could pass for an elementary school. Wide spreading branches of live oak trees, many of them centuries old, intermingled and formed an unbroken canopy shading the sidewalks. The low green bushes along the foundation were bare of flowers now, but come spring, they would burst to life with every shade of pink nature could create.

Lena sat in her car, staring at the building. At the families coming and going. Smiling, laughing together. Speaking in Spanish. Openly. Relaxed. St. Toribio's was a safe place. Lena remembered all too well the withering stares and frowns of disapproval when her parents or grandparents spoke Spanish in public. Her stomach twisted into a knot. Why were her hands trembling in her lap? Why did her heartbeat feel strange in her chest?

She drew in a long steady breath and let it out. *You wanted to do this. Come on. Think of how much better these kids will have it.* She climbed out of the car and stopped to pull her long dark hair up into a ponytail. Dress in work clothes, she'd been told. Expect to do some manual labor. So she was in jeans and a T-shirt she'd only worn at home. It bore the words *Viva La Raza* beneath an upraised fist. She didn't wear it in public because, as racially integrated and liberal as Charleston could be, it was still taken as a challenge and she tried to avoid confrontations with complete strangers.

She tugged the shirt down a bit and tried to pretend she hadn't chosen it just to see Matt's reaction. A smile curled her lips for a moment as she began walking to the center's entrance. He didn't realize how much he gave away with a glance or a physical gesture.

It hadn't changed much. The gorgeous exterior led to a building that was run on a very tight budget. The money went into the services they provided so the same rickety, uncomfortable chairs formed rows in the main waiting room. The check-in desk was the same square hole cut in the wall with a well-worn board serving as the desk. But the shabbiness of it did not hinder the happy babble in the waiting room. Here, everyone knew everyone. Everyone was welcome.

"Lena!"

She turned to see Dr. Rutledge down the hall that led to the medical services wing. She waved and headed down to meet him.

"Eliot, good to see you."

"Finally, I get an *Eliot*. Come on in. We're still painting and setting up."

She stepped into the room the center had cleared for the art room. Sister Agatha and one of the Society Sisters were painting walls in a bright sky blue. Matt was assembling a long worktable in the center of the floor. She ignored the flare of heat that speared her when he looked up and grinned at her.

"Paintbrush or screwdriver?" he asked.

His gaze never left hers. She was tempted to take the screwdriver option because it seemed to come with the side benefit of crawling around on the floor with him. But she'd just had a manicure, and painting seemed less likely to get her a broken nail.

"Painting."

That got her sent to Sister Agatha, who quizzed her on her wall-painting skills on a level that had Lena biting her tongue to keep from reminding her that they were painting a playroom wall, not the Sistine Chapel.

Before too long, the walls were done. While they waited for them to dry, Lena helped piece together the benches for the long table. A multi-cubbyholed shelf was assembled and put in place along the back wall. Once all the furniture was assembled and in place, they began to bring in the boxes of supplies. Several of the children in the waiting room got curious and began to follow the procession down the hall.

"How do you say 'come in' in Spanish?" Matt asked her.

Lena told the children to come in. Matt waved them over to where he was taping a long rectangular space along one of the freshly painted walls. "Do you want to help?" he asked the kids. *"Ayudar?"*

"I speak English," one of them, a little girl about eight or nine, said.

"Of course you do, but my Spanish is terrible, so I like to learn," Matt replied with a smile. "My name is Matt. What's yours?"

"Catherine, but my friends call me Cat."

"So, may I call you Cat then?"

"Sure. What do you need help with?"

"I'm going to need you to round up all the kids you can. Then we'll put some paint on your hands. Tell your parents it will wash right off. I want everyone to put their handprints along this stripe, and then print your name below. That way everyone will know you were one of the first to use this playroom. Does that sound like a good idea?"

"Yes. I'll be right back. I know there are some more kids in the big waiting room."

Lena smiled at him as the little girl hurried out of the room. "The handprints are a sweet idea," she said.

"I've got all sorts of sweet ideas, Ms. Reyes."

Her laugh was cut short by a disapproving noise from Sister Agatha. "Magdalena, I believe the ladies need help with the supplies."

Lena snapped a quick salute at the nun. "Yes, ma'am."

MATT WATCHED WITH a lazy smile as Lena walked away to help with the supplies. One of the Society Sisters was wielding a label maker with all the seriousness of a surgeon. *Speaking of which.* Glancing around, he noticed that Dr. Rutledge was no longer in the room. This left him with a bit of a dilemma since the doctor had driven him to the center. Cat came back, leading a line of children.

"Excellent work!" he told her as he waved the kids to gather around. He looked back over at Lena. She was looking a bit stormy. As if she wasn't going to take being bossed around by Label Maker Lady much longer. "Excuse me, Lena? Can you help me with this?"

"Thank you," she muttered under her breath as she joined the group. A couple of the kids giggled.

"Okay, kiddos. We're going to do handprints inside the strips of tape I have on the wall here," Matt began. He laid out newspaper and bowls. "After you put your prints up, go right to the bathroom and wash your hands. When you come

back, we'll write your name underneath. Everyone understand?"

There were a few frowns and whispers. Lena
spoke up in Spanish, presumably repeating what
he'd said. The smiles that followed her explana-
tion made him smile too. Lena looked…differ-
ent, and he was caught up for a moment. Forcing
his attention to pouring the paint into the various
bowls, he tried to figure out what it was.

"Are you Magdalena Reyes?" Cat asked in a
tone of awe.

Matt looked back up. Lena's smile spread, wide
and genuine across her full lips. "Yes, I am."

An excited little ripple ran through the crowd
of children. Matt cut his eyes back to Lena and
gave her a sideways little smile. "You never told
me you were a celebrity."

Lena spread her hands. "Not at all."

It hit him. Relaxed. That's how she was different. Her guard was down. She was at ease here.
He turned away, wishing he could see her like
this more often. *That is the real Lena.* He put the
paint away and brought out some cheap brushes.
They'd do the job. He patted the bench seat beside
him. "Sit down here," he said to Lena as he stood.
"You paint their hands and I'll help them make
the prints."

Lena said something in Spanish and waved
a hand. The children fell into a neat line. "Help

me with the first one," she said to Matt. "So I'll know how much paint to use."

He painted one of Cat's palms and handed the brush to Lena to do the other. He was barely able to keep his response to the touch of her fingertips against his hidden from the watching children. But she saw the heat of it in his eyes. He knew it because she scowled at him. Then she scowled harder when it made him grin.

As Lena painted palms and he helped the kids press their hands against the wall, he watched her on the sly. A few women her age had come in the room and sat along the bench with her. They were chatting happily in Spanish. Again it struck him how unguarded she was in this environment. His curiosity crept even higher. She was such a puzzle.

The line of children ended and the little girl Cat approached him. "You should do your handprints too, Mr. Matt. You built all this stuff for us."

"You think so?"

He got a chorus of agreement and held his hands out, palms up to Lena. When she looked up at him, he was caught off guard by the look in her eyes. Warmth. Desire. She quickly looked down at the bowls of paint.

"What color?" she asked.

"I like green," he said. He held his breath and readied himself for the electric shock of their hands touching. And a good thing he had. The feel of her palm against the back of his hand, the slow brushstrokes across his palm, were inexcusably and inappropriately too erotic for the current situation. He took in a long breath and let it out slowly as she painted his other palm. *There are children watching. Children. Watching.* As he turned with a jerk to pick his spot on the wall, he thought he saw a little smile of triumph from Lena. She knew exactly what she'd done.

"Well then," he announced as he finished pressing his own palms on the wall. "I think Ms. Reyes should have her handprints up here too. What do you think, kids?"

She flushed as she shot him an evil glare, but a smile played across her lips just the same. As the response from the children died down, she looked at Cat. "I think Catherine here should paint my hands. That way, when new children come in, she can show them how to do it and we can keep adding prints."

Putting his hands on his hips, he let out a laugh and shook his head. She thought she'd gotten him, but really, she'd just given herself away. She must be feeling the same sizzle. "I think that's an excellent idea."

WASHING HER HANDS in the ladies' room sink, Lena couldn't look at herself in the spotty and warped mirror. Her intention of getting back at Matt for all his teasing had backfired. She'd felt his body

tighten as she'd run the paintbrush over his palm.
A quick glance at his dilated pupils had flooded
her with lust. She shook her head and grabbed a
wad of paper towels to dry her hands. Checking
her nails, she frowned. Manual labor and French
manicures did not go well together.

Finally meeting her eyes in the mirror, she
pulled back her shoulders and straightened to her
full five feet four inches. Giving herself a stern
look, she raised a pointing finger. "You hormones
just calm the hell down. You are not in charge
here. I am."

Was she flushed? She leaned closer to the mirror. *No. You look fine. Cool as the proverbial cu-
cumber. Get your ass back in there.* Her stomach
quivered. *Go back in there. He's just another man
trying to get in your pants.*

She left the bathroom, ignoring the whisper in
the back of her mind that some parts of her were
quite on board with the pants thing. That made
her angry. Which was the perfect cure for horny.
She pushed open the door to the playroom. Matt
was sitting on the bench with children surround-
ing him on either side of the table. A line of tin
jars holding crayons and colored pencils ran the
length of the table. Her anger melted away as she
looked at the kids. Chattering away in Spanish
and English, smiling while they drew pictures,
happy. She'd been a part of making this.

A calm sense of pride filled her. Matt looked

up and his gaze met hers. The heat flared again immediately and she looked away. This was not good. Not good at all.

"Ms. Lena," Cat called. "Come sit with us. We're making celebration pictures to hang up."

Lena sat on the bench beside the girl. Cat reminded Lena a bit of herself at that age. Wandering between worlds. Being a Spanish-speaking child at home, but also the English-speaking guide for her relatives out in the world. She was used to talking to adults, to being the go-between.

"Yeah?" she asked. "What are you drawing?"

Cat pointed at the items in her picture. "This is the room with the handprints. That's Mr. Matt. That's the doctor man. That's Sister Agatha." Cat looked over her shoulder and leaned close to whisper. "I'm sort of afraid of her."

Lena laughed. "Me too," she whispered back.

A quick blush colored Cat's cheeks and she turned back to her drawing. "That's you, Ms. Lena. My momma told me that if I make good grades at school, I can go to college like you did."

"It's true," Lena said. Suddenly aware that all the children had stopped talking and were listening to her, she hesitated. This was new. Or at least a new generation. The kids she grew up with knew her story. The first, but certainly not the last, college graduate in her family.

"Ms. Lena?" the boy sitting across from her asked hesitantly in Spanish. "Is it true that you are very, very rich now? And that you were poor just like us when you were little?"

Stunned, Lena said nothing for a moment. Until the boy's face grew worried and he began to stammer out an apology. "It's okay," Lena said soothingly in Spanish. "Yes. I worked very hard in school and got good grades. That helped me go to college. After college, I worked very hard also."

She forced a smile but something was squirming in her gut. Something that felt like shame and guilt. She knew she had money. But rich? She'd never felt rich. Was this how the community here saw her now? As a rich woman? Like one of the Society Sisters who ventured out among the poor once in a while to do a good deed so they could go back to brunching and mimosas? She looked down at her ruined manicure. And mani/pedis at the spa? Had she crossed some line and was no longer seen as a member of this community?

Her face felt numb from the fake smile. She slipped an arm around Cat and gave her a little squeeze. "I need to get back home now," she said. "But I'm going to work on a few more projects around here. So I'm sure I'll see you again, okay?"

"Okay. Thank you for helping us today."

All the children echoed Cat's words and Lena rose on shaky legs. She had to get out of here.

"You are all welcome. Just have fun. That's all I want you to do here. Have fun."

She tried not to hurry as she left the room. She needed to get away. She needed to think about this. She needed to talk to her mother. She needed...

"Lena!"

She stopped on the sidewalk but didn't turn around. Exactly what she did not need. Matt chasing her down. Pressing her lips together, she looked back as Matt caught up to her.

"I need a ride home," he said. "Dr. Rutledge ditched me."

She stared at him. More specifically, she stared at the center of his forehead because she didn't trust herself to look in his eyes. Great. Again with exactly what she didn't need: a forty-minute car ride with him.

"I drew a picture for you," he said in that teasing tone that made her both shiver and want to smack him.

Looking down as he unrolled the paper in his hands, she felt her breath catch. She reached for the drawing. It was a pencil sketch of her in partial profile. "That's..." *Amazing* was the word that faltered on her tongue. She already felt off-kilter about the rich comment and to have him do this seemed to have short-circuited her brain.

"Are you okay?" he asked. His voice sounded

genuinely concerned. Lacking any trace of his usual flirtation or smart-assedness.

She shook her head, trying to jump-start her synapses. "Yeah. I just… I need to go."

His hand caught hers as she turned to leave. "Hold up a minute. Are you okay to drive? What's going on? You aren't acting right."

Jerking her hand away, she scowled at him. "I'm fine."

The bad-boy grin was back. Damn him. "Now, there's the Lena I know. Seriously though, can you give me a ride? Everyone is gone."

She turned on her heel and walked away, fishing in her purse for her keys. "You sit in the seat and keep your mouth shut."

And he did. For about a whole minute. Fairly impressive. "Everyone seemed to know you back there," he said.

She kept her eyes on the road and shrugged.

"Not like 'hey, there's Lena' know you, but like 'oh my God, that's Lena Reyes' know you."

That stirred up the guilty shame slime ball in her gut. "You aren't even making sense and I told you to be quiet and I can pull this car over and kick your ass out anytime I feel like it."

"Are you famous or something?"

"Why would I be famous?"

"That's what I'm asking you."

"No. I am not famous. Go back to being quiet."

"But…"

She flicked on the turn signal and began to slow down.

"Okay. I'll be quiet."

He made it about two minutes this time. "That Catherine was something, huh? Reminded me of a little you."

Despite herself, Lena smiled. Then felt the guilt come back. She should be doing more for the kids out there. Time to stop talking about her. "How'd you end up as an art therapist?"

Silence. She glanced over at Matt. He'd pushed the seat back to make room for his long legs, one arm draped on the headrest. He looked relaxed but the jump of a muscle along his jawline gave him away. She'd hit some nerve. Whether she should jump on that nerve or leave it alone was the question.

"You are amazing with the kids," she said. And meant it.

He made an I-heard-your-words sort of noise. His sudden silence intrigued her. She let it go on for a while as she navigated traffic along Savannah Highway. As they approached the bridge into town, he spoke up.

"My place is on Ashley Avenue near the intersection of Bull."

"Okay," she said slowly. "What's with the silent treatment?"

"You told me to be quiet."

"But you weren't. You were annoying me until

I asked about how you became an art therapist. Then you finally shut your mouth." She crossed the bridge and slowed down as they merged on to Calhoun Street.

"It's complicated," he said.

"How you chose to do art therapy for kids is complicated?"

"Yes, Lena. It is." There was a bit of heat in the words. "Life isn't all apple pie and ice cream just because your parents have money, you know."

She turned on Ashley Avenue. Now he was starting to really irritate her. Rich white man whining was the worst. Standing on third base, crying about a foul ball. "Seriously, dude? I asked a simple, polite question and you are throwing attitude at me. Can you walk from here? Because you can get out of my car now."

He pointed up the street. "It's right there. Just pull over."

She brought the car to a stop in front of a house that looked to have been divided into apartments and put it in Park. But he didn't get out. She looked over at him but he was staring out the window.

"I was sick a lot as a kid. Had really bad asthma. Spent a lot of time in the hospital. It's a scary place for kids."

Lena tilted her head, trying to imagine Matt as a sickly young boy. "But your parents..." she started.

He let out a harsh, angry bark of laughter and shook his head. "Oh no. They had much more important things to do than hang out in a hospital." He shifted in the seat to look at her.

"They just left you? All alone? In the hospital?" She could barely wrap her mind around it.

"When I was in art school, I took a class on art therapy because a girl I wanted to date was taking it. Never did get that date, but it just sort of clicked on something in me and I knew that's what I wanted to do."

Lena blinked as she took in his words. She could understand that. She'd taken her first finance class as a means to learn how to deal with student loan debt and had that same click. Perhaps not quite as humanitarian as helping kids, but she had helped her family and Sadie. And by helping them, they had helped many others.

"That's amazing," she said softly.

The bad-boy grin appeared. "Not as amazing as the story of the famous Lena Reyes."

"Why do you do that?" she snapped.

"Do what?"

"Every time you get real with me, let me see behind the smart-ass persona, you have to ruin it by being all annoying."

"Maybe I really want to know."

"Maybe you should get out of my car. I don't know why I even put up with you."

He didn't get out. He did shift closer and run

a finger along her jawline. She jerked her head away. "Lena. Look at me."

She reluctantly turned to look. He was too close. Too everything. Those eyes. How could such icy blue be so hot?

"This," he said as he took her hand. "This feeling right here is why you put up with me."

He traced his fingers lightly across her palm. The sensation bypassed her brain, going straight from her palm to the very core of her. She could hear her breath coming faster.

She started to say he was crazy. She started to tell him to get out. But his lips were on hers and her hands were in his hair and oh dear God the man could kiss. He pulled her even closer, deepening the kiss. She kissed him back, ignoring the alarms from some distant, rational part of herself.

Right now, she cared for nothing except for how good this felt. How right this felt.

You are kissing a client in broad daylight in public! That thought finally rose above the howls of her libido and she turned her head away. Lifting a shaking hand, she covered her mouth and looked back at him. The smirk was gone. He looked as shell-shocked as she felt.

"Lena," he began.

She shook her head. "No. This didn't happen. Mistake. Never again. Just go on. Get out. Go home."

"I can't do that."

"Yes, you can. This was a horrible mistake, Matt, okay? You are my client. This is beyond unprofessional."

"You're allowed to be human, Lena."

"No," she said quietly, "I'm not."

She turned her head to the window and started the engine. After a moment, he got out of the car.

CHAPTER FOURTEEN

WHEN SHE PULLED into her assigned parking space, she saw he'd left the drawing in the front seat. She caught it between her thumb and index finger and rested it against the steering wheel. It was a very rough sketch, but good enough that anyone would know it was her. A few light lines made up her hair and the shape of her face. The curve of her lips and cheek were more defined. But it was the eyes that he'd focused on. What had she been doing or thinking to have the warmth she saw in the eyes he'd sketched?

Ugh. Dear Jesus. She'd screwed up. Royally. What had she been thinking? *You weren't thinking—that's the whole problem. He gets too close and your brain just shuts down.* She frowned at the sketch and resisted the urge to crumple it into a ball. A long sigh escaped her. She rolled it up and tucked it carefully into her purse.

Kicking off her shoes as soon as she got inside, she scooped up Sass and draped her over a shoulder, the only way Sass would accept being held. She rested her cheek against the sleek orange-red fur and was rewarded with a purr.

"You love me, right, Sass? Even though I manage to screw up everything?"

She took the increase in purr volume as agreement and not an attempt to manipulate an early dinner offering. She let Sass jump off her shoulder onto the couch as she passed through to her bedroom. After taking her bra off with her *La Raza* shirt still on, a skill she never tired of performing, she shimmied into her favorite leggings and went to wash the makeup off her face.

At the mirror, she leaned in close. There was a mark on her chin. She touched it with a hesitant finger. Beard burn. She rifled back through her memory and couldn't come up with another kiss that ever matched the heat she'd felt with Matt.

"You have lost your ever-loving mind, *chica*," she told her reflection.

She washed her face and padded barefoot into the kitchen. Sass came in, weaving between her feet. "Sass. If you kill me, you will starve to death. You know this, right?" She looked at the clock. Almost four. Close enough. "How about this, Sass? You get early dinner if I get early wine time?" Sass meowed. *Perfect. We're all in agreement.*

Two glasses of wine in, her brain helpfully reminded her of the odd feeling she'd felt at the center. The way the kids had been looking at her. That they even knew who she was. She smoothed a hand down her T-shirt. *La Raza.* When had she become that person? Some myth whispered about? Held up as an example by parents? She could easily name at least eight cousins who had advance college degrees. Why her?

The shame wriggled around again, making her skin burn. *Because you're rich.* She sipped the wine. Remembered the look of awe on the boy's face as he'd asked if it were true. She wasn't ashamed of being rich. She was ashamed because while she hadn't forgotten her family, she had forgotten where she came from.

She was sashaying her ass around town, living large in her condo on the waterfront, driving her BMW and making rich white men even richer. Pretending that the color of her skin didn't matter. But it did. If she thought otherwise, all she had to do was remember the time she wore a black dress to an event and was mistaken for the help. She had to consciously govern her expressions so she didn't look angry or threatening. She had to smile and laugh and politely dodge the hot-Latina-momma comments. Hell, she couldn't go to the grocery store in jeans and a T-shirt without seeing the looks. God forbid someone hear her speaking Spanish to a family member in public.

She wasn't a part of the society she moved through. She was merely tolerated because she was useful. On some level, she always knew this but it hadn't bothered her because she was using them just as well. Using them to build her future.

Using them to build the foundation of stability for herself and her family. She'd finally reached that comfortable place. Now what?

"You need to go back," she said out loud. "There's more to be done than putting some coloring books in a room."

She set the wineglass down and stood up so suddenly that Sass scurried off the couch and ran for the bed. "Knock it off, Drama Queen," Lena said irritably. She grabbed a legal pad and a pen from her desk and returned to the couch.

She curled up and balanced the pad on her legs. Uncapping the pen, she stared down at the blank page. *What was the hardest?* She wrote "What I Wished I'd Known" along the top of the page.

How to apply for financial aid and scholarships. Top of the class doesn't mean ready for college if you are in a poor school district. About SAT prep classes. How to write an essay for college applications. She reached for the wineglass and sipped. Walking into her first college class had been the scariest thing she'd ever done. The weight of the expectations of the entire family rode on her shoulders. She added "how to find tutors in college" to the list.

She'd been at the top of every class through elementary school up to the moment she gave the valedictorian speech at high school graduation. Her first freshman semester had yielded a GPA that barely let her hold on to her scholarships. She'd been running scared ever since. She felt her heartbeat speed up. Was that it? The car, the condo? The Broad Street office? Was she still running scared, trying to prove she belonged?

Pushing thoughts of herself aside, she focused on the list. She had contacts. She could make this work. Maybe through the Charleston Center for Women. She scribbled a few names by each of the items and tossed the notebook on the coffee table. Monday. She'd take care of this on Monday. Brushing orange cat hair off her yoga pants, she frowned. The weight that had settled on her chest at the center still remained.

"What?" she asked out loud, dropping her head back to stare at the ceiling. *What was this feeling that wouldn't go away? Guilt?* No, it wasn't guilt. It was hotter than guilt. *Shame. Is that what this is? You should have gone back sooner. You should have always been reaching back.*

She stood and walked to the bedroom. Enough of this. "I'm going to the gym, Sass."

SHE HATED HER GYM. It was too much of a show-up-and-look-pretty kind of place, but it was the only one on the peninsula where she didn't get testosterone poisoning from the lunkheads. She didn't show up to look. She showed up to sweat. She showed up when the weather was too hot or too wet for running outside. When it was dark and she needed to outrun her thoughts. Plugging earbuds in, she cranked up Green Day and started pounding out the miles. As she ran on the treadmill, she kept her eyes focused on the blank TV screen in front of her. Earbuds in, no eye contact kept the men away. She'd had enough of men today. *Man. You had enough of a man today.* She increased her pace. *If you can think, you aren't running fast enough.*

A motion from the free-weights side of the room caught her attention. She flicked her eyes in that direction and felt her stomach drop. *Matt. What was he doing here?* He was spotting for another guy. *Lunkheads.* She forced her focus back to the blank screen but her gaze kept drifting. His friend was cute and certainly well acquainted with the weight machines. They must be here to be looked at. Matt moved to the pull-up bar and began a series of chin-ups. The flex of muscle and the way his tank top revealed brief glimpses of his chest filled her with a sudden lust so strong she almost lost her pacing. She shook her head and slowed the pace a bit as she struggled to regain her focus. But the memory of his mouth on hers came raging back. Along with all the feelings he'd stirred.

Hell. She might as well just go home. This was doing nothing to help her outrun her own thoughts. In fact, it was making it worse. She reached out, intending to hit the cooldown button but stopped as another movement caught her

eye. *Oh, here we go.* A couple of twenty something look-at-us-in-our-two-hundred-dollar-yoga-
outfits women came out of the classroom and
sauntered in the direction of the weight room,
Matt and his friend. Not even going to be subtle
about it. She slowed her pace to watch.

There was a lot of hair flipping and body language going on. Matt's friend was into it. He was
smiling and talking. Laughing. But Matt not so
much. That was interesting. She would have put
money on him hound dogging on such easy prey.
He wasn't rude to them, but he remained seated
on the bench, only made brief eye contact and his
smile was obviously strained politeness at best.
Lena felt a smile touch her lips and a strange sensation in her chest. It felt like…*smugness. Oh my
God. I've turned into one of them.*

She steadied herself and hit the stop button.
Her heart pounded as she straddled the track,
her breath a ragged echo almost lost in the music
that pounded in her ears. *What the hell was that?*
That sense of superiority because the man that
wouldn't flirt with another woman had kissed her
earlier? She didn't play that game. Men weren't
a competitive sport. Head down, she focused on
getting her breathing under control. This day had
certainly gone to shit.

A hand entered her peripheral vision. Matt.
She looked up at his wave. Gave him her best
leave-me-alone glare. He grinned and lifted his

phone. A moment later, the message appeared on her phone's screen.

Lunch. Tomorrow.

She shook her head. No. A moment later, her screen lit up again.

I'll be at the Pineapple Fountain. 1 p.m.

Again she shook her head. He smiled at her. Then he did that thing that guys do. Pointed at his eyes and then at her. *I see you.* The scowl that began to form fell away as he formed his hands in the shape of a heart and pointed at her again. Staring after him as he walked away, she frowned. What on earth? *I see your heart? What was that supposed to mean?*

She grabbed her phone as he left the gym.

I said no.

She got a smiley face back. Damn that man. She suppressed the urge to send him that middle-finger GIF she'd saved the other day. She climbed off the treadmill and wiped her forehead on her sleeve. So infuriating. *Lunch. Tomorrow.* Not even a question mark. Well, he could have lunch all by himself there at the fountain. *Hope it rains on him too.*

"Am I a bad person?"

"No. Why would you even think that?"

Lena swung her legs up on the couch. A long hot shower had done nothing to ease her mind. So she'd sought out her most avid cheerleader. Her mother.

"I was at St. Toribio's today," she said as she rubbed a hand across her eyes. "Now I'm jumbled."

Her mother's voice, sweet and low, murmured in lilting Spanish. "No, my heart. You are not a bad person."

"Then why do I feel like I am?" Lena asked in Spanish. The language that once separated her family from America now seemed like a secret refuge.

"What happened?"

"I don't know. The kids there. They knew me. And treated me like I used to treat the rich white people who came offering charity."

"That's a child's interpretation, Magdalena. The color of a person's skin, the contents of their wallet, those are not the things that define a person."

"You know what I mean."

"No. I don't."

"Why did they all know who I am? Why me? Why not Hannah? Or Sam? Or anyone else in the family? Why me?"

"You know why. You're the most successful. You're the one people look to for what is possible."

A knot twisted in her throat as she fumbled for the wineglass. Her body was already aching from the exertion of the labors of that morning and the half marathon she'd done on the treadmill. Now her heart was aching.

"Mamacita," she whispered. "I feel like I've let everyone down."

Between the sob she pushed down and her mother's pause, Lena saw the truth. She *had* let the community down. She'd hidden her past and her culture so she could move more easily through the white world. Ignored or downplayed her browness. But she'd had to. To survive, to thrive.

"Lena." Her mother's voice soothed her. "You've set a good example. What you're feeling now? Maybe it's just the Lord's way of telling you it's time to give back."

Lena rolled her eyes. The Lord and she hadn't been on speaking terms for quite a while. But she couldn't deny the truth of her mother's words. "I think I'm late on doing that."

"Magdalena. Listen to me. There isn't one of us who doesn't understand the tightrope you've been walking. We knew once you got your balance, you'd turn back to us."

Is that what it was? She'd found her balance? She'd never felt more off balance than she did now. Those kids looking at her. Sadie getting married. Her family pressuring her to find a suitable husband. Matt. She couldn't even think about it all at once without feeling her entire life was out of control. Like Alice down the rabbit hole.

"I'm working on it, Momma," she whispered.

"I know you are. Are you coming to lunch tomorrow?"

Ah. Was she? If she went, she was hiding from Matt and his text demand. If not, then what? Was she going to go out to the fountain at one and let him have the upper hand? She was so tired of thinking.

"I don't think so, Momma. I'm so tired."

"You work too hard. Rest. I love you."

"I love you too, Momma."

Tired. Yes, she was tired. She ended the call and looked at the time. Too late to call Sadie. Not that Sadie would mind but Lena was tired of thinking. She polished off the wine and got to her feet to pour the last of the bottle into the empty glass. Grabbing the container of organic catnip from the top of the fridge, she shook it, bringing Sass running.

"Wanna get slightly toasted, Sass? Yeah?"

She shook some catnip right onto the coffee table. Screw the mess. Raising her wineglass as Sass rolled in the herb, she shook her head. *You've become a crazy cat lady. Hanging out, getting drunk with your cat on a Saturday night. Might as well go get another cat or ten.*

CHAPTER FIFTEEN

MATT LOOKED OVER the various containers on the tiny kitchen counter. Hummus. Pita points. Kalamata olives. Fresh mozzarella cubes.

"Dude. You're going all out, huh?"

He looked up at Dylan and shrugged. "Just the basics." He reached into the fridge and removed a bottle of wine. "Red or white?"

"You're asking me? I'd go with PBR. Is this for that hot little Latina honey from the gym last night?"

Matt shook his head. "Aw, man. Don't do that."

"Do what?"

"That Latina crap. Her name is Lena."

Dylan raised his hands, palms up. "Okay. Got it."

Turning his attention to fitting all the containers in his backpack, Matt held his tongue. Dylan was a nice guy. He lived in the apartment on the ground floor and had got Matt out of the roach-infested shack he'd first rented. But guys were guys. He couldn't stop others from spewing ignorant nonsense, but he could not allow it in his presence.

"So," Dylan asked, opening a container and stealing a chunk of cheese. "You really got a thing for her, huh? Going for the full romantic picnic?"

A grin crossed his face and Matt shook his head. "She's skittish. I'm just trying to get her to even think about me."

"You have women falling at your feet. Those two last night? This one doesn't want you, move on."

"Maybe that's why I like her. Because she won't fall at my feet."

"Don't even tell me you're falling for the hard-to-get routine."

"That's the whole thing," Matt said, slipping the bulging backpack on his shoulders. "She's not playing a game."

"Then she's not interested. Move on."

"*I'm* interested."

Dylan followed him down the stairs. "I'm telling you, man, it's not worth it. If a chick's not into you, don't waste time chasing her down."

Straddling his bike, Matt strapped his helmet on. "I like to run," he said.

As he navigated the backstreets to the harbor, he wondered if Lena would show up. Probably not. But he hoped she would.

He swerved to miss a car backing out of a driveway. The little bits of her he'd seen in the moments when her guard was down only made his curiosity stronger. Behind the strong, cool exterior she showed the world was a woman of great warmth and love. Why did she hide that? What would it take to get her to let down those walls?

And that kiss. He hadn't planned it. He'd simply been unable to leave that car without touching her. And that thing with the paintbrush. She'd been playing with him. She was attracted to him. Her response to the kiss was all the proof he needed. But then the walls had gone back up. Twice as high.

As he reached Waterfront Park, he coasted to a stop and walked the bike along the path to the Pineapple Fountain. His heart rate picked up a little as he approached. *Don't get your hopes up, man. She's not going to show.* His doubt only added to his excitement. How long had it been since he'd felt this way?

Of course she wasn't waiting on him. Checking the time, he saw he was a few minutes early. *Okay, Matt. It's showtime.* Feeling a bit self-conscious, he spread out the blanket and sat down. As he unpacked the picnic, he found himself glancing up at every footstep along the path. He hadn't fully realized how much he wanted her to join him until now. Yeah, he'd probably been a bit too frat boy with his text. He opened the containers and put the bottle of wine down in the center of them. Took a picture. Sent her a text with it attached.

Ms. Reyes, you are cordially invited to join me in a picnic lunch. RSVP.

Nothing. He put the lids back on the containers and lay back on the blanket to watch the clouds drift by. *She's not coming. Probably not even home. You're out here looking like a stood-up idiot.* He smiled up at the sky. Had he ever been stood up before? He lifted his phone.

I have mozzarella. Fresh.

Five minutes later there was still no answer. Maybe she really wasn't even home. He took a picture of the wine and sent that.

Chardonnay.

He set his alarm to go off in thirty minutes and stretched out on the blanket. If she hadn't responded or come out by then, he'd leave. The sun was warm on his face and he closed his eyes. The park was full of sound. People talking. Bits of music. The sound of the water splashing in the fountain. The sound of children playing.

"You got a corkscrew?"

He opened his eyes and smiled up at a scowling Lena. He looked at his phone as he sat up. "Five minutes," he said, showing her the counting-down clock. "I was going to leave."

She sat primly on the corner of the blanket. "Nice to know you have standards."

He took the corkscrew out of his backpack and began opening the bottle. "Thanks for joining me."

"I only came for the wine," she said as she picked through the containers. "And the cheese." She popped a chunk in her mouth.

"Wine and cheese," he said pouring wine into a red Solo cup. He handed it to her. "Duly noted."

"Hummus! And real pita points, not the chips. Why, Mr. Matthews, you do know how to put on a picnic."

He felt a weight he hadn't know existed lift from his chest. He'd made her happy. "But wait, there's more!"

He pretended to not notice her watching him. He felt like a single wrong word or movement would send her storming back to her apartment in a fury. He kept the conversation light and inane. Weather. Mild hospital gossip.

"Why are we here?"

He looked at her. Her dark brown eyes looked directly at him. Into him. Through him. But he couldn't see into her. And he wanted to. How he wanted to. He wanted to get behind that wall. Feel the heat he'd felt when she was in his arms. The care he'd seen in her eyes when she was talking to the children. The warmth and strength he'd felt in her family.

"I wanted to talk about yesterday."

"Yesterday was a mistake. I thought we'd agreed on that." She sat up and began matching lids to containers.

"I don't think it was a mistake."

Her hands stilled and she turned to look at him. "Matt. We can't do this. I'm your financial manager. We cannot, we will not, have a personal relationship. Besides, I'm not in the market for a relationship right now."

He let that last remark go unchallenged. Her family certainly seemed to think she was in the market. "Give my account to Mose, then."

"No. As your financial manager, I can't give you bad advice. I'm the best there is. For me to tell you to go with a brand-new, untested manager would be bad advice."

He grinned at the tone of her voice. Completely professional. "I don't think you believe that. I think Mose would do just fine with my account."

"And what makes you qualified to assess that situation?"

He sat up and leaned closer to her. "Because, Lena, you wouldn't hire anyone you didn't feel could at least match your skills. And I'll even go a little further and say you're the type who is hoping her mentee outshines her one day."

"That's true," she said with a frown. "But it

still doesn't warrant turning your account over to her just because you want to get in my pants."

"And there's the problem, Lena," he said, reaching out to take her hand in his. "I don't want into your pants. I want into your life."

She looked down at his hand but didn't pull away. A good sign. There was no small amount of heat—the bad kind—when she looked up at him. A bad sign. "Does this twaddle work with the sorority girls?"

He let go of her hand. "I'm serious. I don't know the words. I'm a painter, not a poet. I thought I made my feelings clear when I gave you that sketch. I want to know the woman in that drawing. And I want to know this woman who is glaring at me right now. And I want to know the cool aunt who sends her cousins to college. You're like a kaleidoscope, Lena. Every time I look at you, I see something different. I want to know it all."

Her glare softened, but she was still shaking her head. "No, Matt. I can't. First, because of our current business relationship. Second, because it's just not the right time for me to…"

Her words drifted off and the look she gave him was one he'd never have expected to see from her: defeated. He couldn't stand to see it in her eyes. He shrugged and gave her his grin.

"I understand. Had to try though. I've never met a woman like you before, Lena Reyes."

"I can give you some recommendations if you don't feel comfortable continuing with my company."

He began to pack away the picnic leftovers. "No. That's not necessary. I trust you. One hundred percent."

"I'm sorry, Matt."

"Me too."

CHAPTER SIXTEEN

"WHAT DO YOU THINK, Sass? Vietnamese? Thai? Deli?"

Lena scrolled through the list of delivery options on her phone. Sass sat on the coffee table, her head tilted as if she were pondering the decision.

"Sushi?"

Sass meowed at that one and Lena laughed. *Oh dear God, you're sharing jokes with your cat.* Dropping the phone, she brought her hands to cover her face. *What are you doing?* She tried to think of all the reasons she had to turn Matt down this afternoon. Here, now, in the late evening of another Sunday night alone, all her reasons seemed stupid and shallow. She wanted to call Sadie but knew that she was probably tucking Jules into bed and eyeing some grown-up time with Wyatt. Family time.

She sat up and shook her head. "The thing is, Sass," she said aloud, "Matt is a temptation. I'm done with that. I'm done with going through men like Sadie goes through jelly beans. I had my fun. But it's time to grow up. It's time to get serious."

Yes. Yes. But still. Why did her body remember every sensation stirred up by his kiss? The feel of his mouth on hers. His tongue against hers. The scratch of his beard? The heat of his hands on her back? She let her head drop back. *Okay. It was amazing. But you aren't doing the sex-for-sex's-sake stuff anymore.*

Problem was she wanted him. Wanted to feel his hands on her. Wanted to see what was under that frat-boy facade. Wanted to either shock him or be surprised by him. Wanted to see what the heat of that kiss could ignite.

She left-swiped on her phone. She had a long list of restaurants that delivered. A testament to her success. She didn't have time to cook. She could afford takeout every night. *I am an independent woman.* Problem was she wasn't hungry.

Sliding open the door to the balcony, she learned autumn was finally showing up. Cold air cooled her skin and she took in a deep breath and let it out in a frosty mist. Sass peeked out the door and ran back in to the warmth. Leaning on the balcony railing, Lena looked out over the harbor. Through the oak trees, she could see the lights of the Cooper River Bridge and the Yorktown Memorial Museum. A brightly lit sailboat made its way from the harbor up the Cooper River. Loud voices echoed off the walls from the fountain where college kids had gathered to drink and make out.

And she was alone.

No, no, no, you don't do this anymore.

She went back inside and closed the door. Slowly. Deliberately. Making sure Sass was inside. Tomorrow, she would be Lena Reyes, the professional. The perfect one. The role model. Whatever other labels people wanted to attach to her. Tonight, she just wanted to be warm.

"Lena."

Her denial of her actions crumbled as she faced him. He'd opened the door to her quiet knock, despite her hope that he wouldn't. And now, face-to-face with him, she thought she would have doubts, come to her senses. But no. The sight of him in a pair of hiking shorts, shirtless, barefoot, with a palette in hand, the smell of oil paint in the air only inflamed her further. He stepped back as she crossed the threshold.

"What are you doing here?"

"What do you see in my heart?" she asked.

He seemed bigger. More masculine. Maybe it was his bare chest. Wide. Muscled. Covered in light brown hair that her fingers wanted to touch. Silky or crisp? She loved crisp chest hair, the feel of it across her breasts. She locked her gaze with his and those icy blue eyes heated up. He stepped back and shut the door.

"What do I see?" he echoed.

"Yes."

He held out a hand and she took it. He pulled her into the small, sparsely furnished room. There was a table along the wall. Next to it was an easel with a canvas. A landscape, she noted. Placing the palette on the table, he let go of her hand. She watched as he dipped the index fingers of each hand into the paint. Dark red paint.

Her head pounded. Part of her was screaming that this was a mistake. To stop this madness. But part of her was mesmerized by the look in his eyes. Hot. Wild. He lifted his paint-smeared fingers and placed them on either side of her nose, swiping slow streaks to her cheeks.

"I see strength."

The heat his touch generated clashed with the wet chill of the paint. He put a hand under her chin and tilted her face up. His finger went to the palette again. He reached up, placing a fingertip smeared with a brilliant blue in the center of her forehead and smeared a line down to the tip of her nose.

"I see loyalty."

"Matt…"

"Shhhh." He reached one more time for the palette. This time his fingertip found a bright pink. His finger touched her chin immediately below her bottom lip, drawing a gasp from her that grew to a low moan as his finger traced the paint down her chin, throat and to the cleft of her breasts.

"Compassion," he finished. "That's what I see in your heart. A fighter. Fighting for those she loves."

His hands closed in on either side of her face and he kissed her. Slowly, briefly touching his lips to hers as their breath intermingled for a moment before he brought his mouth down on hers, firmly, confidently. Drawing her into his arms. The heat of him against her was almost unbearable and yet she hooked her arms around his shoulders and drew him closer. Her fingers pulled at the band that held his long hair back until it gave way. His hair was like silk beneath her palms.

He pulled his lips away just far enough to whisper, "There are so many things that fascinate me about you."

She felt the old angry defensiveness rise up. "My *exotic* beauty?"

"No. How you came to be where you are. The bond you have with your family. Your drive. Your success. Your humor. That fascinates me."

He kept his eyes locked on hers as he spoke. She'd become adept over her lifetime of spotting the lies. The backpedaling. He was sincere. She felt the tendrils of anger slip.

"That you are here now fascinates me." His hands moved through her hair. Down her arms to her waist. "Why are you here?"

"I'm not sure," she said. She reached out and

pressed her palms to his chest. Crisp. A smile crossed her lips.

He captured her hands and held them between his. "If you aren't sure, then maybe you shouldn't be here."

"It's not that. I want to be here. I'm just not sure what I'm *doing*."

"I think you know exactly what you are doing."

She felt heat rise to her cheeks. They both knew. Why was he making her say it? Guys were usually okay with a random booty call. "I want you," she said in a whisper.

"I got that, but I'm talking about what's going on in that brain of yours. What's changed between super-professional-can't-do-this Lena from this afternoon and showing-up-on-my-doorstep Lena?"

"The sun went down."

"The sun went down?" He let go of her hands and took a step back. "I'm not sure that's a good enough reason. Have you been drinking?"

"No." She stepped toward him. "I'm stone-cold sober."

He backed up a few more feet. She walked to the easel and looked at the landscape he was painting. It was in the early stages but it looked like a marsh scene. "I like your landscapes better than that modern stuff."

"You've made that very clear," he said.

He'd moved close enough that she felt his

breath on her hair. His hands closed on her shoulders and she leaned back against him. "You want me too." she said.

"True."

She turned in his arms. "Then why aren't we naked?"

He laughed and dipped a finger in yellow paint and put two dots above her eyebrows. "Because I want more than naked."

She smiled. *Oh, she could play this game too.* She drew her fingers through the vivid blue paint on the palette. Lifting her hands, her smile grew wider as he lightly grabbed her wrists.

"Lena…"

She slipped her hands free and planted her fingers on his chest, pressing the paint to his skin. Letting her hands move slowly, she traced paint down his abdomen. "There. We're even now." She dipped her fingers into the bright blue paint again and drew a line from his forehead down the slope of his nose and across his lips to his chin. "You look like a Norse god."

Her touch was driving him crazy. She could see it in his eyes, the tightening of his jaw, the slight flare of his nostrils. She smiled and brought her fingers to her chest and smeared the rest of the blue in two vertical lines down her chest, pulling away the shirt collar to reveal her breasts.

"What about the whole inappropriate thing?"

"We'll deal with that tomorrow."

His hands cupped her cheeks, turning her face up to meet his eyes. "I'm not a onetime kind of guy, Lena."

"We'll deal with that tomorrow too."

"I don't have…"

"I do."

"Is this stuff going to wash off?"

Matt traced a line of kisses along her neck. The paint was everywhere. His sheets were probably ruined. And after the amazing sex, he was pretty ruined himself. The hints and tastes he'd gotten of her had proven to be mere shadows of the reality.

"Nope. Should wear off in a week or so."

Matt grinned as Lena sat up in the bed. "Tell me you are lying to me, Charles Beaumont Matthews the *Fifth*, or I will feed your guts to my cat."

"Ow!" he said as she caught his beard in a fist and gave it a tug. Grabbing her wrists, he tried to pull her back down against him but she slipped a leg over and straddled him. "Okay. This works too."

Slipping her wrists free, she laced her fingers with his. "Tell me," she growled.

He grinned as he looked up at her. Naked. Her hair a wild tangle. The stripes he'd painted were now smeared across her cheeks. Her breasts dotted with the paint she'd smeared on him. "God, Lena. You are so incredibly beautiful."

She rolled her eyes in dismissal but not before he caught the fleeting look of something softer there. Letting go of his hands, she sat back on his thighs and traced a lazy hand across his chest. His breath caught. *Round two?* Her eyes locked onto his as she shifted on his thighs, pressing her heat against him. Her fingers continued their light, teasing tour of his chest, now heading south. Then stopped.

"Does it wash off?" she asked.

He groaned. "Maybe. I think so."

Her fingers began to move again, millimeter by maddening millimeter. His hips flexed. And her fingers stopped again. "You think?"

"I have turpentine if it doesn't."

She was off him like a shot. "Turpentine?" she screeched. "Turpentine? This paint better wash off with soap and water, *pendajo.*"

She stormed from the room, leaving a stream of enraged Spanish behind her. He scrambled from the bed with a grin. She made him crazy. Hearing the shower turn on, he grabbed a couple of clean towels on his way. Expecting more anger, he stopped in the doorway.

"It'll wash off," he said. "I was just teasing you. A little soap and water."

She turned her head and gave him a sultry smile. "Promise?"

He set the towels down and caught her cheek in his hand. "I'll wash it off myself."

"Oh, that sounds fun."

Jerking the shower curtain open, he gave her a smart smack on the butt. "In with you."

She twisted and turned under the water. It was all he could do to keep his mind on the task of getting the paint off. Yes, it would wash off but he wasn't going to take any chances with delaying the job. She'd kill him if she had to go to work in the morning with paint on her face. She grabbed the bottle of body soap.

"Guess I should be glad it isn't some dude-bro stuff, huh?"

"Don't be insulting." He poured soap into his palms and pulled her closer. "Close your eyes."

Gently, he washed the smeared lines of paint from her face. The movement of his fingers over the curves of her cheeks seemed more intimate than their lovemaking. She opened her eyes and the dark depth of them mesmerized him for a moment.

"Is it coming off?"

"Yes," he managed to choke out as he concentrated on soaping down her shoulders, chest and belly. "I think that's all of it," he said, and turned her into the water.

She rinsed off and turned back round, pulling him under the spray. "Your turn," she said with a wicked smile.

He groaned as she began soaping his face and

chest with slow, deliberate strokes. Forced himself to remain still under her touch.

"All done," she finally said.

He turned quickly into the water, rinsing as fast as he could. Lena's arms circled around him. He felt her hot mouth press kisses along his spine. Turning, he pulled her into his arms and pressed her against the shower wall.

"We can stay here," she said.

"Hot water won't hold up that long," he said with real regret. But it was the truth—they were about ten seconds away from ice water raining down on them. "I'm going to dry you off and take you back to my bed."

"I CAN'T STAY all night."

"If you did, you might kill me," he said. "You can stay as long as you want."

Lena didn't answer but snuggled up to his body, draping an arm and leg across him. He felt so good. So warm. So solid. "Thank you," she whispered against his chest.

He shifted and wrapped his arms around her shoulders, pulling her even closer. "For what?"

"Not throwing me out when I showed up here."

"Should I have?"

"No. I knew what I was doing. What I wanted."

"I hope you got at least that," he teased.

"And some. That was pretty amazing."

"Art makes everything better."

She growled deep down in her throat. It had been sexy as sin. Both the going on and the washing off. "You've made a believer out of me."

"I want us to get to know each other. Like normal people. Go on dates. Meet each other's friends."

"I don't think that's going to happen."

"Make it happen. Tell me you don't feel it. That you aren't just as attracted to me."

"Oh, I felt it. But sex is just sex."

"What I feel is more than sex. And I think it is for you too."

He let go of her and rolled over on his back. Acutely feeling the loss of his warmth, Lena propped up on an elbow and looked down at him. "Don't pout. It's unbecoming."

"I'm not pouting. I'm confused."

"About what?"

"What comes next."

"Does there have to be a next?"

He tilted her face up to look in her eyes. "I want there to be a next. Go on a date with me, Lena. A real date. I have a showing this week. Come with me."

"Matt. I can't…"

"You can. Turn my account over to Mose. Or cut me loose as a client. I don't care. I want to give us a chance."

She pushed away. "There is no us, Matt."

"I want there to be."

She rolled out of bed and gathered her scattered clothes. Once dressed, she looked at him. "But there won't be."

"Why? Tell me one reason other than this whole business thing."

She hesitated. Pressed her lips together even as doubt flickered within her. She let out a long breath and shook her head. "We're too different."

"That's where you're wrong. I don't think we're very different at all."

She raised an eyebrow. "You don't? Why not?" *This should be interesting. This rich white man thinking we have so much in common.*

"Go on a date with me and I'll tell you."

A frustrated half growl rolled from her throat. "You are the most conceited, irritating, and... and..."

"Handsome?"

"Basta!"

He scrambled off the bed and caught her at the door, draped in the bed sheet. "Wait. Let me walk you to your car."

"No."

He grinned. "A good-night kiss?"

"I think you had enough kisses."

"See you Wednesday night then?"

"I can't on Wednesday. Sadie and I have dinner every week. It's sacrosanct."

The evil-bad-boy-Viking-about-to-ravage-amilkmaid grin surfaced. "So, you will go out with me, just not on Wednesday?"

Every part of her was screaming to walk away now. Let it be a warm memory of the best sex she'd ever had. Yet there was a tiny little part of her that was curious. Because he might have come from money, but he didn't have any. She'd seen his finances. He had sky-high student-loan debt. The kind a person gets when their family made too much money for student aid and scholarships. The kind you get when your family doesn't fund your college education. *What exactly did he think they had in common?*

"What time on Wednesday?" The words fell out of her mouth as if by accident. Her only saving grace was that he looked so surprised he didn't even tease her about it.

"Seven. At the Unitarian Church."

She arched an eyebrow at him. "Our first date is going to be at a church?"

His hand swept her hair back and he placed a lingering kiss on her forehead. "We can beg forgiveness for our sins. Now, let me get dressed and walk you to your car."

"It's okay. You don't have to."

"But I want to."

CHAPTER SEVENTEEN

"OH. MY. GOD. Why are you so slow?"

The coffeemaker didn't reply. Lena needed more than a cup of coffee. She needed another five hours of sleep. She'd stared at her ceiling for hours after returning home from Matt's apartment. Feeling exactly how cold and lonely her bed was. Wondering what she'd gotten herself into. Coming up with a plan that was a little more professional than "Hey, I slept with a client so here's his account."

"Finally," she said as she grabbed her giant travel cup. Downing half the coffee in a single guzzle, she moved toward the door, gathering her purse and phone as she went. "I'm going to work, Sass. Do not climb the curtains again or no more catnip for you."

Chloe and Mose were already at the office when she arrived. "Good," she said as she walked through the lobby. "I have a couple phone calls to make, and then I need to talk to you both."

"Good morning to you too, boss," Mose said.

Stopping to refill her cup in the tiny space they called the kitchen, Lena waved a hand in Mose's general direction. She wasn't awake enough yet to even pretend to be polite.

"Rough night?" Chloe asked, innuendo dripping from each word.

That got them a middle finger as Lena went into her office and shut the door. She finished the coffee as her computer booted up. Finally, the caffeine began to hit her nervous system and she didn't quite feel like stabbing anyone anymore.

Rough night. Last night had been anything but rough. Amazing. Hot. She felt as if she should have burns from the heat. Pulling up her client list, she shook her head. Last night was last night. *Now it's time to do business.* She scanned through the list of clients. She needed one more. She couldn't just hand Matt alone over to Mose. She'd figure that out in a hot minute. *Ah. There we go. Perfect.* She reached for the phone.

"Logan? It's Lena Reyes. Sorry for calling you so early, I know you work late but I had a question for you."

"Shoot," Logan said. "I'm mostly up."

"I'm making some changes here and want to promote Moseley from my assistant to an associate partner. I want to turn a couple accounts over to her to manage and yours is one of them. I need your consent."

"Uh, sure. That'd be fine."

"Great. Thanks. We'll send you a formal letter later."

Lena sat back after ending the call. *Are you sure Mose is ready? Wanting to bang a client was not a good reason to give a promotion. Two promotions.* She looked around the office. Her degrees on the wall. A few pictures of her receiving various awards. Here she sat with an office on Broad Street, some of the most powerful men and women in the city on her client list, and yet she was still afraid it would all disappear at any second.

"Time to stop being a coward," she muttered under her breath. Pushing back from the desk, she stood and walked out to the hall. Mose's office door was open. "Mose. I'd like to talk to you in my office please." She turned her head toward the lobby. "You too, Chloe."

They came in giving each other side glances. They both looked worried. "It's not bad," Lena said. "Sit down and stop side-eyeing each other."

Once she returned to her chair, she drew in a deep breath. "It was pointed out to me the other day that I can be a bit of a control freak."

"Is that person still alive?" Chloe asked.

"Shit," Mose said, elbowing Chloe. "She's going to jail. That's what this is about."

"No one is going to jail. God. Stop it. I can take constructive criticism." She could feel the heat across her cheeks. The snickering giggles from her employees only made it worse. "Okay. I get it. Here's the deal. I want to make some changes."

That got them to stop laughing. "Mose, I've received permission to turn over two accounts to you. I want to promote you to associate partner. Let you handle these accounts and as you feel comfortable, you can start building your own client list."

"Yes!" Mose said with a fist pump.

Lena smiled. Matt had been right about this. Seeing Mose grow and learn had been one of the most rewarding parts of her work. It was past time for this. Time to let her fly.

"So," she continued, turning her attention to Chloe. "That means I'm losing my assistant. I'd like to promote you to be the assistant for both of us. We'll hire a new office manager and once we have him or her trained, you can move into your new position. If you want to, that is."

"Absolutely," Chloe said.

"What brought all this on?" Mose asked.

"It's overdue. Should have done it months ago. You're both more than ready."

"Which accounts am I getting?"

"Logan Rutledge and Matt's," Lena said, straining to keep her tone casual. As if she'd just randomly chosen two accounts. Mose and Chloe went back to side-eyeing each other. "What?"

Chloe held out a hand, palm up, to Mose. "Twenty dollars."

Lena glared at them. "What?"

"You slept with him!" Chloe blurted out. "Didn't you? Come on, Lena. Oh my God, how was it?"

She glared harder. Added her patented single-eyebrow arch. And they were still giggling in their chairs like teenage girls. "Get out of here," she said.

"Please," Chloe begged, clasping her hands together. "Please, please, please tell us. He's so gorgeous."

"I am not discussing my sex life with you," Lena said prissily. "Get out. I have work to do. And *you* need to hire a new office manager."

As they left the room, still grousing about not getting any juicy details, Lena shook her head and smiled. She couldn't give details. If she started talking about last night, she'd end up right back at Matt's door like a stray cat. *Focus.*

Settling in to her Monday routine of checking any developments in the financial world over the weekend and making a list of actions to take, she began to feel more in control. More like herself. *Was that the problem? That Matt turned her upside down and inside out and she didn't feel in control?* Maybe she was a complete control freak. She made a face. No, she wasn't. She'd just turned over a huge hunk of control to Mose and Chloe. *Because of Matt.*

"Shut up," she said out loud.

Pulling up her list of contacts, she turned her attention to the next item on her agenda for the day. St. Toribio's. Where to start?

"Lena. It's so good to hear from you."

"Hi, Doris. I know. It's been too long. I had a quick question."

Doris Manigault was the Director for Diversity at Lowcounty College. She'd been there when Lena had been a student needing guidance through the alien environment of higher education.

"Make it a long question. I always have time for you."

"I was out at the mission over the weekend. St. Toribio's. Are you familiar with it?"

"Yes. The Catholic mission?"

"That's it. Well, I didn't know this but apparently, some of my mother's generation have been holding me up as an example to the kids out there."

"As they should."

That made Lena smile. Doris was the sole reason she'd survived the first semester. "I got to thinking about how lost and confused I was that first year. How much you helped me. I'd like to... I don't know... It's a rough idea, but I'd like to try to get together some professional women to either do some talks or workshops. Things like how to apply for financial aid. How to write an application essay. How to find the academic assistance they may need."

There was a long pause on the other end of the phone. Lena felt a bit of panic begin to creep in. Maybe this was stupid. Thankful she had presented it to Doris first because she knew Doris wouldn't judge her, she drew in a breath. "Is it…"

"No. No! Oh, honey. This is brilliant. I was just writing down names. I have all sorts of people we can get together for something like this."

"Wonderful. Another thought I had was more of an economic issue than diversity issue. I thought we could talk about the difficulty of beginning your first professional, white-collar job when you are from a history of laborers or blue-collar workers."

"Yes! Lena. Are you committed to this? Because we can make it into something really good and potentially huge."

She sat back, a grin on her lips. How committed was she? "I'm in. Completely."

"Me too. You have others you are reaching out to?"

"Yes."

"Okay, you talk to your people, I'll talk to my people and we'll set up a strategy meeting."

"Perfect. I'll get back to you tomorrow."

Ending the call, Lena set her phone down slowly, carefully. There was a light, wild emotion spinning through her. It felt good and she didn't want it to go away. How long had it been since she'd truly been happy? Well before Lito, her beloved grandfather, died.

Feelings of happiness led to thoughts of Matt. That was a happy of another sort. She frowned and did a Google search for the Unitarian Church. Upcoming events. What had she gotten herself into? Contemporary Art in a Historic City. *Ugh. More of his Pollock-y stuff. Smears and drips.* Another feeling began to rise. Along with the memory of his fingers drawing lines of paint across her face. His painted face above her. *Okay. That had been hot. Can't lie about that. Fires like that burn out quick though, Lena. Watch your heart.*

A single rap on the door preceded Mose. "Hey, boss, I wanted to… You okay?"

"Yeah. Fine. What's up?"

Glad for the distraction from her own thoughts, she settled in to listen and answer Mose's questions about transferring the accounts. *Focus on this transition. Focus on getting this new project off the ground.* Matt was a distraction she didn't need at the moment, no matter how tempting.

THE SOUND OF THE "Imperial March" was so unexpected, Matt didn't realize it was his phone. Then his heart sank. His father. He lifted the phone from the bedside table and squinted. *What?* He could think of no good reason for his father to be calling him. From his personal line, which meant it wasn't his assistant.

Scrubbing a hand across his face, he thought about dismissing the call. He didn't want to talk to his father. He wanted to continue to wallow in bed, remembering how it had felt with Lena in it beside him. After she'd left, he'd spent half the night painting in something close to euphoria. It had been a long time since he'd painted with that passion. Talking to his father would only ruin it.

He answered the call. It might be important. Maybe his mother or one of his sisters. "Morning, Dad," he said as cheerfully as he could muster as he rolled to sit on the edge of the bed.

"The day is half-gone already."

"I'm good. Thanks for asking. How are you?"

"Your grandfather's ninetieth birthday celebration is this Saturday. You will be required to attend. I've made your travel plans. My assistant will email you the details. Cut your damn hair before you show up. And leave your attitude in Charleston."

"Wow," Matt said, but his father had already ended the call. He wanted to be furious but it was all so old. He'd spent half his life in a rage-fueled campaign against his father, and he was tired of it. But his dad had either never noticed that Matt had stopped playing the game or he didn't care.

He checked the time. Eleven. Not too bad. He

yawned and shuffled to the kitchen to make coffee. It was going to be a light day he saw as he checked the calendar on the kitchen wall. Art therapy at the hospital from two until four. A wine and paint at seven. Perfect. Grabbing the coffee decanter before it was finished brewing, he held a cup under the stream of coffee.

The anger came back, nibbling at the corners of his postsex postpainting high. *Who does that? Calls and just demands that you be somewhere? No respect for your time or life?* He shook his head, trying to clear the thoughts. *Doesn't mean you have to jump.* The anger, the frustration, everything fell away as he approached the easel. He'd set aside the marsh scene he'd been working on for this. Casting a critical eye over the painting, he smoothed down his beard and sipped more coffee. *Lena.* He'd painted this portrait like a man possessed. He'd *had* to capture that look. The hot, dark passion in her eyes when he'd painted the streaks across her face. *Fighter* he would title it.

It was more of an art nouveau style than he usually used for portraits, but it captured the lines of her face and hair perfectly. The streaks of paint contrasting with the black of her hair. The eyes. He hadn't quite gotten the look in her eyes. The rounded cheeks, the full lips half-opened, yes, those were perfect. He finished off the coffee and poured a second cup before returning to the painting and dipping his brush in the paint. Just a little bit more.

An hour later, he sat in a chair, stuffing cold leftover pizza into his face, hoping it wasn't too old and wishing he had another couple of hours to work on the portrait. His phone signaled a Face-Time request. His sister Susie. Probably backing up his father's call. The old one-two punch. The face of his four-year-old niece, Lila, appeared on his screen. *Emotional blackmail. Great.*

"Hey, squirt," he said. "What's up?"

"Momma says you are coming to visit me this weekend," she said.

Damn it. Trying to keep the irritation out of his expression and words, he shook his head a little. "I'm not sure, Lila. Your grandfather just told me about it this morning. I'm going to have to check my schedule."

Her sweet face grew serious as she drew her lips together in a double pout. "But you haven't visited me since Christmas. And that was way back when I was just a baby."

"But we see each other all the time on the phone," he reminded her.

"But I can't hug a phone, Uncle Matt!"

She had him there.

"Pleeeaaase!" she begged.

"Okay. I will come see you this weekend."

He put a little stress on the *you* for the benefit

of her mother, who he knew was near enough to hear. Sure enough, the phone was taken from his niece and his sister's face appeared.

"For God's sake, Matt. Just come to the party. Show your face. Sing "Happy Birthday." The old man is freaking ninety. Ignore Dad like you always do."

"I said I'd be there. I'll be there."

"Thank you. You know it puts all of us in an awkward position when people start asking about you."

"Why? Why is it so awkward to say I'm living in Charleston? That I'm an artist and an art therapist? You guys act as though I'm a male stripper or something."

"You know what I mean."

"And you know what I mean."

She sighed and rolled her eyes. "So you'll be there?"

"Yes. Tell dear old dad you did your familial duty. But don't use Lila anymore. She's a child, not a tool."

He ended the call with a rough stab of a finger. He and Susie usually could pretend to tolerate each other. But involving an innocent four-year-old infuriated him. Another reason to stay far away. He wanted kids and he wasn't going to let them grow up in that toxic atmosphere.

Jumping in the shower, his irritation melted away with the memories of Lena standing under the spray while he washed the paint away. Grinning, he hurriedly washed his hair and beard. He had enough time. Barely.

NOT AS MUCH time as he thought. By the time he'd parked his bike on the sidewalk outside Reyes Financial Services, he had less than thirty minutes to get back across town to the hospital. Pushing through the door, he was greeted with an exceedingly knowing grin from Chloe.

"Why, Mr. Matthews," she said archly. "What a pleasant surprise. Flowers?"

He grinned and half perched on the edge of her desk, bringing the little bouquet—mostly daisies, baby's breath and greenery—up to his nose. "And here I thought you blondes were supposed to be rather dim."

"No, blond men are the dim ones. So tell me are the flowers for Mose to congratulate her on taking over your account? Or...?"

She left the *or* hanging in the air with a wicked grin. He felt his cheeks going a bit warm. Surely Lena hadn't kissed and told. They must have guessed. He remembered Mose teasing Lena that time.

"I think you know exactly who they are for."

"If it's Lena, and it better be, she is out of the office for a meeting. But I'll be happy to give them to her for you along with any message."

He handed over the flowers, a part of him glad
Lena wasn't there.

"Wednesday," he said as he stood.

"Wednesday?"

"She'll know what it means."

CHAPTER EIGHTEEN

BUTTERFLIES ROUGHLY THE size of pterodactyls were colliding in her gut and her hands were trembling. Lena put them in her lap and smiled. She and Doris Manigault had gathered four women interested in developing a program for the college-bound kids of St. Toribio. Public speaking had never been her strong point. Doris finished introducing everyone and turned back to Lena. The five other women were watching her, waiting. Clearing her throat, she put her hands on the table, palms down. She'd thought she'd have more time, but everyone was so excited about the idea they'd agreed to meet after work on Tuesday.

"First, thank you all for coming. I think we're all clear on the overall goal—to put together a program that can be presented at least once a year, more if needed." She cleared her throat again. They were all just sitting there. Staring at her. She laced her fingers together. Took a deep breath. "Okay. I'm no good with making speeches and stuff, so I'm just going to spit it all out and we can sort it out."

Doris nodded. "Basics," she said.

"Yes. Basics. Going to college is a norm for a lot of families, but in the immigrant community, it may not be. Everything is new territory for them. Deciding on a college. How to apply for financial aid. Writing the essay. Preparing for the SATs."

Heads were now nodding and one woman, Andrea, was taking notes. "Exactly," Doris echoed. "Also, college readiness. Many of the students I work with struggle in their first semesters because even though they were in the top ten at high school, we all know school districts are not created equally."

"I work in the financial aid office at North Charleston Technical College. I can put together something on the different types of financial aid," Andrea said.

"Great, thank you," Lena said.

"I think in addition to the talks, we should have some literature printed up," Doris added. "So the kids could take it home. And would we be able to leave it there for them to pick up when they are there?"

"Yes," Lena said. "I can arrange that and keep track of the supply."

"I can help with the SAT information," another woman said. "I'm a librarian. I have a great list of free tutoring and online resources for preparing."

Doris clicked the pen and began writing on a yellow legal tablet. "Okay. So far, Andrea, you'll put together financial aid information. Erin, you'll do the SATs. What else?"

"Writing the essay. Deciding on a college," Lena said.

"I can do the essay part. I have a degree in journalism and do freelance writing on the side."

"Alyssa for the essay," Doris said as she wrote it down.

"I guess that leaves me for the deciding which college," the last woman said with a smile.

"Is that okay, Lauren?" Doris asked her.

"I got five kids through four different colleges," she said with a laugh. "Different kids need different things. I got pretty good at helping them identify what would be a good match for them."

Lena sat back in the chair. The butterflies were gone. "This is great. Thank you all for this. I'll get in touch with the people at St. Toribio and coordinate things with them. I'll be telling my personal story as part of the program."

"Perfect," Doris said. "Can we meet again here next week? Is that enough time to get the initial information together?"

Everyone agreed. Lena got up to shake hands and thank them each for coming. She was slightly stunned. She'd had an idea and now here she was making it happen. Like a real grown-up. A warm hand cupped her shoulder. Doris.

"This is going to be a really good thing we're doing, Lena. I'm so happy you reached out."

"I can hardly believe it's going to be real."

"Oh, it's going to be real. You're just getting started. I see in your eyes how much you like this. This helping people stuff gets addictive."

"I believe that. This all started with a small project I got roped into doing and when I saw how just a little thing could positively impact so many people, it felt really good."

Doris laughed. "You're hooked already."

Lena felt the smile on her face all the way down to her core. *Yep, I'm hooked. This is some serious feel-good stuff.*

"WHAT IN THE hell is a fried pig's ear? Please tell me that means something else in fancy restaurant talk."

Lena smiled at Sadie's horrified expression. Harvest was about the fanciest restaurant they'd been to in all their years of Wednesday-night dinners. But it was in walking distance of the Unitarian Church and she'd be damned if she was going to find parking twice tonight.

"I'm pretty sure it's a pig's ear," she said.

"So they what? Just chop it off and drop it in the deep fryer? And people are just too afraid to say how gross it is because they don't want to be the one pointing out the emperor is naked?"

"Maybe it tastes good. We should try it."

Sadie shook her head. "I can't. I'm just pictur-

JANET LEE NYE   237

ing all these poor little pigs wandering around earless."

"God shouldn't have made them so tasty."

"Why are we going all fancy tonight?" Sadie asked, raising her eyebrows. "Or should I ask why are *you* all fancy tonight?"

Lena tried for a casual tone. "I have a thing after."

"A thing?"

Lena met Sadie's gaze. "A thing," she said firmly.

"A date?"

Her emotions betrayed her. "Maybe," she muttered, pretending she wasn't hiding behind the menu. A little quiver shook her inside as she thought about what had happened Sunday night and the very real possibility of it happening again.

The tip of Sadie's index finger touched the top of the menu and forced it down to the table. "You have a date and you didn't tell me?"

"It's weird. And complicated."

Sadie laughed. "Anything involving you is going to be complicated."

"What are you saying? That I'm high maintenance or something?"

"Nice try at diverting the topic of discussion, but no go. Who is he? Details. I need all the details."

"There are no details. He's just this guy. Rather annoying, actually."

"Oh please. It's Wednesday. You're in a sexy little dress and high heels."

"I think I'm going to get the shrimp and grits. Have you decided yet?"

"Oh. My. God."

Lena looked up at Sadie's shocked face. "What?"

"It's that guy. That Viking guy? Isn't it?"

There was no hiding the blush that spread across her face. She tried a scowl. "Maybe."

Sadie did a little happy dance in her seat and clapped her hands. "Tell me. How'd this come to be?"

Lena sipped her wine. "He asked me."

How did this come to be? That she was sitting here, wearing heels and makeup, with her insides quivering in anticipation? The waiter appeared at the table. Grateful for the interruption, Lena gave him her order while Sadie decided what she wanted.

"Didn't you want a pig's ear?" she teased.

Sadie looked up at the waiter with such a horrified face that Lena almost spewed wine across the table. She swallowed and then laughed. A real laugh. *Can dress us up but you still can't take us anywhere.* The thought turned her laughter into giggles. Sadie glared at her across the table but her lips were pressed together against her own laughter.

Lena dabbed at the corners of her eyes. "Stop it. You're going to ruin my makeup."

"What's gotten into you?"

"I need to talk to you about something important," Lena said as the waiter left.

"What? How to tell your family you're dating a white guy while they're still conducting Hispanic Bachelor auditions?"

"They aren't doing that anymore."

"Then why did your mother ask Wyatt if he knew any Hispanic police officers?"

"She. Did. Not." Lena ground her teeth against the rush of very bad words that wanted to fly out. Harvest was a small place and there were others seated very close. "She told me she'd put an end to that nonsense."

"Tell her you're dating this guy."

"We aren't dating. We have this…this thing."

"Uh-huh?"

"Listen. I'm putting together a series of talks out at St. Toribio's. For the kids starting high school. I want you to participate."

Sadie made a face. "I give money. I don't do things. Write yourself a check."

"It's going to be basically a what-I-wish-I'd-known-back-then kind of thing. How to apply for college, stuff like that."

"And what would I teach them? How to be a

maid? I didn't go to college, Lena. I don't have anything to offer them."

"That's exactly why you should be involved. I'm not some dewy-eyed do-gooder who thinks she's going to save the world, Sades. Some of these kids won't go to college. But not going to college doesn't mean not becoming successful. That's what you have to offer them. An example of hard work and not giving up."

Sadie made a face. "I'll think about it."

"I didn't ask if you wanted to do it. I said you were doing it."

Sadie sat back as the waiter delivered their dinner. After he'd left, she picked up her wineglass. "Only if you give me the details on the Viking. I've never seen you so blushy about a man before."

THE VIKING. LENA paused as she entered the church. A fairly large crowd was milling around, looking at the art, but her gaze went immediately to Matt. Sadie had that right. Tall, blond, broad shouldered, he did look like a Viking, especially with his long hair tied back with a length of leather and that beard. He was dressed in poor-artist chic. Khaki pants, a blue work shirt with the sleeves rolled up over those very nice forearms. Her hand went to her chin and a hot rush raced through her as she remembered the burn that beard had left on her skin.

The heat intensified when he turned and looked

directly at her. Even from across the room, she could see the hot spark in his eyes. With a grin that seemed almost feral, he headed straight for her, his eyes never leaving her.

"Thank God, you're here," he whispered in her ear as he looped an arm around her waist, sending a delicious thrill through her. "Save me."

"Save you from what?"

"These people. Inane blither. All of them trying to remember enough Art History 101 to pontificate properly."

Lena snorted out a laugh, then clapped a hand over her mouth. Looking around the room, she laughed again. A much more ladylike laugh though. Because it was true. The crowd was ever so properly dressed and ever so properly discussing the art. They all looked so serious.

"These are your people, Matt. You should know how to talk to them."

"I don't want to talk to them. That's the problem."

She swayed, lightly bumping against him. "Let's get out of here then."

His eyes were hot and his bad boy grin at full power when he looked over at her. "And go where?"

"Anywhere."

He sighed. "As much as I want to, I can't right this minute. I need these people."

She matched his sigh. "I understand." Snatching a wineglass from the tray carried by a passing server, she showed him she had a bad-girl grin of her own. "Let's booze, schmooze and vamoose."

"Is that your strategy?"

"Watch me."

WATCH ME. As if he could take his eyes off her. Grabbing his own glass of wine, he followed. She moved around the room with a precision that awed him. Her instincts were perfect. First she chatted up the wives of the men with the deepest pockets. Then she played coquette as some of the old goats flirted with her. She made it look easy. Effortless. He chatted halfheartedly with a few of the other artists while watching Lena work the room.

It only looked like she was casually perusing the displayed art. She turned her dark eyes in his direction and made a discreet motion with her hand that he interpreted as "give me a minute, then come over." He nodded.

"Ah," she said a moment later as he approached the small group clustered around his painting. "Here's the artist. Matt, I was just telling everyone that you're about to become the next Pollock."

"I don't know about that," he said slowly as the others turned to stare at him. *What had she been telling them?*

"Well, you might not, but I do," Lena said

brightly. She smiled at the three couples standing with them. "So humble, but look at this. It's almost alive."

Matt almost choked on his wine. He managed to keep from laughing. She was spreading it on rather thick, but from the look in their eyes, they were buying it. All of them were glancing between him, Lena and the painting.

"Lena!"

Everyone turned as Dr. Rutledge approached them.

"Eliot," Lena practically purred, an evil little glint appearing in her eyes. "I was just telling these wonderful people about Matt's work. How he's about to explode in the art world."

The doctor turned an appraising glance at Matt, one corner of his mouth lifting in a quick smile. He caught Lena's verbal pitch as smoothly as if they'd planned it. "Indeed. I'm trying my best to leave some of it for others, but it's difficult." He motioned to the painting. "Every new piece I see, I like more than the previous one. My wife is going to take away my checkbook soon."

"You've been very generous in your support," Matt said.

"I've been very selfish in my support," Eliot said. He lifted a finger at the others. "I only invest my money in a sure bet."

"Do you have a card?" one of the men asked.

"THAT WAS A thing of beauty," he said.

Lena sipped her reward—a blush martini at Kaminsky's—and winked at him. "I know a thing or two." She dipped a finger into the whipped cream on the slice of key lime pie Matt was eating and licked it off.

His eyes followed her movement, and then met hers. "You can't be doing things like that in public."

She held his gaze as she slowly, deliberately, reached out and scooped up another fingerful of cream and, this time, sucked it off her finger. "Do what?"

"You're killing me here."

"Torturing maybe, but not killing."

He pulled the plate closer and placed a protective arm in front of it. "I offered to buy you a pie but you said no."

"Greedy."

"But really. Where'd you learn to work a crowd like that?"

She shrugged. "Watching. Listening. You rich people are amazingly predictable."

He gestured at himself with his fork. "I am not rich."

She rolled her eyes. "Rule number one, you all pretend like you aren't rich. Rule number two, you're all afraid if you don't do or say what other rich people are doing and saying that they will think you aren't rich like them. Rule number three, don't ever be the first one to do something new. Only the richest white male with the most influence is allowed to do something new first. Then everyone has to do it because he did."

Matt stared at her, forkful of pie midway to his open mouth. She reached out, closed her fingers around his wrist and guided the fork to her mouth. She closed her eyes. May have moaned a bit. He was still staring at her when she opened her eyes.

"What?"

"That's…that's brilliant," he stammered.

She laughed. "I swore you were going to say bullshit."

"No. It's dead-on."

"I know. This is why you, Charles Beaumont Matthews the Fifth, make me curious. How did a long-haired, bearded artist fall out of your family tree?"

A look crossed his face. Not quite annoyance, not quite anger. It was gone as quickly as it appeared. That grin came back. "I don't want to talk about my family. I want to talk about where we can find a can or two of whipped cream at this time of night."

She lifted her eyebrow and finished her martini in a few long swallows. "I believe I have a can in my fridge."

He put down the fork. "Then why are we still here?"

"IT'S COLD OUT HERE," Matt said as he stepped out on the balcony. Lena had slipped out of her bed, and when she didn't return, he'd gone looking for her.

"Winter's coming," she said. "Or it'll be in the nineties next week. Never can tell with Charleston weather."

He put his arms around her, pulling her against him. "What are you doing?" he murmured in her ear. Their lovemaking had been as amazing as the first time but she seemed a bit distant now.

"I like to watch the ships go by in the harbor," she said. She lifted her hands to his arms and tilted her head back against his chest.

"Do you want me to leave?"

She turned in his arms. "No. I mean, I don't expect you to stay if you don't want to…" Her words trailed off. "But, hell, Matt. What are we doing?"

"That's not a discussion to be had out here freezing. Come back inside."

He took her by the hand and led her back inside. Sliding the door shut, he felt something sharp on his foot. Lena's cat dashed through the closing door to hide under the couch. Which was better than the cold death stare the thing had been giving him since they arrived. Which was a shame because he liked cats.

Back in the warm bed, with Lena curled up in his arms, he felt both at peace and a bit nervous. *What are we doing?* It sounded suspiciously close to an initial approach of a the-sex-was-great-but-goodbye-now speech. A speech he did not want to hear.

"I know what I'm doing," he said. "I'm getting to know a fascinating woman and discovering more amazing things about her every minute."

"Is that what we're doing? Getting to know each other? Are we dating? Sex buddies? What?"

"What do you want us to be?"

She rolled away from him and stared up at the ceiling. "It's just complicated. I'm not very good at the dating stuff."

"Then we won't date. We'll just go be in the same places at the same time a lot."

"You are just full of solutions."

He turned on his side and brushed her hair away from her face. "If that was true, I wouldn't be going back home this weekend. I'd be somewhere at the same time with you."

That got her attention. "You don't want to go home?"

"I want to see my nieces. But I'm not going home. I've been ordered home."

She propped up on an elbow. "Ordered?"

"Something like that." He didn't want to talk to her about his family. It didn't show a good side of him. It showed the bitterness he was still trying to work out of his system. He wanted her to see the Matt he was trying to be. Not the Matt he had been.

"Something like that? What does that mean?"

He rolled onto his back and put his forearm across his eyes. "My family and I don't see eye to eye on my life choices."

"Oh, that's better. Except that it isn't. What's the truth?"

He moved his arm and looked at her. "My family hates me."

A puzzled frown appeared on her face. It was so genuine it made his heart ache a little bit. She shook her head.

"I don't understand. *Hates* you?"

"Okay. *Hate* might be a strong word. They don't like me. And I'm not overly fond of them. Except my older sister, Charlotte. We get along great."

Lena sat up and propped the pillows on the headboard behind her. "How can you not like your family?"

He craned to look over at her. Sighed. "Everything you've said about me is true, Lena. Spoiled, rich, trust-fund brat. But those things come with expectations. And I didn't meet their expectations."

"How?"

He sat up and pulled her into his arms. "Lena, I could start listing those right now and not finish until the sun comes up. I don't want to talk about it."

The look she gave him, long and speculative,

sent a flicker of worry through him. She was close to her family. He'd seen that at the hospital. And as annoyed as she said she was with them, she loved them. *What must it have been like? To be raised with such support and love?*

"I'd like to meet your family," he said impulsively. Then laughed as her expression turned into one of incredulous horror.

"That's not funny," she said, pulling the sheet up over her breasts and tucking it under her arms.

"Why? Because I'm white?"

"That's the least of my worries."

"What then?"

"That they'll think we're serious. They'll have the church picked out and have you enrolled in conversion classes—you aren't already Catholic, are you?—before the lunch table is even cleared off."

"Sorry. Not Catholic. Worse, one of those starchy Methodists. So, your family is doing the Hispanic-guy setups because…?"

She scowled at him, so he gave her his baddest bad-boy grin. "Because they are stuck in their ways."

"Come on, Lena, take me home to meet your family. I'll be good."

"Not yet," she said.

"Progress," he replied.

Sass hopped up at the end of the bed and they

looked at her. She sat down and stared. Lena held a hand out. "Come here, Sass. It's okay."

"I don't think she likes me," Matt said.

Sass's head swiveled to him and her ears went high and pointed forward. She took a tentative step forward.

"It's not you. She's a spoiled-rotten feline, that's all. Come here, Sass."

Matt turned to look at Lena, who made a quiet beckoning sound. Sass took another step and he looked back at her. She froze. He looked at Lena again. "Pretty sure it's me."

"No, she's coming."

He turned to see the cat marching up the bed now, her eyes intent on him. "She's not going to kill me, is she?"

"She's a cat, Matt. Not a tiger."

"Whoa. Okay. Hi there, Sass," Matt said as Sass stepped up and sat on his stomach, staring at him. He looked to Lena. "Does she like ear scratches?"

"Of course."

"Ow!"

"Oh my God! Sass!"

Lena leaned forward and grabbed the cat from his stomach as he clamped his hands over his beard. "She attacked me!"

"She was playing with your beard." Lena let the cat go and fell forward, laughing. "She thought it was a toy."

"Your cat attacked my face!"

"Your beard. You kept whipping it around so much swiveling your head like that, so it probably looked like a new toy."

He cast a doubtful eye at Sass, who was sitting back at the bottom of the bed. She lifted a paw and licked at it delicately. "Does that mean she likes me?"

Lena sat up and wiped the tears from her eyes. "Yes. She likes you. I'm sure your family likes you too, Matt. Have you tried to talk to them? I mean, it's been a while since you left home, right? Maybe they are regretting things they did also?"

He smiled at her earnest tone of voice. Little did she know. "Maybe."

"Talk to them when you go home. Maybe they are. You won't know until you try."

CHAPTER NINETEEN

SATURDAY MORNING, MATT leaned against the window at the Charleston Airport, losing a battle with his mother. "I don't want you to send the car. I can take the metro. It's faster."

"Nonsense. I won't have you dragging up the drive like some homeless bum."

He rolled his eyes. "Have the car pick me up at the metro stop then. What are you afraid of? That the neighbors might realize we know how to walk?"

"The driver will be waiting to meet your flight. Today is about your grandfather, not how much you hate us all."

"I don't hate…"

But she'd already hung up. He threw his backpack in an empty chair and slumped down next to it. *Next time, just pull a Nancy Reagan. Just say no.* Turning his phone over in his hands, he thought about calling Lena. Just to hear her voice. A smile touched his lips. He was already learning so much about her. Like how when she was completely relaxed, a tiny tinge of an accent appeared in her words. And that she could swear in Spanish raunchily enough to make a priest faint. She could make him laugh until his ribs hurt. And kissing her was like nothing he'd ever experienced before. Being with her was like a refuge. Even with that crazy cat of hers trying to rip his face off.

He tucked the phone away. No. Calling her now would be a bad idea. Dealing with his family didn't bring out the best in him. And he wasn't blameless in the situation.

He didn't hate his family as his mother frequently accused; he just didn't like them. Except Charlotte. His oldest sister had been away at college for most of his bad years and she was a little more understanding and forgiving. She'd had a lot of pressure placed on her as the firstborn. She had been required to be perfect, to be pretty, to be properly refined and to catch a suitable rich husband and begin providing grandchildren. She'd done those things, but on her own terms.

Susanna, the middle child, was worse than his mother in some ways. Of course, she'd been front and center at his rebellion and being only two years older, they'd been in high school together. He'd embarrassed her too many times for her to forgive him. He sighed. High school had been a long time ago and as much as he wished they'd let go of the grudges, it didn't seem like they would.

The phone vibrated in the outer pocket of the backpack. He pulled it out. A text from Lena.

Safe travels. Have fun. Talk to them.

Reading the words, he felt a heavy sadness press down on him. Have fun. Had he ever had fun with his family? How could he ever explain this to Lena? He'd seen her family. In droves, they showed up to visit her little cousin in the hospital. Loud, loving, warm. He typed out a few replies, deleting them all before settling on a simple lie.

I will try. Thanks.

OF COURSE THERE was a driver waiting for him. Holding a sign. *For God's sake.* The only thing surprising was that he wasn't dressed in a black suit. It crossed his mind to just walk by and get on the metro but he slowed his steps. Part of the reason he'd agreed to this trip was to try to make amends.

"Hey," he said. "I'm Charles Matthews." The driver looked him over, clearly skeptical. "I can show you my ID if you'd like."

"No, sir, that's quite all right. Do you have baggage to claim?"

Matt smiled. Yeah, he had baggage. "No," he said, shaking his head.

"Very good, sir, if you'll follow me."

The backseat of the car made him feel claustro-phobic. The dark leather, the tinted window be-tween him and the driver—all of it reminded him of too many car rides trapped in the back with his father, enduring a lecture. The constant tone of disappointment and disapproval. Matt plugged in his earbuds and cranked up the music, watched the scenery roll by and thought about Lena.

Smiling, he sent her a text.

Landed safely. Miss your scowl already.

A moment later, she sent him a picture of her-self scowling fiercely. He felt the tension and claustrophobic feelings slip away as he laughed. *I could fall in love with her.* The thought cut short his laughter and the phone slipped from his hand. It was true. He could. Whether he should or not remained to be seen. Grabbing the phone before it hit the floor, he sent her a grin emoji. *Focus on what you're doing here, man. You should take her advice and try to fix this stuff with your family. Then you can figure out what to do about Lena.*

Too soon, the car turned up the circular drive and glided to a stop in front of the large Victorian. Blue-and-white trim and soaring rooflines un-changed since his earliest memories. Climbing out, he felt the bite of wind and cold. Back in Charleston, autumn was barely tapping at the door but here winter was already making its presence known. The respite from the feelings of suffocation Lena's text had given him faded away. *Twenty-four hours. You can do this. You get to sleep for at least eight of them.* Hooking the backpack over a shoulder, he started up the wide front porch.

"Matt's home!"

His mood brightened. Charlotte. "Chuck!" he teased as he met her on the porch.

"Beau!"

She hugged him. Charlotte didn't fool around with her hugs. She came in fast and tight. He closed his arms around her and lifted her off her feet. When he set her back down, she reached up and ran her hands through his hair and beard. Snorted out a laugh. "Dad's gonna shit a brick."

"Won't be the first time," Matt said. He gestured at the front door. "What's the mood?"

"The usual. Mom's on a rampage. Everyone is incompetent. We're purposely trying to embarrass her. Three of the caterer's waitstaff have been reduced to tears. One quit. Called Mom a crazy old bitch. It was awesome."

"Tell me you got it on camera."

"Nope. Happened too quick. Heads-up, Susie is in there being Mom Junior. Dad's hiding in his office."

"So, essentially, nothing's changed at all."

"Nope. Welcome back to the asylum."

The front door opened and his mother leaned out. "Charles. Where is your luggage?"

"Hi, Mom. Nice to see you."

"You didn't even bring a suit? I suppose you think you are going to attend your grandfather's ninetieth birthday party in that?"

"I have some pants and a shirt. Figured I'd borrow one of Dad's ties."

He followed her into the house. Inside was the usual preparty bustle. Catering staff scurrying around, setting up tables and laying out place settings. His mother's decorator had her own staff hard at work with flower arrangements and candles. He steered clear of that side of the house.

"Mom, I was wondering if I could…"

She looked at him, then past him. "No!" she screeched. "Not there. I told you people not to put flowers in that room." Pushing past him, muttering under her breath, she stormed into the formal dining room.

Okay. Should have known better. Not a good time. He took some deep breaths, trying to let go of the irritation. He was going to try to make some amends this weekend. They weren't going to come to him. He'd have to get them to sit down together at some point. He headed up the staircase to the second level and his old room.

It had been stripped of any hint of him and turned into a guest room, but it was where he stayed when home. Tossing the backpack in a chair, he toed off his shoes and flopped down on the bed. His phone vibrated in his shirt pocket. Charlotte.

You are not allowed to hide up there.

I'm taking a nap. Need to be fresh for tonight.

I have a flask of cinnamon whiskey on the back porch.

On my way.

He stopped at his father's closed office door. Maybe he should do this after a wee sip or two from Charlotte's flask. Shaking his head, he lightly knocked once on the door. *Good old Dad would love to smell alcohol on his breath.* There was a gruff sound from behind the door that he took for permission to enter the sacred chamber. He turned the doorknob, hating the way his heart rate picked up and he felt like he was fresh from the principal's office.

"Hi. Just wanted to let you know I was here. Thanks for the plane tickets."

His father looked up and pulled reading glasses from his face. When Matt was a boy, his father seemed a giant. Ten feet tall, hands like catcher's mitts and a voice loud enough to shake the foundations of the earth. As an adult, he was a sedentary man heading into his senior years. He wasn't even six feet tall. The hands were soft from turning pages in books all day. Only the voice remained. Gravelly, abrupt.

"I thought I told you to cut that hair."

"I trimmed the beard," Matt said, stroking a hand down his chin, falling against his will into the habit of goading his father.

"Always the smart-ass. Thought you'd outgrow that."

"Dad. I want to talk to you and Mom at some point before I leave tomorrow."

Replacing the glasses, his father returned to the book on the desk. "We aren't lending you money."

Fury, white-hot and oh so familiar, flared within him. He'd never asked them for a penny. Ever. The door opened behind him.

"Matt. Come on. Susie's here," Charlotte said. She caught his hand and pulled him from the room. Out in the hall, she looped an arm around his waist. "Why do you do that?"

"Do what?"

"Keep hitting yourself in the head with the same club and expecting it not to hurt."

He pulled away. "Is Susie really here because I'd rather not deal with her right now. Where's that flask?"

They sneaked out through the basement door, heading down the paved garden walkway to the hidden gazebo that overlooked the woods behind the property. Huddled together on the bench, they passed the flask back and forth a few times.

"How do you do it?" he asked.

"Deal with them every day?"

"Yeah."

"I can't change them, Matt. They will always be exactly who they are. I can only change how I let them impact me."

"I want to tell them I'm sorry," he blurted out. Charlotte had that effect on him. She'd been more than his big sister. She'd been more of a loving, motherly influence than his own mother. "I know I was a terrible son for a long time. But I'm tired of the dance."

"And you want to know if they'd be receptive to this?"

"Yeah."

Charlotte took a sip from the flask and handed it to him. "Bald truth? No. I don't think they will be. They are so…so…inflexible."

"So I should forget about it?"

"I didn't say that. If you want to apologize to them for your own peace of mind, to make amends, then do it. If you want to do it to change how they treat you, you're going to be disappointed."

"But what if I want both?"

Charlotte shrugged. "Won't get either or both if you don't even try."

"Are you two drinking?"

Susie's voice climbed several shocked octaves. Matt and Charlotte slid lower on the bench. Charlotte pressed her face against Matt's shoulder to hold back the giggles. Susie appeared on the gazebo steps. She was a perfect miniature of their mother. Blond hair tastefully tinted and shaped into an acceptable helmet around her face. Powder blue suit with a white blouse and black pearls. Black pumps with two-inch heels. She put her hands on her hips and Matt lost it. He began giggling, which made Charlotte giggle harder.

"I swear, Charles. You aren't even home ten minutes and you're causing trouble. Why don't you grow up already?"

He pointed at Charlotte. "It was her," he wheezed out. Drawing in a huge breath, he tried to stop laughing.

"It was," Charlotte said, wiping at her streaming eyes. She held up the flask. "Mine."

"Well. I'm going to tell Mother."

The threat sent Matt and Charlotte back into a laughing fit. After Susie stomped away, Matt grabbed the flask and took another sip.

"Home sweet home," Charlotte said.

"Think she'll really tell?"

"No. Mom's on a rampage. Even Susie isn't going to throw gasoline on that fire. Come on. Let's go find some food."

CHAPTER TWENTY

HIS MOTHER'S PARTIES always followed the same protocol. Cocktail hour for the family that was essentially a wardrobe inspection and a briefing on the important guests. Matt finished ironing his dress shirt and put it on while it was still hot. Moving to the mirror, he tied the tie in a neat knot, adjusting it at his throat as if he did it every morning. Stepping back, he looked at himself. Nodded. Should pass inspection. *Crap. His hair.* He scrounged around in his backpack and found a hair band. Perfect. He scooped his hair up into a neat man bun.

He took a grinning selfie and sent it to Lena.

I clean up okay.

No immediate response. He took a deep breath. Okay. Showtime. He was going to behave. He was going to be charming. He was going to control his smart-ass mouth. After everyone had left, he'd sit down with his parents and tell them what he came to say. Charlotte was right—their response didn't really matter. It'd be great if they could begin to heal this rift, but if not, he'd tried.

Halfway down the stairs, the phone buzzed.

That man bun is so hot. Have you talked to your parents?

He stopped on the staircase and began typing out a response.

Not yet. Soon. When I get home, I'll let you watch me put it up.

Charlotte came running down the stairs and snatched the phone from his hand before he could hit Send.

"Baby brother! Lena? Who is this? You have a girlfriend?"

He took the phone back and sent the text. "Lena is… I don't know what she is yet. Don't say anything to anyone. It's very new."

Charlotte mimed zipping her lips but she gave him one of her giant hugs. "I hope it works out. I want to see you happy, Beau."

"Don't make me up, Chuck."

She groaned. "Still as horrible as when you made it up, dork."

Their mother appeared at the bottom of the stairs. "Will you two stop wasting time and get down here."

Following her into the formal living room, Matt looked around. His father lounged back on the sofa with Susie beside him. Grandfather sat in the side chair, looking older and frailer than Matt remembered. A pang hit his heart. He missed his grandmother. She had been an artist also and had encouraged his talents. Against the wishes of everyone else in the family. There was still not a small amount of resentment that she'd put the bulk of her estate in a trust for him.

But he was going to be the penitent son. "Grandfather," he said respectfully, approaching the old man and holding out a hand. "Happy birthday. Happy to be home to help you celebrate."

The old man pretended to squint up at him. "Susannah? Is that you? Can't tell with all that hair."

Matt pressed his lips together as Susie and his father snickered from the sofa. He turned to them with a smile. "Suz, you need to tend to your chin hairs. Must be out of control if Granddad here is mistaking me for you."

"Enough," his mother barked out. "I swear to God, can we just pretend to get along for one night?"

Charlotte made a drinking motion from behind the sofa and crossed her eyes. Matt ignored her and turned to his mother. "I'm sorry. I'll behave. I promise."

At the ring of a bell, the maid carried in a tray of champagne flutes. After they'd each taken one, his father got to his feet. "Happy birthday to my mentor, my leader, my father. May we have many more years of your knowledge and guidance."

They all raised their glasses and called out, "Happy birthday."

"Now that that's over," his mother began. Matt met Charlotte's eye and she shook her head. "Matt, you haven't been around much, but I'm sure you remember who the partners are at the firm."

"Pretty much," he said.

"There are several new wives," she continued with a disapproving sniff. "Harley Bennett married that little blonde secretary of his, Eva. And Edward Cooper married his…"

"Mistress," Charlotte supplied the word. She grinned at Matt. "She was a Vegas showgirl."

"Lola?"

"No, Kelly. You'll know who she is. Slamming hot."

"Both of you, stop. No need to rummage in the gutter with Edward."

Matt dipped his head. "Yes ma'am."

THE PARTY WAS a mind-numbing whirl of faces and fake smiles. Matt moved restlessly around the perimeter, nursing the same glass of champagne he'd used for his father's toast. It was all too much. The inane banter, the insincere compliments were almost physically painful to him. Watching his grandfather puff up under the fawning made him want to run screaming back to Charleston.

A hand closed around his biceps, squeezing tight. "Why, Matt, never in a million years would I have thought I'd see you here."

He turned toward the familiar voice with a forced smile. "Bitsy," he said before kissing her on both cheeks. "I wouldn't miss Grandfather's ninetieth birthday."

Her eyes moved over him hungrily. "You're looking rather…dangerous."

She did all but lick her lips. He gave her a grin. She did lick her lips then. "Dangerous as a newborn kitten," he said.

She lifted his left hand. "Still unattached I see."

He pulled his hand away. Bitsy and her parents had decided that he was going to marry her when they were seniors in high school. Bitsy went off to college to get a degree in flower arranging or something. Matt had fled the scene. One of his many sins.

He pointed at the rock hanging off her fingers. "I see you aren't."

She gave him a smug, superior smile. "I found a real man."

"Congratulations. I wish you happiness."

"I'm sure I will be. Donald is a junior partner at—"

"Excuse me. Sorry, Bitsy, but my Grandfather is trying to get my attention."

He slipped away. He was sorry he'd just run off all those years ago instead of telling her he didn't love her and didn't want to marry her. But not sorry enough to listen to her try to prove how much better her life was without him. He grabbed a fresh glass of champagne and sat down, unasked, next to his grandfather.

"Escaped her clutches again, son?" the old man said.

"Barely. How're you enjoying your party?"

"Bah. I'd rather be reading a book. All these people. Not one of them has spoken to me since I retired. They don't care."

"I care."

"Do you? You ran away from us fast enough."

"I know. I didn't know what else to do. But I did care about you all. You and Grandmother. Maybe I didn't appreciate it back then, but I know how much work you did to provide us with all the advantages that we took for granted."

The look in his grandfather's eyes was one Matt had never seen before: respect. He shut his mouth before he said anything to ruin the moment.

The old man nodded and clasped Matt's forearm for a moment. "I'm sorry your father is a bit of a dick. And I didn't choose your mother. That was your father's doing. And don't ever tell anyone I said that or I'll deny it and cut you out of my will."

Matt laughed. "You can cut me out, Grandfather. I'm doing okay."

"I know you are."

"Oh?"

"I keep up. I know you're something of the hotshot down there in Charleston. Your grandmother would be proud."

Matt blinked. A lump rose in his throat even as his heart warmed at the words. "Thank you, sir," he said in a thick voice. "I miss her."

"Me too, Matt. Me too."

And then Matt did something he'd never done before in his life. He reached out and took his grandfather's hand. Gave it a gentle squeeze.

He took in a deep breath and looked around the room. Charlotte was deep in conversation with Kelly, the former Vegas showgirl who was indeed slamming hot. Susie was huddled in a corner with Bitsy and some other woman, casting dour glances at Charlotte and Kelly before murmuring what were surely not compliments. His father was working the men in the room, his hearty fake laugh bouncing off the walls. His mother was flitting about with her party smile on, but her eyes were sharp and constantly moving, looking for the waitstaff to make a mistake.

He suddenly remembered what Lena had said about rich people. That everyone was afraid to do something different unless the richest, most influential man in the society did it first. Was that what was wrong with his family? They were all acting out the roles they thought they were supposed to play? Could it be that under all that icy armor, they were looking for someone to make the first move? A new feeling rose in his gut. *Hope. This might actually work. He'd take that first step and maybe they were ready to let go of the past as much as he was.*

AFTER THE GUESTS had all left—several hours after Grandfather had taken his leave—Matt cornered his parents in the family room where they were enjoying a postparty cocktail.

"May I talk to you about something?" he asked from the door. He half hoped they would say no. Plead the late hour. Something. Anything. He stood straighter. *No. You will do this.* He crossed the room to the bar and splashed some club soda in a glass.

"What is it now, Charles?" his mother asked. "I have a headache and I'm not in the mood for any of your…"

"Bullshit," his father finished for her.

Matt pulled the armchair around so he was facing them and sat down. "I wanted to apologize."

A brief look of surprise crossed their faces before they each settled into their neutral states. Bored for his father and slightly annoyed for his mother. He took a deep breath.

"I know I wasn't an easy child. I was terrible, in fact. The things I did. I don't know why I did them. I don't know why I was so angry and rebellious. I just was. And I hurt you both. It must have seemed like I was disrespecting everything you'd done for us. I'm sorry."

They exchanged puzzled looks. "Well," his father said. "Okay. I appreciate that."

"You were always an ungrateful child," his mother began. She hushed when her husband placed a hand over hers.

"He's apologized, Anne. He's admitted his mistake and apologized. Let it go now."

"Thank you," Matt said. This was the first time his father had stood up to his mother on his behalf. "I want to try to get past all these feelings we have from what happened back then. Start again. Try to be a family."

"Law school?" his father asked. But his tone was questioning, not commanding, another first.

"No," he said quietly, shaking his head. "I love what I do. I'm very close to creating my own nonprofit to bring art therapy to kids who really need it."

"I'm trying to understand this," his father said.

"Here's how I see it. When Grandfather took over the firm, he modernized it, brought it into the twentieth century. When you took over, you put your own mark on the firm. You expanded the reach and brought it into the digital age. You each took it and made it your own. That's all I'm trying to do. Build something of my own."

His father sat back, nodding. Matt's heart was beating hard. He'd never opened himself up to them like this before. His mother's silence did not bode well. But his father's quiet appraisal did. He held eye contact.

"That I can understand. And respect."

"Thank you, sir," Matt said, letting out a breath and feeling a weight lift. He looked to his mother. "Mother?"

"If your father forgives you, then so shall I."

Not exactly the Hallmark moment he was looking for, but he'd take it. "Thank you." He wanted to add an "I love you" to that but the peace seemed too fragile for it. He stood and moved the chair back. "Good night."

"Good night, son," his father said.

Matt froze. When was the last time his father had called him son? Fifteen? Twenty years? This was going to be okay. They were going to be okay. The war was over.

CHAPTER TWENTY-ONE

"WHO KEEPS TEXTING YOU?"

Lena stuffed her phone in her bra and looked over at her mother. "Work stuff," she mumbled.

"On a Sunday?" Aunt Paula asked, her voice dripping with horrified disapproval.

"There is no weekend in the financial world."

She returned to her assigned task of cutting fruit for sangria. It was a full-family Sunday. Everyone was there or on the way. Lena may have been an only child, but her aunts and uncles had provided her with a multitude of cousins. They had all grown up living either with each other or next door to each other depending on the job market. Now another generation was being added, one baby at a time.

Her mother set down more oranges. "I've never seen you smile at work stuff like that before."

Lena looked up into her mother's knowing eyes and felt her stomach drop. "Good news always makes me smile." Saying a quick, silent prayer for lying to her mother on a Sunday, Lena put down the knife and dropped the chopped fruit into waiting pitchers.

"That didn't look like a business smile," her mother pressed. "That looked like a personal smile."

"A personal smile? What in the heck is that even supposed to mean? Oh, look! Jules is here!"

That worked. Ana went running to greet Jules. Her first granddaughter. Never mind there was no blood or legalities behind it yet—Ana didn't need any of that. Lena caught Sadie's eye and made a face.

"What's wrong?" Sadie asked as she sidled up next to Lena at the kitchen counter.

"Mom's getting suspicious."

"Ha. Good luck trying to hide anything from her. The FBI should hire her. I swear she can smell a secret on anyone."

"Where's Wyatt?"

"Out on a case. He said he'd swing by if he finishes up in time."

"See, Mamacita," Lena said as Ana came back in the kitchen with her arm draped around Jules's shoulders. "Wyatt is working today also."

"And I'll bet he's not smiling at his phone every ten minutes."

"Only when I send him cute texts," Sadie said with a not so innocent smile.

Lena gave her a death glare, but her mother had already moved her attention to Jules. "Thanks. Get me in trouble."

"So," Sadie purred as she reached for a knife

to help with the fruit. "Who's got you smiling at your phone?"

"Shut up," Lena hissed, looking around. "Any of them could be anywhere."

"Now you're just getting paranoid."

Voices rose from the front room as more people arrived. "I'm not paranoid," Lena said, using the noise as cover. "They are up to something."

"Paranoid," Sadie said in a singsong voice.

"Lena! Sadie! Hi!"

Lena looked up at her cousin Dan. "Hey, Dan, what's up? I didn't know you'd be here today."

"Yeah, Mom said it was all-family day or else. And I don't do 'or else' with her."

"I know what you mean," Lena said with a laugh. Dan's wife, Juana, came in the kitchen, followed by a group of men. She gave Sadie a sidelong glance. "Wow. Hi, Juana. And company."

Juana looked slightly embarrassed as she motioned to the four guys who stood behind her. All tall, midtwenties to early thirties, Hispanic. Surprise, surprise. "These are my brothers. They're visiting from out of town."

"Oh? Out of town from where?" Lena asked.

The men looked at their toes and Juana blushed. "Mount Pleasant," she mumbled and glanced around. "Estrella asked them."

Lena stared. Sadie hip bumped her. "Technically, Lena, Mount Pleasant *is* another town."

Lena put the knife down. Slowly. Deliberately. Before she stabbed someone with it. She wiped her hands on the dishtowel and plucked her phone from her bra. *Oh, they all looked up for that. Estrella is dead. Dead.* "Excuse me. I have some business to attend to."

Up in the guest room, she resisted the urge to slam the door. Instead, she kicked her shoes off against the wall and flopped down on the bed. There was a message from Matt.

At airport. Will be back in Charleston in a couple hours. Would like to see you tonight.

She dropped the phone to her chest and stared at the ceiling. There was about to be a major skirmish in the War of the Aunties. Blood might be drawn. She wasn't sure if she wanted Matt to see her postfamily drama. She lifted the phone.

Out at my parents' in Edisto. Don't know when I'll get home.

The door opened and she quickly hid the phone. It was just Sadie. "You see what I'm talking about now? Four? They rounded up four poor guys and had them come out here to see if poor, pathetic, dried-up, old spinster me might be able to entice one of them. They've given up on setting me up. They're doing cattle calls now."

"Scoot over," Sadie said, and plopped down beside her on the bed. "That was…uh…pretty obvious."

"That was humiliating. It's like they're down to 'Are you brown? Do you have a penis and a pulse?' I'm going to kill Estrella."

Sadie giggled. "Next, they'll be bussing them in from Hanahan."

"It's not funny."

"Yes, it is. Want me to suggest they just do full-out auditions? We'll make up questions for them to answer."

"Dancing," Lena said, "I want them to have to dance."

"Definitely dancing. Maybe a talent portion?"

"Yes. I want a husband who can sing."

"Oh! A tuxedo competition. See how well they clean up."

"Swimsuits!" Lena said, lifting her hand.

"Underwear!" Sadie said. They both were giggling now.

"With bowties on!"

Lena wiped at her streaming eyes and rested her head on Sadie's shoulder. "Thanks, sis."

"Anytime. So, what's up with the Viking?"

Lena shrugged. "I don't know. He's different than any guy I've dated."

"You're dating?"

"Technically, no. We're just in the same place at the same time sometimes."

"Holy cats, Lena. You are so weird."

"I know, it's…" She glanced at the door. "He scares me a little."

"Scares you how?"

Lena smiled. Street Sadie had shown up in a heartbeat, ready to take on anyone who threatened those she loved. "Not like that. But like…" Her words trailed off. *Scared* wasn't exactly the right word.

Sadie pressed her cheek to the top of Lena's head. She lowered her voice to a whisper. "Do you think he might be the one?"

"He could be. Sadie. I just never met a man like him. He's nothing like he appears. There are layers and layers to him. And he's so talented. And he wants to do something good in this world."

"Sounds like you're moving toward the big *l* word there, Lena."

Her insides went icy cold and a slippery feeling squirmed in her gut. *Is that what falling in love feels like? Exciting? Terrifying?* Before she could answer or think about it further, the bedroom door opened.

"There you are," Ana said from the doorway.

"We were talking," Lena said, sitting up in the bed.

"You are being rude. Ignoring your guests."

Lena stared, openmouthed, at her mother. Even

Sadie's hand on her arm couldn't stem the rise of fury. "They are not *my* guests," she hissed. "They are Estrella's guests. She can entertain them. And you all are being rude to me. Dragging these poor men here."

Sadie rolled off the bed. "I think I'll just go see what Jules is doing."

There was a long silence after Sadie deserted her. Lena crossed her arms against her chest but didn't lower her eyes. She matched her mother, glare to glare. She felt like a petulant child, but seriously. They'd had this conversation. Her mother had promised to put an end to this nonsense.

"Magdalena," Ana said with a sigh. She came to sit on the edge of the bed. "We just want what's best for you."

"I know that, Mom. But I can find my own husband."

"Can you? You don't seem to be doing too well in that department. When was the last time you dated a man more than a few weeks?"

Lena felt her face burn. Just because she was picky didn't mean she couldn't sustain a relationship. "That has nothing to do with anything. If I know it's not working out, I move on. I'm not staying with a man just to have a man."

"It's because you date white men."

"What?" The word fell out of her mouth. She stared at her mother, barely believing the words she'd spoken. "What did you just say?"

"I'm sorry. I know how it sounds, but Lena, listen to me. You need a man who understands you. Understands the extra challenges you and your family face every day."

"I can't believe you just said that, Mother. What does skin color have to do with understanding people? You and Poppa taught me better than that."

But even as the words left her mouth, they rang sanctimonious in her ears. She'd thought things about Matt that weren't far from what her mother was saying. Shame burned hot and cold in her gut.

"It isn't racist. I'm not saying that some people are better than others based on skin color. I'm just saying a Hispanic man will understand the challenges you have."

"I don't have any challenges that I haven't handled all by myself."

Lena scrambled off the bed. Her heart was pounding even as an icy cold washed over her. Her stomach felt like a tight fist. Her mother was holding up a mirror to all the things Lena tried to pretend didn't exist. Because on the flip side of overcoming challenges was the assumption by some that you were given an easier path because of those challenges. And the implication that she hadn't earned her accomplishments by her own talent and not some bar lowered for her was infuriating.

"Lena." Her mother's voice was low and calm as she rose to her feet. "Tell me, then, why you won't go to the grocery store in sweatpants and a T-shirt. Tell me why you won't speak in Spanish when you are in public. Tell me why you feel you need to be perfectly put together at all times."

Lena pressed her lips together. "That's just how I am. I don't like to look sloppy." The excuse came out sounding weak and they all knew it.

Ana stood and threw her hands up. "Fine. Keep believing that. You think because all those rich white people let you take care of their money, invite you to their fancy parties, have you over to dinner, that they don't see your brown skin? Tell me, Lena, when you are at those fancy parties, how many other people of color are there?"

"What are you saying, Momma? That I've only achieved the success I have because white people are keeping me around as some sort of token. That I'm their pet brown person? Because that is a lie. I know people think that, but I was given no special treatment. And it's insulting to me to say so."

"No, Lena. You are taking this all wrong. It has nothing to do with them or you or the hard work you've done. It's about having a safe place from the world. About having someone who completely understands without needing explanations."

"I have to go. I can't even with this discussion." Grabbing her shoes, she stomped barefoot down the staircase. Ignoring the people gathered in the large living room area, she headed straight for the door. And got her hand on the doorknob…

"Magdalena Teresa Reyes! You stop right there," her mother ordered, in Spanish, from the staircase. "We are going to finish this discussion. We can finish it here or in private, but it is going to be finished."

Oh, she was pulling out the big guns. One, she three-named her. Two, she was speaking in Spanish, which meant she was extra mad. Three, she was fully ready to have this out in front of everyone, including the four poor, innocent bachelors. Well, fine.

Turning around, she glared around the room. *"Tu y tu,"* she said, pointing at Paula and Estrella. She snapped her fingers. *"Vámonos."*

She headed back up the staircase, brushing past her mother. When all three of the older women were behind the closed door of her room, Lena pointed at them.

"Enough," she said. "All of this foolishness stops right now. It's not only extremely irritating and rude to me, but to these poor men that you are dragging here and throwing at me."

"Lena, we just want…" her mother began in a more consolatory tone than Lena expected.

But she was not consoled. "I know what you want. To make it easier for me. Well, I don't want easy. I want to be madly, crazy in love with my future husband. Nothing's ever been easy for me. And what's more, you're wrong. Just because someone isn't Hispanic doesn't mean they can't understand me. Look at Sadie. And while I'm thinking about it, look at that guy I dated in high school. He was one hundred percent Mexican, but did he understand me? No! He hit me."

"That's not the same," Paula began. "Just because that one boy—"

"Excuse me. I hate to be rude, but I am not *asking* any of you. I am *telling* you. No more of this."

Paula and Estrella looked at her murderously. Never before had she raised her voice to one of her elders. Heart pounding, she pressed her lips together to keep from babbling out apologies. She had to stand her ground on this. And as for her mother… Now her lips were pressed together in a clear attempt to keep from crying. She couldn't believe her mother had said such things to her.

The door opened and Sadie quietly slipped in. She took one look at Lena and stepped between her and the women. "I don't know what's going on, but let's give Lena some room here, okay? Everyone can just cool down before things are said."

Estrella snorted. "Things have already been said."

With that, she and Paula left the room. Ana approached her daughter and touched her cheek. "I know you are angry, Lena. But you think about what I said. You'll know it's true."

Lena turned her head away, sending tears spilling down her cheeks. Why did this hurt so badly? It wasn't the fixing up. It was her mother's words on race. It felt like an attack. Not on her, but on…

"Lena, what happened?" Sadie asked, pulling her into an embrace.

"My mother is a horrible person," Lena managed between shuddering sighs as she tried to force back the tears.

"She is not a horrible person and you know it."

Pulling away, Lena found some tissue and wiped at her eyes. *Matt.* The image of him appeared crystal clear in her mind's eye. It felt like an attack on him. She lifted her hand to cover her mouth. *All those things. All those horrible things you thought about Matt. Rich white boy. Frat boy.*

"What?" Sadie demanded.

"Oh my God, Sades," she whispered. "I'm racist."

A look of complete confusion spread across Sadie's face. "What? Huh? How did we get from your family setting you up to you being racist?"

Lena sank down on the edge of the bed. "My mother. I was mad at her because she said I shouldn't be dating white guys. That I should date and marry a Hispanic man because he would understand me. And I said she was being racist."

Sadie sat down beside her and took her hand. "Okay," she said slowly. "Go on."

"But I did the same thing. When I met Matt. I assumed he was all these really bad things simply because he was white and came from a wealthy family. That's racism, right?"

Sadie shrugged. "Maybe. A bit. I don't know, Lena. Sometimes white guys who come from money can be sort of dickish."

"Sure they can, but that's not everyone. And it doesn't mean I should start from that assumption."

Sadie flopped back on the bed. "I see what you're saying. I wouldn't say you are racist. Maybe it's more of a case of realizing a stereotype isn't always true? I mean, if you were racist would you be feeling bad about it? Or would a real racist even consider the question?"

Lena flopped back too. "Now my head hurts. I don't know."

After a long beat of silence, Sadie spoke. "You have real feelings for this guy. That's why it hurt so much."

A lump rose in Lena's throat and she tried to swallow it down. *Maybe. But now she knew she'd never get her family's blessing.* "It feels so fragile, Sadie. Like if I make one wrong move, it's all going to break into a million pieces."

"What's going to break, honey?"

She wiped at the tears running down her cheeks and into her ears. "My heart," she whispered.

Sadie's hand closed around hers and squeezed.

There was a tentative knock on the door and Lena let out a muffled groan. She was done with people.

"Momma Sadie?"

Sadie propped up on her elbows. "Come on in, Jules."

Lena hurriedly wiped her face.

"What are you doing? Is Abuelita mad?"

"We're staring at the ceiling," Sadie said. She moved over on the bed. "Come stare with us."

Jules squeezed in between the two of them and they all stared at the ceiling. "But is she mad?" Jules whispered.

"Maybe a little. It's okay. People get mad. She's not mad at you."

They stared at the ceiling some more.

"This is boring," Jules said. "Why are we doing this?"

"Because my brain broke and I can't do anything else," Lena said.

"If your brain broke, you wouldn't be able to talk," Jules countered.

"True."

"The tamales are ready," Jules said. "Want me to bring you some?"

"Can you just grab a pitcher of sangria?" Lena asked.

Sadie stood up. "Come on, Jules. Let's raid the kitchen and we'll bring back food and have a picnic."

After they left, Lena looked at her phone. Matt must be in the air because there were no new texts. Her finger hovered over the phone for a moment before she began to peck out letters.

Can't tonight. Might be late getting back from Edisto.

She wanted to add more but couldn't pin down a single thought. Hitting Send, she dropped the phone on the bed. This was a big, fat mess. Rolling to her side, she brought her legs up. *You just need a nap. That's all. This will all make sense once you've had some tamales and some sangria and a nap.*

Sadie came back, balancing a plate in one hand, a pitcher in the other and a couple of red Solo cups between her teeth. She was alone. Good. Not that she didn't love Jules. She wasn't quite up to an inquisitive nine-year-old at the moment. The scent of her mother's corn-husk-wrapped chorizo tamales propelled her out of the bed.

"Where's Jules?"

"Playing with the other kids. We're boring."

Sadie sat on the floor and poured them each a healthy shot of sangria. She pulled a handful of napkins from the front of her shirt.

"Eww," Lena said.

"I only have so many hands."

Lena pulled back the husk and bit into the tamale, a little moan of pleasure escaping her. Say what you will about her meddling mother and aunties, they could cook. "How's the mood down there?" she asked around a mouthful.

"I don't think anyone really noticed anything. Y'all are always yelling at each other. Your mom and aunts are playing it cool."

They gorged on tamales in silence. *I should go down there. Apologize for yelling at them. But they deserved it.*

"So tell me what's going on with this guy. How'd he go from annoying the general hell out of you to maybe being the one?"

Lena washed down the last bite with a healthy swig of sangria. *How did this happen?* "I don't think I even realized how I felt about him until my mother started her rant about not dating white guys." She clapped a hand over her mouth and stared at Sadie.

"What?"

"Oh. My. God. Do you think I just like him now because my mom doesn't want me to? Am I adolescent rebelling here?"

"Give me your phone," Sadie demanded, holding her hand out.

"Why?"

"Give it to me."

Lena handed it over. "Hey! Stop. How'd you get my password?"

Twisting away from Lena's grabbing hands,

Sadie laughed. "Like I haven't watched you unlock this phone a billion times. Oh? Frat Boy? Is that him?"

"Don't look at those!"

"I'm going to assume it is then. Shouldn't you change that to something more sensitive? Like his name?"

"Seriously, don't scroll through those. It's personal."

"I'm not reading them. I'm just looking at them."

Lena leaned back against the bed and poured more wine. *No. This wasn't new.* She'd known there was something different about Matt from the time she'd bumped into him at the Pineapple Fountain and told him why she wouldn't accept his apology. She'd never had a man be truly grateful for enlightenment. That was when she really knew, in her heart, that he wasn't what she thought him to be.

Sadie handed the phone back. "One. No, this isn't a reaction to your mom. Two. You two are beyond cute together. Three. That man is hot as sin on Sunday."

"But what do I do now?"

"I don't know. Are you going to get drunk on sangria and spend the night here? I can have Wyatt pick Jules up so I can stay with you."

"No. I have an early meeting in the morning. I need to apologize to my mother and get out of here before they make me mad again."

CHAPTER TWENTY-TWO

MATT CHECKED HIS phone for about the millionth time. He'd had no response to the text he'd sent Lena yesterday after his plane had landed. She'd said she was staying late at her parents but that was the last he'd heard. *Dude. It's Monday. She has a job. Stop checking your phone like a...* Stuffing the phone back in his pocket with a grimace, he straddled his bike and pulled on the helmet. *Lovesick puppy* were the words he'd shut down.

He needed to focus. He had a lot to do today. A shift at the hospital and two private lessons. Plus, he needed to get a couple more of his abstracts ready for a showing. Lena's and Eliot's one-two sales punch at the church had cleared out several of his larger works. Which led him to the other thing on his to-do list: meet with the hospital's social worker to identify the neediest of elementary schools so he could begin approaching the school district about bringing art therapy into the classroom. And he was only halfway done with the written proposal on that project.

In other words, man, get your head out of the clouds and focus. He steered the bike out into the street, where focus was definitely needed. He felt good. He'd dreaded the trip home but it had turned out to be a good thing. He felt like the black cloud that hung over his relationship with his parents had lifted. Maybe things weren't perfect, but much improved. The weight of his guilt had lifted and for the first time in a long time, he felt he had his family back.

As he set up the art table in the playroom and the kids began to show up for the session, he looked around. A cold wisp of dread drifted through him. "Where's Clarissa?" he asked. Always a dangerous question with the cancer kids.

One of the boys spoke up. "She went home. Her labs were good."

He was relieved, but still he'd seen the looks on all their faces. His question had reminded them that they might not go home one day. They'd seen enough of their fellow patients not go home. Mentally kicking himself, he made a note to check in with the unit's charge nurse to get updates if he'd been gone awhile.

He got the kids started on their choice of projects and circled the table, encouraging and helping out where necessary. His phone buzzed and he stepped back to check it. A smile crossed his face. Lena.

Sorry. Crazy day. Glad you made it home okay.

He looked at the words for a while. The message seemed rather flat. The teasing was gone.

It's all good. I was going to offer to cook dinner for you tonight.

A shocked face emoji showed up.

You can cook? On top of all your other skills?

I can demonstrate any skill set at your demand.

He looked up to check on the kids. They were all involved in their projects. Except Keesha. She was watching him. If she was smiling, it was hidden by the mask that she wore to protect her fragile immune system. Her eyebrows were raised almost to her forehead. His phone buzzed again.

I'll make up a list. Seven?

He sent back a thumbs-up.
"Mr. Matt?"
"Whatcha need, Keesha?"
"Were you talking to your girlfriend?"
He tucked the phone back into his shirt pocket. Time to start being more careful. These kids noticed everything. "Just a friend," he said.

"Oh. Because I heard two of the nurses wondering if you had a girlfriend, so I can tell them if you don't. I think they would be your girlfriends if you wanted."

He managed to keep a straight face. "That's okay. I like to get my own girlfriends."

"Okay, but I can tell them if you want."

"That's okay. You don't need to do that."

"Ow! YOU PINCHED ME!"

Lena grinned and took a sip of wine. "I couldn't help it."

And she couldn't. All broad shoulders and tight abs, hair up in a messy, sexy man bun standing in her kitchen unpacking a paper bag of food that wasn't in little boxes already cooked, he couldn't be real.

"I had to see if you were real or if I'm dreaming."

Matt rubbed his backside. "I think you're supposed to pinch yourself to see if you're dreaming."

"Oh? Is that how it works? Sorry."

"Not sorry."

"Not a bit."

"Make yourself useful then. I'm going to need a cutting board. And a pot. A big pot. And a baking sheet."

Lena blinked and shook her head. "Did you

start speaking Mandarin or something? Because
I don't even know what you just said."

Matt moved around the small kitchen, opening cabinets. He found the cutting board. "How
do you not know how to cook?"

"How do you know how to cook?"

"Pots?"

She sighed and set down the wineglass. Bend-
ing, she pulled the nest of pots she'd received as a
housewarming gift from…someone. Probably her
mother. "For someone who offered to make me
dinner, you sure are demanding a lot. I thought
I'd be on the couch, feet up, drinking wine and
watching you prance around the kitchen wearing
nothing but an apron."

"Okay, now you are dreaming." He took the
largest pot from the nest. "Put those away and
I'll teach you how to make a *tagine*."

"Like a Moroccan *tagine*?"

"See? You know how to cook."

"I know how to order off a menu. How do you
know how to make it?"

He pulled a knife from the little block thing
that was also an almost-pristine housewarming
gift and set it on the cutting board. "There's this
new thing, you may have heard of it, called the
internet."

"I thought that was for shopping without leaving the house."

He stared at her. "Come on, do you really not know how to cook?"

"Okay. All right. Yes. I was forced labor in my mother's kitchen all my life. I just don't like to…" She stopped. She didn't like to cook for one.

"Good. Because this is a little labor intensive, so dust off your chopping skills and rustle up another cutting board."

"How was your trip home?" she asked minutes later as they stood side by side at the counter. "Is this okay for the onions? Smaller?"

"That's fine. It was an interesting trip."

"Interesting good or interesting bad?"

He shrugged. "I talked to my parents. Things are better now."

She put a handful of dates on the chopping board. After the dustup with her mother and aunts Sunday, she wasn't sure what her relationship status was with her own family. She'd spoken to her mother and apologized, but she'd left Estrella and Paula alone. They were the ones behind the most egregious of fix-ups. She was still mad at them.

"Why'd you lie to me?" Matt asked, pulling her out of her thoughts.

"What? I didn't lie to you."

He motioned to the neat piles of chopped onions, dates and apricots. "You handle that knife like a professional."

"If I had a penny for every tamale I had to roll, I'd never have to work again. You grow up in a Mexican household with about a million extended family members either living with you or next door. Food prep is military-level precision."

"Sounds pretty awesome, actually."

"You still haven't told me much about your visit. Did the talk with your parents go well?"

He put down the knife and leaned against the counter. "I did it, Lena. Your family is amazing. Everything I wish mine had been. I think the talk went well. They accepted my apology and we reached some neutral ground. But…"

She looked into his eyes and saw real pain there. Putting the knife down, she reached up to put her hands on his cheeks. "But what, Matt?"

He shrugged. "We'll never have the type of love that your family has for each other."

She frowned at him. "I'm having a hard time understanding this."

"I don't know what it is, Lena. The way we were raised. Tradition. We just aren't the demonstrative type. At least my parents aren't. My older sister and I get along amazingly well."

She held her tongue. Families were different. His wasn't the hugging and kissing and teasing type. Didn't mean they were bad. "I'm sure it isn't that bad," she said.

He picked up the knife with a laugh. Bumped her hip with his. "Because you have the best family."

"I don't know about that," she said slowly. She

wanted to continue this discussion, but it seemed to be a sore spot. He was trying to make things right with his parents. *Give him some space.* Time to change the subject.

"So, what did you have, like, a cook and a maid to serve you? Did your father sit at the head of the table and ring a bell?"

He stared at her, openmouthed for a moment before he laughed. A big, free laugh that sounded wonderful bouncing around the small kitchen.

"You've been watching too many movies, Lena."

She spread her hands. "I don't know how rich people act. You're saying your mother cooked?"

Matt set the pot on the burner and turned the heat on, still chuckling. "God forbid. She'd break a nail or something and the other ladies would talk about her behind her back. We had a maid. She usually made us lunch if we were home and cooked dinner before she left."

"See? I wasn't wrong. Did she teach you all this?"

"Okay. Point. No, I learned this on my own. When I was in college, I found that for good, cheap food, the small family-run, hole-in-the-wall restaurants were the best bet. Ate at all kinds. Moroccan, Ethiopian, Indian, Thai, Lebanese. Got to know the spices. Started experimenting."

"Now I'm starving. Thai. Drool."

He dropped the onion into the heated oil and

began stirring. "Noted. Next time, I'll make you my *tom gah kai*."

"Slow down there, Bobby Flay," she said. "You trying to get lucky?"

He caught her around the waist with one arm and pulled her against him. "I'm already lucky." He kissed her forehead.

She looked up into his impossible blue eyes, her breath frozen in her chest. Sadie's teasing words came back to her. *The l word. It's happening. You are falling for him.* She felt her mouth open but no words came out. The look in his eyes changed. From teasing to something warmer. Hotter. His hands went to her cheeks and he kissed her. Slowly, deeply. Until she was clinging to him, lost to everything except the feel of him, the taste of him, the…

"The onions!"

Matt grabbed the pot off the burner and stirred. "Not burned. Barely."

Lucky onions. She was burning right down to ash. "Whew," she said shakily. "Better toss the chicken in there."

"You are too dangerous to have in the kitchen." Matt pointed at her wineglass with the spoon. "Take your wine, pour me a glass and go sit down. I'll just toss all this together and get it simmering."

She let her gaze move from his eyes all the way

down to his feet and back up. "And how long does it need to simmer?"

"Not long enough for me to do what I'm going to do to you. But long enough to get started."

MATT TUCKED HIS hands behind his head and smiled up at the ceiling. His belly was full of good food, his body still humming from good loving. Lena's hand lightly smacked his chest.

"Look at you grinning like the Cheshire Cat."

He caught her hand and brought it to his lips. "You make me smile, Lena."

She wiggled over and propped herself on his chest, looking down at him. "You are an entirely unfair human being, Matt."

"What? How am I unfair?"

"You look like a Viking god come to life. You can cook. You got the skills to match that hound-dog swagger. What's a girl supposed to do with you?"

Love me. The words sprang into his mind unbidden. He let out a slow breath as he looked into her dark eyes. This close, he could see flecks of darker brown within the brown. He lifted her heavy black hair and let it sift through his fingers. He was falling in love with her.

"Keep me?"

He meant it as a bit of joke, to interrupt the nearly overwhelming urge to blurt out that word. The one word he was afraid would send her running for the hills. But her look turned speculative. *She's thinking the same thing.* The word hung there unsaid between the two of them. *Say it, man. She's waiting for you.*

"Meow!"

The moment broke as they turned to look at Sassy, who'd jumped on the bed and was glaring at them both. "Sass, what do you think? Should we keep him?"

The cat turned and showed them her cat butt. Matt laughed and pulled Lena down into his arms. "I think that's a no from the Sassinator."

"Actually, it's a sign of trust when a cat does that. But I think I forgot to feed her."

She sat up and as she slid from the bed, he caught her hand. "Lena. We have something here."

She sank to the edge of the mattress. "I know," she whispered as if she were afraid to say the words too loudly.

He nodded. "We going to see it through?"

"I think we should."

He grinned as a light, happy feeling filled him. "Can we say were dating now?"

She stood and made a swirling motion with her finger at the bed. "After those shenanigans? I think that earns an advance to dating level."

"Hmm. Now I'm going to have to top that to advance to the next level?"

She turned with a laugh but not before he saw

the flare of heat in her eyes. "I can't imagine. I might not survive."

"Oh, you'll survive."

"Come to Edisto with me for lunch on Sunday."

Matt pushed her back on the bed and stared down into her eyes. The look on her face: regret tinged with slight horror, led him to believe she'd just blurted that out without thinking.

"What did you just say?"

"I don't know. I claim insanity. You drove me insane with all these orgasms."

"You want me to meet your family."

"I shouldn't. They'll kill you. It will be a horrible mess. They'll hate me forever and, oh my God, Matt, what are we doing?"

"This Sunday? Because I am so there. Lena. Do you know how much I want to be part of your life? Your family? The love I saw in the hospital? It's like I was starving and didn't know for what until I saw that."

She went still and silent, and he could feel her heart pounding against his ribs. She brought a hand up to cover her mouth. Tears rolled from her eyes. But he didn't think they were bad tears.

Matt leaned in and kissed the twin tears from her cheeks. "It's okay," he whispered. "It's okay. Let's just feel this. We don't have to say anything."

CHAPTER TWENTY-THREE

"I'M GOING TO need to you and Wyatt to come to lunch at my parents' this weekend."

Sadie's eyebrows rose as she swallowed the chunk of salmon sashimi she'd just stuffed in her face. "Any particular reason?"

Pushing her lips out in a pout, Lena hedged. "Because I want you to."

Sadie pointed her chopsticks at Lena. "Uh-uh. Need. You said you needed us to be there. Why? What do you need protection from? Are the aunties still being crazy?"

"No. I just… Matt's coming." She forced the words out as quickly as she could and prepared herself for the consequences.

Lowering the chopsticks to the plate slowly, Sadie stared. "Did you just say what I thought you said?"

"Yes. Don't make a big thing about it. He wants to meet the family. Hang out. He's under the impression that we're fun or something."

"Oh," Sadie said casually as she took a sip of wine. "Okay. No big deal. Just you bringing home the first guy you've ever brought home, and a white guy at that. And you're going to drop him dead center in the Hispanic Bachelor Parade. Yeah, that's going to be just fine."

Lena covered her face with her hands and groaned. "What have I done?"

"Lost your mind would be my guess."

"What should I do? Just show up? Give my mom a warning? I don't even know how this happened."

Sadie dragged a bit of salmon through the wasabi and shrugged. "Were you naked? That's a lesson I learned. Never agree to do anything while naked."

Lena felt her face go hot. That's exactly what it was. He'd tricked her! Plying her with home-made Moroccan food and wine. Making love to her until her brain melted. "This is all his fault."

"Sure it is," Sadie said cheerfully. "So, what I want to know—is this Sunday an all-family Sunday or just your family Sunday?"

Horror wrapped its cold fingers around Lena's heart and squeezed. "All family was last week," she stammered through cold lips. "We never have it twice in a row."

"Well then," Sadie said. "I wouldn't tell your mother about bringing Matt over because she'll sound the alarm and y'all will be walking into an ambush."

"I have to tell her. I can't just show up with him."

"Call her on the way."

Using the chopsticks, Lena pushed the bits of sashimi around on the plate. She wasn't really hungry anymore. This was going to make it real. She and Matt were skirting around the issue but they were falling in love. She knew she was at least. She was pretty sure Matt was. If she took him home and her parents were okay with it, then there would be no more barriers for her to put up. She'd have to own up to her feelings.

"You and Wyatt have to get there first. We're going to need a cushion. My parents won't kill me if Wyatt is there."

"Your parents aren't going to kill you."

"MY PARENTS ARE going to kill me." Lena leaned forward and put her forehead on the steering wheel.

Matt put his hand on her back and patted. "No, they won't. They'll kill me before they kill you."

Sitting up, she drew in a deep breath. "Okay. Hold on. Time to make the call."

"Make the call?"

"I can't just show up with you. That will make my mother mad. But I can't give her enough warning to gather all my aunts and cousins." She lifted her phone and held a finger to her lips.

"*Bueno*, Mamacita. I'm just leaving town now. I wanted to let you know I'm bringing a friend with me. Is that okay?"

Matt grinned at her. It was strange to see her

like this. Nervous. Unsure. She was usually so confident and decisive. She turned those dark brown eyes in his direction as she listened to her mother.

"No. Matt. Yes. Maybe. Momma…"

His grin faded and for the first time, a thread of worry wound around him. *Was this a good idea? Lena's family means everything to her.* What if they rejected him? Would he lose her? He would never make her choose. His worry deepened as she switched to low, rapid Spanish.

"Everything okay?" he asked when she ended the call.

"She's mad because I didn't tell her sooner. She only made meat loaf and thinks it isn't suitable to serve to a guest."

Relief flooded through him and he laughed. "I like meat loaf."

Lena glanced in the side mirror and pulled away from the curb. "You love meat loaf. Meat loaf is your favorite meal ever."

"Absolutely."

Lena had spent the drive filling him in on every member of the family who might be there. Too many names to keep straight. Her father, Carl, was a retired construction foreman. Her mother, Ana, was a homemaker and an amateur photographer. They were the most important names. The others, he would learn later.

"Wow," he said as Lena pulled into the driveway of a gorgeous redbrick house. Centuries-old oak trees framed the roofline. The front porch was deep and spanned the entire length of the house. There were rocking chairs and two hanging swings. "This is nice."

"Okay. No one is here yet except Sadie and Wyatt. I wanted you to meet the parents before the entire family descends."

The nerves returned. Leaning forward, he pulled a gift bag from his backpack. "Chardonnay," he said. "A hostess gift for your mother. Yes or no?"

"Yes. If she won't drink it, I will. Ready?"

"As I'll ever be."

He followed her up the porch and through the empty front room to the kitchen. "We made it," Lena called out.

He stepped into the kitchen and glanced around. Sadie, he remembered. She owned the guy maids business. She slipped off the tall stool.

"Matt," she said, coming to shake his hand. "It's good to see you again."

Lena's mother turned her head to look at Sadie and one eyebrow rose in a perfect arch. He had to resist the temptation to laugh. Nice to know where Lena got that from.

"Mr. and Mrs. Reyes, it's a pleasure to meet you. I'm Charles Matthews." He crossed the room to shake hands.

They seemed like nice people. Welcoming. He

was waved into a seat beside Sadie and her fiancé, Wyatt.

"So. Sadie," Mrs. Reyes asked archly, "you two
have met?"

"Uh," Sadie said, shooting Lena a look. "Yes.
Lena introduced us. Matt is putting together a
charity to help kids through art. I donated some
money."

"Matt set up the art room project at St. Toribio's," Lena added.

"That wasn't just me, now. Dr. Rutledge had
the initial idea," Matt said.

Ana looked from Matt to Sadie to Lena. One
corner of her mouth quirked up in a smile. "I
heard about that. Very good thing for the kids."

Matt lifted the gift bag. "For you," he said.

The sound of several car doors slamming shut
broke the awkward moment. Mr. Reyes stood and
clapped Matt on the shoulder. "You are welcome
here, son."

The touch. The words. Matt blinked as a warm
feeling flowed into a hole he didn't even realize
was within him. "Thank you," he managed to
choke out.

A corkscrew appeared on the counter in front
of him. Ana patted his hand. "Make yourself useful and open the wine."

As Mr. Reyes left the room to greet the arriv-
ing family and Ana turned back to her cooking,

Lena sidled up next to him. "See? No problem," she whispered. "Unless…"

"Unless what," he whispered back.

Sadie grabbed wineglasses and began to serve the wine. "So, Mamacita. Are Paula and Estrella coming?"

Lena turned with a murderous glare but Sadie and Ana only laughed. "Unless *that*," she hissed.

Ana made a rude noise and took her glass of wine from the counter. "If you aren't helping, get out."

Matt rolled up his sleeves. "I can help."

The look he got from Ana made his insides freeze. *Oh hell.*

Sadie got up. "Do you need those potatoes peeled?"

Lena put her hand in Matt's. "Come on. Ava is here. I'm sure she'd love to see you again."

In the front room, he pulled her to a stop. "Did I say something wrong?"

"No. Don't worry about it. It's a generation thing. Women cook. Men go sit at the creek and have a beer while they pretend to fish." She went up on tiptoe to give him a quick kiss. "They like you."

"So far, so good."

It was good. As more of the family arrived, it got louder and happier. Matt relaxed enough to enjoy himself. The weather was perfect and he found himself sitting on the back-porch steps watching the small herd of children running and screaming with laughter across the yard. From the open kitchen window, he could hear the women laughing and talking. Occasionally bickering. The bickering was in Spanish and he wondered if it was about him. The door behind him opened and Wyatt came out to sit next to him.

"It's quite overwhelming at first. But you get used to it."

"How long have you known the family?"

"Not long. Since last summer when I met Sadie. You'll be fine. Just treat Lena like she's a princess and try not to let the aunts spook you. It's their job to disapprove of everything. Like those two old guys in the *Muppets* opera balcony."

"Aw, man," Matt said with a laugh. "Why'd you do that? Now that's what I'm going to picture when I see them."

A little girl with long black hair appeared at the edge of the woods. "Dad!" she yelled across the yard. "Alligator!"

Wyatt rose and hurried across the yard. Matt followed him.

"Everyone, back in the house," Wyatt called out. "Just for a few minutes. Go on."

They reached the path. "It jumped up on the bank and grabbed the fish Uncle Luis caught. It's just sitting there."

"Okay, Jules," Wyatt said calmly. "Go on up

to the house. I'm sure the alligator is long gone by now."

"Are you going to shoot it?"

"No. I'm not going to shoot it. Get in the house."

"Wow," Matt said as they rounded the final curve of the path before it opened out into a clearing. Mr. Reyes and three other men were standing behind camp chairs watching the alligator watch them. "That's a big one."

"Six foot at least," Wyatt said as he walked forward slowly.

"Got your gun, Wyatt?" Mr. Reyes asked. "He isn't scaring away."

Wyatt leaned forward and unstrapped a handgun from an ankle strap. "Yeah, got it. He's not budging?"

"Nope. We yelled and stood up. Luis threw a bottle near him. Just standing there like he's trying to decide who's the slowest runner."

"That'd be you, Carl," Wyatt joked.

Matt edged closer, fascinated. He'd never seen a wild alligator this close before. "I thought they were afraid of people."

"Not this one," Mr. Reyes—Carl—said. He held out an arm, barring Matt from getting closer. "Careful, son, they can be very fast."

Wyatt picked up one of the camp chairs and held it in front of him at ground level. As he took a few steps forward, the gator turned to look at him. "Go on, Mr. Gator," Wyatt said in a loud voice.

Instead of retreating back to the water, the gator quickly ran left around Wyatt, toward the men. Matt jumped in front of the men and grabbed a chair. Swinging it like a golf club, he made a threatening enough move to scare the gator away, back toward the creek. Wyatt scrambled out of the way as it hit the water with a loud splash.

Matt dropped the chair. He looked at Wyatt and they both began laughing. "Dude. You just scared away a giant alligator."

"With a chair."

The others joined in with more adrenaline-relieving laughter. Carl shook Matt's hand. "That was impressive."

"Good to know all those golf lessons came in handy after all."

The men began gathering their fishing poles and beers. "Let's give that gator some breathing room."

LENA LOOKED OVER at Matt as they idled at a stop-light. "Dinner went well."

"It did. I like your family more than I thought I would."

"You didn't think you'd like them?"

"Don't get your feathers all ruffled. I thought it might take a while for them to warm up to me or that I might feel out of place. But none of that happened."

He plucked her hand from the steering wheel and kissed it.

"My place or yours?" she asked, squeezing his fingers.

"Yours. Always yours. I take the extra steps in the morning, not you."

"Did you really scare that alligator away by yourself?"

"Yep."

"My dad is sold on you now, you know."

"I hope so. I saved his life. What about your mother?"

"I think she's fine. We'll see over the next few days if I get a phone call or not."

She hit the gas pedal, heading toward the harbor. Matt's hand lightly covered hers on the stick shift. "I really do like your family, Lena."

"We can be a hot mess."

"Maybe. But…" His words trailed off as he tried to put words to the feelings he'd experienced that afternoon.

"But what?"

"I could feel the love. The love you have for each other despite all the annoying things that families do to each other."

It wasn't new to him, exactly. He had friends. Buddies from college who he'd tag along home with over holidays. He'd seen loving families.

But there was something about Lena's family. The possibility that he could be part of it. It was scary and exciting. Meeting a woman like Lena was a miracle in itself. Her family was a dream he'd never imagined.

"Yeah." Lena cut across his thoughts. "You say that now. Wait until they get used to you and there is three-naming and screaming and people stomping out in huffs. And all the crying that comes with the apologies. You saw everyone on their best behavior."

She pulled the car into her assigned parking spot and put it in Park. Matt turned and leaned toward her. "Will they have a chance to get used to me?"

Her eyes went wide before a sultry smile crossed her lips. "You trying to bail out on me, Frat Boy?"

He kissed her tenderly. "Never."

CHAPTER TWENTY-FOUR

"Now he wants me to meet his parents." Sadie's fork clanged off the plate as it fell from her hand. Lena frowned at her. "Close your mouth. There's food in there, and frankly, it's disgusting. I might vomit in your plate."

Sadie clamped her mouth shut and chewed hurriedly. Her throat worked as she swallowed. "What did you just say to me?"

"I mean, not, like, *meet the parents*," she made finger quotes around the words. "But meet them. They're coming to Kiawah Island. His father has some sort of business thing. He's having dinner with them and wants me to come."

"Okay. Wait. Back this horse up a bit. He's met your parents. Now you're meeting his parents? What exactly is going on here?"

Lena put her elbows on the table and put her hands over her face with a groan. "I don't know."

But she did know. Beyond the insanely hot sex, he made her laugh. He moved her to tears with his stories of the kids he helped. He had zero issues with her bank statement. True, he was from a family whose bank statement probably made hers look like chump change, but even some of those types did not like a woman with her own money. She was falling crazy in love. And that never ended well.

"Do you want to meet them?"

She peeked out through her fingers. Sadie was sitting back in the booth, wineglass pressed to her lips, frowning at her. "I don't know."

"Okay," Sadie said briskly, downing the wine. She reached for the bottle and poured more. "You are freaking me out here. Who are you and where is Lena? *I don't know?* That's all you have? No. I am not the grown-up here. You. You are the grown-up."

Lena topped off her own wineglass. Screw it. If she had to Uber back to town and get her car tomorrow, she'd do it. "I don't…" She stopped as Sadie shook a finger at her. Rubbing her forehead, Lena sighed. "I know. It's crazy. I feel like I've run off the end of one of those moving sidewalk things. My life seemed normal, but now it's all out of control and I'm just flailing around trying to get my balance."

"You're in love."

"No. I'm not. Yet."

"Yes, you are. You just haven't admitted it."

Scowling, Lena took a sip of wine. "I thought you weren't going to be the grown-up."

"Okay, I'll be the teenager. How's the sex?"

She felt her face go hot as the woman in the

booth behind Sadie turned to look at them. "Can you at least lower your voice?"

Sadie looked over her shoulder. "If you saw this guy, you'd know why I had to ask."

"Sadie!"

"Sorry, Mom. Now. What were we talking about? Meeting his parents? Do you want to? Sister truth."

She made a face. "Sort of but not really. No matter how we frame it, I'm the girl he's dating and I'm meeting his parents. That's loaded all by itself. But then, he and his parents haven't had the best relationship and they all kissed and made up when he went home a few weeks ago, so he's eager to go and continue with that healing process."

"What does Matt think your relationship is?"

Lena plucked a crayon out of the mason jar and began doodling a flower on the white paper covering the table. The best reason to make the trek to South Windermere and the Med Deli. Second best was their shrimp and grits. "I don't think he's thought about it. He was dreading their visit before and now he's looking forward to it."

"Have you said anything to him?" Sadie took a crayon out too and began doodling on her side of the table. "This is fun. I should get one of those adult coloring books."

"No. Not directly. I've asked him a thousand times if he's sure they won't mind me coming to their family dinner. And he always says it'll be fine."

Dropping the crayon back in the jar, Sadie reached across the table to still Lena's hand. "Lena. Look at me. Family is the most important thing to you. Even now when they are driving you insane. If Matt's been estranged from his family and is trying to reconnect, you need to support him."

Lena sat up straight and tapped the crayon on the table. "I didn't think about it that way." A slight bit of self-recrimination rose in her gut. She should have. She'd watched Sadie sever the bond with the mother who had severed her parental rights, condemning Sadie to a lifetime in foster care. Watched as she reconnected with her half brother and, recently, with her half sisters. Josh, the man Sadie considered her brother of the heart, was just now getting to know the sister he'd been separated from since they were children.

Sadie's fingers curled around hers. "I can see what you're thinking. Don't feel bad about it. It's not in your normal to need to reconnect with family."

"Doesn't change the fact that it didn't even occur to me even after watching you and Josh struggle for years with it. I'm sorry I'm such a horrible friend."

"Oh. My. God," Sadie said, rolling her eyes. "Stop with the Catholic drama."

"Guilt. Catholic guilt."

"Oh! Are you going to go to confession and tell Father Greg what you and Matt have been doing? How much detail do you have to give? Can I go just to watch his face when he comes out of the booth thing?"

She arched her eyebrow. "You mean the confessional?"

"Whatever. If it's that important to Matt, I think you should go."

"Yeah. I guess so. I've never had to meet parents before. It's so weird."

"We picked a wedding date."

"Well, okay, next subject. That's great. When?"

"April first."

"Please tell me you are kidding."

"Nope. It's the first Saturday in April and apparently, people don't like getting married on that day so everything is available."

Lena shrugged. "And it'll be easy to remember. But you know my mother is going to be in panic mode the entire time. She'll be terrified y'all will turn around at the end and yell April fools."

"We're doing a Fool for Love theme."

"Oh sheesh. That's too corny to even comprehend."

"Jules came up with it."

"So a nine-year-old is planning your wedding?"

"Pretty much. Better her than me. She's way more stylish than I'll ever be."

"Great. Send her to my house to dress me for dinner with the parents."

STANDING IN THE walk-in closet with Sass winding around her ankles, Lena flicked through dresses. Too short. Too sexy. Too bright. Maybe. Too business. Maybe. She slipped one of the maybes from the hanger and wiggled into it.

The emerald green was a good color on her. The hem hit at exactly one inch below her knees, so that was good. She frowned and leaned forward. The girls certainly were on display. Shaking her head, she unzipped the dress.

"Why didn't you tell me I dress like a hoochie momma, Sass?"

At the back of the closet, she found the dress she'd worn to her grandfather's funeral. *What would Lito think of Matt?* She smiled in spite of the sadness that filled her. Missing Lito was a part of her she would carry to her own grave. She lifted the dress from the hanger and carried it to the bedroom. Sitting on the edge of the bed, she held the dress pressed to her chest for a moment. *I think he would love Matt.* She could picture them, sitting by the creek together.

She pulled the dress on and smoothed down the skirt. She'd thought putting it on would make her sad, stir up memories of that awful day. But it didn't. She felt like Lito was with her. As if the dress had summoned his spirit. Black wasn't her best color, but she could add a pop of brightness with a necklace.

"Oh, Lito," she whispered at her reflection. "I wish you were here and could go with me tonight."

Because she was scared. Terrified. Meeting his parents had been an abstract problem until now, when she had to face the reality that she would be face-to-face with them in less than two hours. She knew nothing of them except that they came from old money and his father was a lawyer at a prestigious firm in Washington, DC. She wanted to like them. And wanted them to like her.

There was a quiet knock at the door and her heart rate shot up. Matt was here. She padded barefoot to let him in. "I don't know if I can do this," she said.

"You'll be fine," Matt said. He took her hands and lifted them, his gaze running over her. "You look amazing."

"So do you. Damn, you clean up pretty good."

He'd put his hair up in a neat man bun and trimmed his beard. The black suit was perfectly tailored and the blue shirt he'd paired it with brought out the ice in his blue eyes. He opened the jacket and pulled two ties from the inside pocket.

"Which do you think? I never can pick a decent tie."

Lena took them and held them each against

the shirt. The feel of his chest beneath her fingers sent her heart rate up again. "Why don't we just stay home? Order Chinese and get naked?" She draped one of the ties around his neck. "This one."

"Are you still nervous?"

"Yes. Are you sure they'll be okay with it?"

"Lena. I've already told them. They know you are coming. They are looking forward to meeting you."

"Really? They said that?"

"Not in so many words. Please don't be worried. It's just dinner with my parents."

"Okay. Let me finish getting ready."

Just dinner with his parents. Little did he know. She'd spent most of the day looking up dinner etiquette sites online. What if it was one of those super fancy places and she used the wrong fork? She could fake her way through the high-society parties easily enough. Even when having dinner with clients, it was business, not personal. She had very little firsthand experience being with people of Matt's parents' social status. She didn't want to embarrass herself.

"What do you think?" She did a slow twirl. She'd added a black-and-blue beaded necklace with a matching bracelet. Her nice diamond earrings. Sensible two-inch black heels.

"You look great."

"The black is okay? Should I wear something with color?"

Matt put his hands on her shoulders to hold her in place. "No. I think you are beautiful. Stop worrying. It's going to be fine."

"But what if I say something stupid?"

He kissed her gently. "Just be you, Lena. Just be the woman I love."

She went still at his words. Everything went away. Her nerves. His parents. Everything. She looked deep into his eyes. "Do you?" she whispered.

"I love you, Magdalena Reyes."

A smile crossed her lips. "I love you too, Frat Boy."

He pulled her closer and held her against his chest. "I've been wanting to say that for a while now."

"What took you so long?"

"I thought you'd run away as fast as your Jimmy Choos would allow."

She pushed back. "I'm not sure how I feel about a man who knows what Jimmy Choos are."

He laughed and took her hand. "Too late. You love me. And I have two sisters. Come on. It's a long drive."

THE OCEAN ROOM on Kiawah was perhaps the fanciest restaurant Lena had ever been to, but it was just a restaurant. She could do a restaurant.

Order some food. Eat with the utensils they bring you. Try not to spill anything on you. Or others. The nerves crept back.

"Ready?" Matt asked as he opened the car door and held a hand out to her.

Put on your big-girl panties and deal with this. You know how to schmooze rich people. You've spent your entire career doing it. Drawing in a slow breath, she placed her hand in Matt's and stepped from the car. "Piece of cake."

"That's the spirit."

He tucked her arm into his as they walked up the wide porch. "Now I feel like we're going to prom or something," she said with a laugh that sounded a little too giggly to her ear. "We need a code."

"A code?"

"For if I start babbling inanely."

"Oh. Okay. Let me think."

"Quick. We're here. Are your parents here? Are we early? We haven't kept them waiting, have we?"

"Is that Mose over there?" Matt asked.

"Where?" Lena gasped, looking around.

"It's the code."

Tipping her head back, Lena laughed. "That is perfect."

Matt pulled her away from the door and gave her a quick kiss. "You just keep smiling and laughing like that, beautiful lady."

She looked up at him and put her hands to his cheeks. "You are so going to get lucky when this is over."

He took her hands in his and lifted one to his lips. "I'm already lucky."

The swell of love and happiness sent her floating on a little cloud of euphoria that allowed no nerves to intrude as he led her inside the restaurant. She was in love. With the most awesome man she'd ever met. And he loved her. Everything else was just minutiae.

"They're waiting in the bar. We'll have drinks first," Matt said.

"Okay." Her happy little cloud sank a bit. Her hand tightened around Matt's forearm as he stopped in the doorway and scanned the room.

"There they are."

He steered her to a couple sitting at one of the little armchair arrangements in the bar area. She smiled. Matt looked much like his father. His father's hair had gone to gray, but he had the same blue eyes and she could see the shape of Matt's nose and lips in his face. His mother was a prettily preserved blonde. Petite and perfectly dressed in a delicate shade of pink Versace. Her Louboutins put Lena's poor Jimmy Choos to shame.

Matt's hand slipped around her waist. "Mom, Dad, this is Lena Reyes."

Showtime. Lena stepped forward and smiled as Matt's father stood. "It's such a pleasure to meet you both. Mr. Matthews. Mrs. Matthews." She shook hands all around.

"Please have a seat," Mr. Matthews said.

After they settled in their chairs, there was more polite chitchat. Matt asked about their trip. The weather. Lena smiled and nodded. A lot. Mr. Matthews made a discreet motion with his hand and a waiter appeared instantaneously.

"Are you ready to order?"

"Yes. I'll have a martini. Your finest chardonnay for my wife. Charles? Lena?"

Lena reached for the menu and scanned it quickly as Matt said, "I'll have a glass of the chardonnay also."

Lena smiled up at the waiter. "The Strawberry Airmail sounds good."

Mrs. Matthews leaned over to tap at a spot on the drink menu. "That one sounds good also."

Lena's eyes dropped to where she'd pointed and she froze. Tequila. Jalapeno syrup. Mezcal. *Breathe. Maybe she just likes margaritas. Don't be paranoid.* Peripherally aware of the silence and the waiter poised to take her order, Lena shook her head and smiled. "Oh, I'm not much for tequila. I think the Strawberry Airmail will do just fine."

"I hear your artwork is doing quite well," Mr. Matthews said to Matt.

Lena clasped her hands in her lap, willing her heart rate to drop. The smile on her lips seemed frozen. *Let it go. Ignore it.* But, part of her screamed silently. *But nothing. Suck it up, buttercup.* Tuning back in to the conversation, she heard Matt self-deprecatingly giving Eliot Rutledge credit for his success.

"Matt," she said gently. "While Eliot may have elevated your presence in the art world, people aren't buying your art because of him. It's because your work is amazing."

"Do you have an art background then, Lena?" Mrs. Matthews asked.

"No. ma'am. I just know what I like."

"Ah, I see. Well, art is the most subjective form of human expression there is."

"One could say that about any artistic endeavor," Mr. Matthews interjected with a dry, humorless laugh.

Lena gratefully took her drink from the returning waiter and took a healthy sip. Nodding, she gave him a thumbs-up. "Wonderful," she said. Catching Mrs. Matthews's frown, she widened her smile. "Perfect choice for me."

Matt's hand rested on her shoulder with a gentle squeeze. "Lena is definitely a champagne sort of woman."

"Mmm," Mrs. Matthews said as she took a delicate sip of her wine. "Remind me, Lena, what exactly is it that you do?"

Okay. She wants to play the high-society card. Lena took another sip of the cocktail—it really was quite delicious—and smiled. "I make poor people comfortable, rich people wealthy and wealthy people adore me."

Mr. Matthews laughed. A real laugh, not one of those fake polite laughs. But his wife looked like her wine had turned to vinegar. "I'm sorry, I don't understand that."

"Lena is a financial manager," Matt said. "The best. I was lucky to get a spot with her partner."

"Well, the best in Charleston. What an accomplishment."

An awkward silent moment fell. Mr. Matthews raised his hand again and the waiter appeared like magic. Rich, white, male power. Must be nice. "I think we're ready to move to our table now."

As they were led to the table, Matt kept Lena back a few paces. "What's going on?" he whispered.

"Your mother hates me," she whispered back.

"No, she doesn't. She's like this with everyone. Don't take it personally."

"No, this isn't like everyone. Didn't you tell them?"

"Tell them what?"

"That I'm Mexican. For God's sake, Matt. Tell me you didn't spring this on them."

He stared at her, openmouthed, much like the time she'd told him why his little joke at the art gallery was so insulting. "She asked about your last name, I told her your family was Hispanic.

She was just asking. Lena. Believe me, it doesn't matter to them."

"Really?"

He frowned. "Of course. They aren't like that. They aren't prejudiced."

"You're sure of that? Because your mother was…"

"She's always like this, Lena. Don't take it personally. She's not a warm cuddly kind of woman."

"Charles? Lena? Are you coming?"

His mother's smile and voice was sugar sweet and Lena knew she should just walk away right now. Take Matt with her. But she also knew how he was struggling to rebuild his relationship with his parents. The relationship he'd destroyed with his rebellion and anger. If she asked him to make a choice, she'd lose him. And despite his mother apparently winding up to be a total bitch, Matt wasn't like that at all. The best she could hope for was that he'd see it too and make the right choice.

"Is there a problem?" Mrs. Matthews asked as Lena and Matt took their seats.

"Oh no," Lena said with a smile. "I was just telling Matt how beautiful I thought your dress is. Versace?"

"I believe so. I can't keep track."

"I'm not going to talk shoes and dresses," Mr. Matthews said. He pointed at Lena. "What's your current top recommendation for diversification of a stagnant account?"

Lena leaned forward with a smile. "Depends. Are you looking for fast gain or solid long-term growth?"

"Your advice?"

She paused while the server brought water and the menus. Listened intently to the specials. She was going to order the most expensive food this place had to offer.

"To answer your question, sir, I can't make a recommendation based solely on that single fact. My answer would be much different for a twenty-year-old than it would be for a fifty-year-old."

Mr. Matthews laughed and clapped Matt on the shoulder. "I like this one. She answers like a lawyer."

Matt covered her hand with his. "Good. I'm pretty fond of her myself."

Lena distracted herself with the menu. *Lobster bisque and filet mignon.* She looked up at the faces around her. Matt was reading the menu. His father was eyeing her thoughtfully. His mother looked like she was grinding her teeth down to the gums. *Leftover crap from Matt's teenage years or fear of half-Mexican grandbabies?* It had been so long since she'd had to play this game at this level. Sure, she got the side eye and rude remarks from knuckle-dragging, mouth-breathing idiots from time to time, but that was life. She'd found the higher the social status, the more willing to play the we-don't-see-race game.

They ignored it not because they didn't have their prejudices, they just didn't want to be rude. And she'd used it to her advantage. But she didn't want to play games with Matt's family. She loved him and wanted to be a part of his entire life. Not the cause for another rift.

She sipped more of the champagne cocktail. He had fit in perfectly with her family. She'd been relieved to get glowing reviews from her parents. They were on board. Looking at the trap Matt had unknowingly placed her in made her squirm a little. She'd done almost the same to Matt. She'd told her parents his name and let them figure out he was white. But she had no rift with her family. She wasn't trying to make amends with them. Matt was. Just as Hannah had told her parents up front, before they'd met him, that her fiancé was African American, Matt had told his parents her background. And here she sat, wondering what his mother's silence on receiving the information really meant. The best she could do was ignore the little volleys being lobbed by his mother and have a long talk with him later.

After placing their orders, Mr. Matthews turned his attention back to Lena. Where had she attended college? How she'd come to a career in finance. Him, she knew how to handle. The only color men like him saw was green. His questions revealed that he had a good working knowledge of finance, but was not an expert. She was able to answer him honestly and respectfully without sugarcoating anything.

"Charles, stop badgering the woman about money. She's not at work now."

Lena smiled. "It's okay. Get me started on money talk and I'll blabber all night long."

"What about your family, dear? Matt told me you're an only child?"

"Yes. But I have quite an extended family with lots of cousins, so I never really felt like an only child."

"Really? Is that unusual?"

Lena managed to keep her expression in polite society mode. Her inner face was rolling its eyes. *Here we go.* "Unusual?"

"No disrespect, but aren't Hispanic families usually quite large?"

Lena met her eyes unflinchingly. Her mother had fertility problems and she was the miracle baby she was told she'd never have. But Mrs. Matthews had no right to that information. "No. Families come in all sizes. No matter…" Acrid tones of anger tainted her words even though she'd tried not to let it show.

"Is that Mose?" Matt asked, taking Lena's hand in his.

His parents turned to look in the direction he

was pointing, but Lena looked at him. He shook his head and leaned close.

"Don't let her bait you."

Her fury was burning brighter. She wasn't going to sit here and take this. Mrs. Matthews was not some clueless person tripping over her own ignorance. She was being deliberately hurtful.

"She's doing it on purpose," she mouthed back. She turned to face his mother.

"I'm sorry, Mrs. Matthews, have I done or said something to offend you?"

"No. I'm sorry, Lena," Mrs. Matthews said in a not-sorry-at-all tone of voice, "But you need to understand something. What my son needs to understand. This is just not how we do things in our family."

"Not. How. You. Do. What?"

"Anne," Mr. Matthews said. "What are you doing?"

"Charles," his mother said, her gaze hot on Lena's as she motioned to Matt. "He's always tried to find ways to shock us, to embarrass us. You seem like a very nice young lady, and it is wrong for him to do this…"

"Mom!"

"Anne, stop this right now. Lena, this is not how…"

"No," Mrs. Matthews said, staring at Matt. "It isn't right. Charles, this is a new low for you. To bring her here, let her think she'd have a place in our family. I'm ashamed of you for treating her like this."

"New low?" Matt choked out. "This is a new low for *you*, Mother."

"Lena, please," Mr. Matthews said. "There is a misunderstanding here."

Lena picked the napkin off her lap and slowly placed it on the table. She reached for her purse with shock-numb fingers and pushed back in her chair. "I'll be leaving now."

Matt put his hand over hers. "Lena. Don't go. This is just a misunderstanding. Mother, apologize."

She slipped her hand away from his. "This is not a misunderstanding. Goodbye."

She vaguely heard Matt calling for her as she crossed the restaurant floor. *Head high. Back straight. Strong, confident strides. Ignore the tears. You can cry later. Don't give any of them the satisfaction.*

He caught up to her at the car. "Lena, wait. I'm so sorry. I had no idea she'd act like that."

She pulled open the car door. "Well. You should have."

"Yes. I should have. I was all caught up in them being so accepting of my apology, that I thought… I don't know, that they were accepting me."

"Ms. Reyes."

She turned to see Matt's father approaching them. Her glare should have burned him to the ground.

"I apologize for my wife's inexcusable behavior. This is not who we are. She's angry at Charles, not you. I know that doesn't make it better or right, but I wanted to tell you I am sorry she acted this way."

Biting down on the conciliatory words that wanted to smooth down the whole situation, Lena nodded. Apologies didn't matter. The words were said. They could never be unsaid.

"I hear you," she said. He'd been nice. It was the least she could give him.

Get in. Drive away. Leave him and his complete bitch mother behind. She looked over the car at Matt. He had no right to stand there looking like a kicked puppy. "Get in," she said curtly and climbed into the car.

He came around and slid into the passenger's seat as she started the engine. "Lena…"

"Don't talk to me."

CHAPTER TWENTY-FIVE

IT WAS GOING to be a long, uncomfortable ride back to Charleston. Matt clenched his jaw and lightly bounced his head off the headrest. *Idiot. How could you be so stupid? They will never accept you. Accept the things you love. Whether it's art or a woman.* Shame burned through him. He'd done this. He should have realized what she was planning when she asked about Lena's name. His stupidity had placed Lena squarely in his mother's crosshairs. The worst part was that he knew his mother wasn't like this, but she'd done it just to hurt him. She had attacked Lena for the sole purpose of hurting him. This was all his fault.

They reached the intersection of Main Road and Savannah Highway. Instead of the right turn that would take them into downtown Charleston, Lena continued straight across Savannah to Bees Ferry Road.

"Where…"

"Not one word."

Her tone was still deadly and he slumped against the car door. He'd messed everything up. Maybe his parents were right. He was a screwup.

He didn't even know how to begin to apologize for the horrible things his mother had said. Or his role in allowing them to be said. Lena was right. He was every label she'd stuck on him. Trustafarian. Frat boy.

Soon, they were on the Interstate, heading west. He had no idea where they were going but kept his mouth shut. He was about to get dumped. And it was probably going to be epic. Propping his elbow against the window, he covered his eyes. Wherever she was going, he hoped it wasn't too far. He just wanted it to be over. The shame he felt and the fury at his mother and the disappointment of his failed attempt to mend fences with his parents was enough. Lena was about to break his heart and there was nothing he could do or say.

The car came to a hard stop and he opened his eyes. It was dark but a handful of streetlights illuminated a small trio of single-wide mobile homes that had clearly seen better days. Lena got out of the car and he followed. Down the long road, he could see similar clusters of trailers.

"This," Lena said, taking a few steps into the weedy grass and spreading her arms. "This is where I grew up. In that trailer, right there."

Her voice was low and quiet, humming with pride and fury. Matt pushed his hands in his pockets and forced himself to keep quiet and listen. It was all he could do.

"My grandfather crossed the border at fifteen. He became a citizen at twenty-five. My mother was a second-generation American citizen. My grandparents, my parents, my aunts and uncles, they all worked. In the fields. On roofs. Planting gardens for uptight rich white people who don't want to see us, but they sure did want to use us for cheap labor. Any and every job they could find from sunrise to sundown. With one goal in mind—to get me through college. Get all the kids through college And they did it. Twelve of us. To college thanks to their sweat and blood."

"My mother is an ass," he said.

"No! Your mother is a bigot." She advanced on him and stabbed a finger in his chest. "*You* are an ass, Charles Beaumont Matthews the goddamn Fifth. Telling me to stay there and listen to that racist bullshit coming out of her mouth. You think because you come down here out of your rich white world to play with us, that you are enlightened somehow. You aren't. If you were, you would have known that your parents would never accept a brown person in their family."

Her words stung. Possibly more than his imminent loss of her love. He hadn't thought he was just playing in her world. He thought he was just living his life, doing the things he loved. He nodded. "I should have."

"Take a good look at this place, Matt. I pulled my family out of here. I built my business. I built that house on Edisto for them. I paid cash for my condo and that fancy car you just dragged yourself out of. I did that. From here. The only work your mother ever did was making sure the right sperm hit the right egg so she could win the genetic lottery and end up in another, even richer white family. You tell her to go to hell. You tell her she is so far beneath my brown, overbreeding family that I don't give a damn what she thinks. I know who I am. I know where I'm from."

She stared at him. Even now, even when he'd screwed up beyond anything he'd ever screwed up before, and that was a lot, his heart filled with an aching love for her. Everything she said was one of the many things he loved about her. That strength, that courage. She'd created an entire life.

"I know you do," he said quietly.

She turned away and walked toward the car. "Get in the car."

"I'll call a cab."

"Don't be an idiot. No cab is going to come for you in this neighborhood. Get in the car before you get yourself killed."

BACK IN HER CONDO, Lena kicked off her shoes and stripped out of her fancy dress as she crossed to the bedroom. Her hands were still shaking in impotent fury. She held on to that rage. *How could he? How could he?* Because the instant the rage left, the pain was going to come. A pain she didn't want to feel because it meant his mother had won. She'd gotten to her, inflicted a wound with her hateful words.

She pulled on her most comfortable leggings and a T-shirt. Poured an extra-large glass of wine. Sat on the couch. *How had she been so completely wrong?* The rage collapsed under sheer exhaustion. Every day. Sass jumped up beside her and leaned against her, purring. As if she could sense the bubble of pain that was welling up within Lena.

She fumbled for her phone.

"I need you," she whispered, her voice breaking on the words.

"I'm on the way," Sadie answered.

Thirty minutes later, she was letting Sadie in. She'd managed to wash off her makeup without looking at herself in the mirror but the sight of her best friend rolling through the door with a bag full of sushi, a couple of bottles of wine and her favorite salted-caramel-dark-chocolate bars knocked down the last wall and the tears came.

"Come on," Sadie murmured as she wrapped her arms around Lena. "Sit down."

How long they sat on the couch, Lena sobbing and Sadie just quietly holding her and passing the occasional tissue, Lena had no idea.

"I hate this," she wailed once the tears had slowed to a trickle.

"I know you do. Blow your nose."

Lena went to the kitchen—much better than the bathroom with its mirrors—and blew her nose. Splashing cold water on her face, she dreaded what her eyes were going to look like in the morning. She returned to the couch and curled back up in the shelter of Sadie's arms.

"I'm going out on a limb here and guess meeting the parents didn't go well?"

"It was horrible."

"Do I have to go beat anyone up?"

Lena pushed away and turned to sit facing Sadie. "No. Although if his mother got bitch slapped by a random stranger, I wouldn't feel bad about it."

"What happened?"

Lena shook her head and grabbed for the wineglass. *What had happened?* "It was like a nightmare unfolding in slow motion, Sades. I knew exactly what was going to happen but I was trying to ignore it. Trying to give them the benefit of the doubt for Matt's sake."

"And?"

"First of all, I kept asking him if his parents were okay with meeting me. And he said yes."

Sadie raised her hand. "Okay, dumb question here. Did he not tell them you weren't Buffy from Kappa Phi?"

"He said his mother asked about my last name and he told her I was Hispanic. He said she left it at that. It's all okay until a brown person comes home."

"Okay. So what happened?"

"His father was actually nice. It was his mother. She got completely nasty. Then she accused Matt of using me to shock them."

"Holy hell," Sadie said slowly. "What happened then?"

"I started to leave, but Matt tried to stop me, was making excuses for her. I left after that."

"You just walked out?"

"Yep."

"Have you spoken to Matt? What's he got to say about this?"

"He came with me. I took him to the trailer park. Told him his mother was a bigot and my family was way better than his any day and his mother wasn't fit to wipe my feet on."

"So you let him off easy, then?"

Lena covered her face with her hands. Tears streamed between her fingers. "I can't believe I thought it would be different," she whispered.

"You thought it'd be different? How?"

"That he'd told them. That it wouldn't matter."

"It shouldn't have. That's where I'm confused. He told them you were Hispanic. His dad was being a nice guy. Then his mother pulls this crap out of the blue? What did Matt say?"

"Not much. I think he knew there was nothing he could say. He just apologized and listened to me yell at him."

"So, it was completely unexpected on his part too?"

"He should have known. He knows her. She's his freaking mother for God's sake."

"You thought your parents would freak out if you brought a white man home and they adore him. Come on, Lena. Eat something. You're hungry. Enough wine."

Sadie slid off the couch to sit on the floor in front of the coffee table. She moved Lena's wineglass to her side of the table and began to pull trays of sushi out of the bag. Lena sat beside her.

"How'd you get all this and still get here so fast?"

"I bought it this afternoon."

Lena popped a small salmon roll in her mouth and chewed. Her stomach raged to life. It'd been a long, stressful day since the tiny salad she'd had for lunch. Sass hopped up on the table, her whiskers twitching. "Thanks for your confidence in me."

"I didn't forget you, Ms. Sassy Pants," Sadie said, placing a bit of tuna sashimi on the table. Sass grabbed it and ran into the kitchen.

"I hope she eats that instead of hiding it somewhere for me to find later."

"Eat."

It felt good to let it all go for a minute. Sitting on the floor with Sadie beside her, scarfing down sushi felt like home. A smile crossed her face and she nudged Sadie with an elbow.

"Remember the first time I took you to eat sushi and you were horrified."

"I remember telling you man had discovered fire so we didn't have to eat our food raw."

"How long ago was that?"

"Geez. I don't know. It was right before I quit working for Marcus. So, I had to be eighteen or so."

"Long time ago. We've been through a lot together."

"And look at us now. Still sitting on the floor, eating sushi."

"You and those basic avocado rolls."

"Hey! I've added tuna to my menu."

Lena leaned against her friend. "This hurts so bad, Sades," she whispered.

"I know."

"It's more than just Matt and his parents though. It's me. I'm starting to think my mother is right. I should just stick with Hispanic men."

Sadie turned and propped her elbow on the couch cushion. "Oh?"

Lena swirled a chopstick through the glob of untouched wasabi on her tray, trying to coalesce her thoughts. "I don't know if I can put it into words. It's all a jumbled-up knot in my brain."

"Then just start talking. We'll figure it all out. We always do."

"It started when I went out to the St. Toribio mission. The kids there knew me. Knew about me. I'm some sort of role model to them and I never knew it. Because I never went back."

"But you are going back now. You helped with that art project and now you're setting up more programs to reach back and help others up."

"Yeah. I know."

"But?"

"It's always there, no matter what I do. No matter how much money I make or how many charities I fund. How many people I make millionaires. It's always there. Almost every time I meet someone for the first time, I can see the quick little surprise in their eyes. And I smile and pretend I didn't see it. But it's there."

Sadie turned to face her, her eyes troubled, her lips pressed together. "I didn't know this."

Reaching across the table, Lena snagged her glass of wine. This was more painful that losing Matt. "It's like I have different halves. I'm one person with my family. It's easy. I don't have to worry or think or pretend I don't see these things. But here in town and in my business, I have to walk this line. They know I'm Hispanic but I have to be careful not to be *too Hispanic*." She stopped to take a deep sip of wine to ease the painful knot in her throat. "I'm tired. I think that's what it is. I'm just tired of it, Sadie."

Sadie took the wine from her hand and took her own gulp. She draped an arm around Lena's shoulders and pulled her close. "Is it kind of like the tired I get of people asking me if I 'test out' the Crew before hiring them?"

"Yeah, but you can control that. If people don't know you run the Crew, you don't get asked. I can't hide my skin."

"True. People suck."

"People are the suckiest."

"We're going to need bigger wineglasses," Sadie said as she rose to her feet.

Lena stared at her freshly manicured nails while she waited. Manicures. Pedicures. Two-hundred-dollar haircuts. Tastefully classy designer clothes. All the things she used to arm herself against the looks. And none of it mattered. It'd been a long time since reality had reached up and smacked her upside her head. She hadn't been ready for it this time. Sadie returned with two large brandy snifters. "Those aren't…"

"Do you care?"

"Not really."

"Up on the couch. I'm getting too damn old to sit on the floor," Sadie said as she twisted open a fresh bottle of wine and poured a generous amount into the snifters.

"I just don't know what to do."

"About Matt or people sucking?"

"The latter."

"I can't help you with that unfortunately. But don't keep this to yourself, Lena. I'm your best friend, sister. If you're hurting or mad, please come to me. Even I can't do anything but listen. I want to be there for you. And I think you and Matt need to sit down and talk."

"No, that's over. It's done."

"Why? Because his mother was a bitch?"

"My mother was right. I need to stick with guys who will understand me."

"Last week," Sadie said slowly, sipping more wine. "Wyatt asked me to go to a PTA meeting with him and Jules. I had a complete meltdown panic attack. He had no idea what was wrong."

"Me either," Lena said, tossing Sass another bit of sashimi.

"School and PTA are nostalgic to him. He grew up in a house in the suburbs with his mother and sister. He was in Boy Scouts. All that stuff. School was a happy place for him. To me, it means being the outsider. Being the freak foster kid who didn't have a family. Social workers. Guidance counselors. Just because we're both white doesn't mean we understand each other all the time."

"This is different."

"Not from where I'm looking at it. And get that look off your face. You've told me plenty of things I didn't want to hear. It doesn't matter who you end up with, Lena, you're going to be different. What if your Hispanic guy is a first-generation Puerto Rican? Think y'all are going to have the same experiences?"

"That's not what I mean."

"What do you mean then? That because Matt is white and comes from money he won't understand? Well, suck it up, buttercup. That's called being in a relationship. I'll give you that being with someone from another culture adds another layer of difficulty but no one is exempt from having to work on a relationship."

Lena drank more wine. "Go home. I don't want to talk to you anymore."

"Don't tell me what to do."

Sadie got up and went rummaging in the kitchen.

"Get out of my kitchen too."

Returning with a bottle of Fireball whiskey in her hand, Sadie slammed two shot glasses down on the table. "Stop being a whiny-ass princess. Sister truth time."

"I'm not drinking that."

Sadie glared at her. "You will drink this. You will tell me the truth. I don't care how many shots I gotta shove down your throat. You don't get to play this game with me."

Lena watched as Sadie poured a hefty shot in each glass. She considered continuing to refuse but the look in Sadie's eyes hinted that she'd probably hold her down and pour the whiskey down her throat.

She took the offered glass. "I don't like you anymore."

Sitting on the coffee table across from her, Sadie clinked her glass against Lena's. "You don't like having the tables turned on you. Brat. Drink. Sister truth."

Lena threw back the shot. "Phew. That's got bite."

Sadie slowly wiped her lips. "Question—do you love him?"

"No."

Sadie stood up slowly. "You just lied to me. You've never lied to me before."

Lena watched with growing alarm as Sadie gathered up the remains of the sushi and put it in the fridge. When she came back to the living room, she picked up her purse.

"Wait. Stop. Sades, I'm sorry. I promise. I won't lie again."

Sadie turned and Lena was shocked at the fury in her eyes. "Over the years, you've told me some really hard truths about myself. You've ripped my rationalizations to shreds and thrown them back in my face. And I never, ever, once lied to you. Because I knew you were the one person who loved me enough to tell me the truth. Now when it's your turn to hear some truth, you are going to lie?"

Lena felt tears gather in her eyes. Her heart and stomach writhed in shame and fear. "Sadie," she whispered. "I'm sorry. You're right. I'm being a spoiled brat. That's part of my problem. Don't leave. Please."

Sadie dropped the purse and Lena let out a sigh of relief. "Yes, you are a brat. High maintenance and oversensitive too."

She opened her mouth to protest but snapped it shut.

"Yeah," Sadie said. "Keep it shut." She crossed to the table and poured two more shots. "No more lies."

Lena took the shot and raised it. "No more lies."

Sadie curled up in the corner of the couch. "Question—do you love him?"

Lena sat facing Sadie. Sass hopped up between them. "Yes," she said, holding her hand out to Sass. Who sniffed it and went to sit on Sadie's lap. *Traitor.*

"Then talk to him. It sounds like his mother's problem is really with him and she just used you to hurt him."

"That's part of the problem. You know what family means to me. I know my family fights a lot, but we love each other. How can I get serious about a guy who doesn't have that love for family?"

"Doesn't he?"

"What do you mean?"

"Didn't you say he was trying to make amends with his family? That's why you went with him over your misgivings?"

"Yes."

Sadie shrugged and spread her hands. "Talk to Matt. Give him a chance."

"I don't know if I can. That was…pretty awful. What she did."

"Matt isn't like his mother."

"But she's his *mother*. She'll be part of his life."

"Where does Matt fall in the category of people you can be one hundred percent yourself with? And we're still under sister-truth rules."

Leaning over, Lena snagged the brandy snifter full of wine. Where indeed did he fall? She knew the answer. She took a sip to hide her trembling lips but the tears splashed down her cheeks. "On your side," she whispered.

"Then talk to him. If you have so few people who love you one hundred percent for being exactly who you are, then you can't afford to be throwing them aside because other people are idiots."

"I don't like you very much right now."

"Fine. Now we're equal. I didn't like you very much when you told me I had to face my mother after she abandoned me to foster care and left me twisting in the wind. But it set me free. Let me love Wyatt. So there."

CHAPTER TWENTY-SIX

HE STARED AT the expanse of white as his fury rose. *How could she?* The same question had been circling his brain since the disastrous dinner. He wasn't sure what was worse. His fury at his mother or his sense of betrayal. He'd gone to them. Begged their forgiveness. And they'd accepted his apology. Agreed to begin fixing their family. And all the while, she'd been lying. Scheming a way to slide that knife between his ribs. To make him pay—for what? Being embarrassed at her garden-club meetings?

He dropped the brush he held on the table. This wasn't going to happen today. As he reached for the palette to clear it of the paint he'd set out, his gaze fell on the dab of ocher-red paint. He scooped up the paint with a one-inch brush and made a broad, thick swipe against the white canvas. Staring at the bloody streak stirred something in him. The cyclone of emotions—rage, loss, regret—now came together. He grabbed the tube of ocher and squeezed a large dollop on the palette. His fingers flexed on the brush handle, automatically finding the balance; the very feel of it in his hand centered him. Rage. Another red, twisting streak crossed the canvas. Thick, stark, twisted lines of pure rage.

How dare she?

Lena. Lost to him forever now.

Groping for the paints, he added black and white to the palette. Thick ropy strokes of black crossed and mingled with the red in an opposing arc. He poured his feelings into the act of creation. The lines of the art were as twisted and intermingled as his tangle of emotions. Mixing the black and white to a slate gray, he filled in the holes between his anger and pain with the bleakness of loss.

A tentative knock on the door drew him out of the painting. He glanced at the clock. It'd been an hour. He put the palette and brush down, rubbing at the cramping in the arch between thumb and index fingers. He grabbed a rag and wiped his hands as he crossed to open the door.

The fury returned and his eyes narrowed. "What do you want?"

"To apologize," his father said.

Matt stood with one hand on the door, the other on the wall. *Slam it. Just slam it in his face.*

"I would deserve that," his father said as if he could read his thoughts. Maybe he could see them on his face. "If you shut that door and never spoke to us again. We'd deserve that."

"I'm not the one you should be apologizing to.

In fact, you don't need to apologize at all. Get your wife to apologize. To Lena. That was the most despicable thing she's ever done, and you and I both know she can be vindictive. But to take it out on Lena? To use her as a weapon against me? No. I'm done."

Even with his fury pounding through him, Matt recognized the truth in his words. He'd never have a place in his family again. He'd be expected to show up for important events to keep up appearances, and right now, he wasn't even sure if he'd do that. The small twinge of pain was swept away by weariness. *So tired of dealing with this crap.*

"May I come in?"

His father's voice was soft and respectful, a tone he'd not heard ever in his entire life from the man.

"Son?"

Matt turned away with a heavy huff and retreated to his painting. "Say what you have to say and get out."

He kept his back to his father as he concentrated on cleaning the brushes he'd used. *Deep breaths. Let him have his say and move on.*

"I came to apologize to you, Charles. I should have realized how angry your mother was. When you were up for your grandfather's party and we talked, I thought we had all agreed to start with a clean slate."

"Yeah, well, so did I."

His father moved to look at the painting. "This is…powerful. You always were talented, Charles."

In spite of his anger, the words stirred something in him. He set a brush down carefully and looked at his father. "You've never told me that before."

Glancing around the small room, his father motioned at the two armchairs off to the side that served as his living room. "Can we sit down?"

"Sure. I'll have the maid bring us lunch."

Settling into the better-looking of the two chairs, his father shot him a look. "Don't ruin it. I have something I want to say."

"Fine," Matt said, throwing himself into the other chair. "Say it."

"I was wrong. I see that now. When you were having your difficulties, I was feeling much the way you were then. I'd just taken over the firm. I had two generations of expectations weighing down on me. I wanted to make the company my own."

"And you did."

"Yes, but now I see that you, with your art, were only trying to do the same thing. Leave your mark in this world. It was never going to be the firm. And that angered me back then. Because I'd dutifully just followed along with what was expected of me. I'd never considered the fact that

I could have chosen to do something else. If I'd only had the courage to rebel like you did."

Sitting straighter, Matt turned to face the man. "In all fairness, back then, I didn't have a clue what I was rebelling against. I just knew I didn't want to be a lawyer. Live the life I watched you living."

"I see that now. I only wish I'd seen it sooner. We might not have lost all those years."

Matt nodded and swallowed down a lump in his throat. "Thank you for saying that."

"Now, about your mother."

Emphatically shaking his head, Matt raised a hand. "No. I'm not even going to discuss it. Thank you for accepting my life choice and respecting it, but I am in no way about to forgive her for what she did."

"I'm not going to ask you to. After you two left, I asked her what was wrong with her. The thing is that I never realized how much of an impact it had on her when you acted out in high school and then left. I had the firm. I was respected for that. All she has is her society friends. And apparently, they were very unkind to her about this. She felt a laughingstock."

"No. She's my mother. She should have told them to shut the hell up. It shouldn't have mattered if a few rich old biddies gossiped about me. It's not like I killed anyone drunk driving like what's-her-name's kid that got off scot-free due to his father's deep pockets and team of lawyers."

Leaning forward, clasping his hands and staring down at the floor, his father nodded. "You're right." He sounded so very tired. He looked up. "I'm very proud of you. You've built a good life that's of service to others. I understand if you don't want to be involved with the family. But I'll also be sorry."

Matt rubbed his face and leaned back in the chair. *Shit. What he'd always wanted. His father's acceptance. And it had cost him Lena.*

"I love her, Dad."

"How can I help make this right, then?"

Shrugging, Matt lifted his hands palms up. "There's no making it right. If you were Lena, would you ever want anything to do with us? Our family? She thinks we're a bunch of racists."

"Can't say I blame her after that. But you know—right? That isn't true. Your mother just grabbed the lowest hanging fruit to attack you with."

"That doesn't even matter. Doesn't matter why she did it. She did it. There isn't any taking the words back. The damage is done."

"I am sorry. I like her. She's very smart and must be very good at what she does to be so well respected."

"You checked her out?" He shouldn't have been surprised, but still it angered him.

His father raised a hand and smiled. "Just looked at her firm's website. I was curious. You'd never brought a woman for us to meet before."

The anger faded under the weight of sorrow. *Fat lot of good it did.* "That's a mistake I'll never make again."

"I am sorry," his father said as he rose to his feet. "If I can do anything to try to fix this, tell me, Matt. I will."

Shaking his head, Matt stood. "I don't think there is. No taking it back now."

"I'm guessing you won't be coming up for Thanksgiving or Christmas?"

"I can't, Dad. I can't even think about looking at her right now. I'd say things and, once again, ruin everything for everyone."

His father's hand squeezed his shoulder. "I understand. But you and me? We're good?"

Were they? Matt nodded and realized he was glad his father had come. They still had a way to go, but they'd each grown up a bit. "Yeah, we're good."

"Thank you," his father said before pulling Matt into an embrace. As he hooked his arms around his father, Matt tried to remember the last time he'd hugged the man. *Twenty years? Twenty-five?* He stepped back with a lump in his throat. *Never too old for your father's approval to mean something to you.*

After his father left, he returned to the painting. The pain felt manageable now that he'd poured most of it onto the canvas. He pulled another tube of paint from the box and added it to the palette. Twirling a brush between his fingers, he thought about the portrait he'd painted of Lena after the first night they'd been together. How he'd struggled to capture the expression in her eyes. His fingers stilled on the brush and he dipped it lightly into the yellow paint. Began adding small patches of yellow to the angry reds and despairing blacks, brightening the edges of gray.

CHAPTER TWENTY-SEVEN

THE GATHERING THIS Sunday was small and Lena was grateful for that. Her head still hadn't forgiven her for the shots. She'd poured the rest of the bottle down the kitchen sink while Sadie laughed. Hangover and heartbreak notwithstanding, she'd made it out to Edisto early enough to attend the 10:00 a.m. mass with her parents.

Father Greg was talking about forgiveness. Almost made her believe it wasn't a coincidence.

After church, she sat on a stool at the large granite-topped island in the kitchen, chopping whatever vegetable her mother put in front of her. Her father sat across from her, slicing fruit for sangria. Lena watched as her parents teased and talked while they prepared the meal. Her mother had her lighter skin and straight black hair. Her father was darker, mostly from a lifetime spent as a roofer, and his black hair, now shot through with gray, was curly when he let it get a little long. A wistful longing flooded her heart.

This is what she wanted. A home that, regardless of how much money there was, was always full of love, laughter and family. She wanted to have kids. Lots of them. Four. Maybe five. She wanted to have her cousins come over and to sit on the porch sipping sangria while the kids all played together, growing up as close as brothers and sisters, just as their parents had done.

Her mother's arm slipped lightly across her shoulders. "What's wrong, Lena?" she asked.

Turning into the warmth of her mother's touch, Lena let the tears loose, half-horrified of her loss of control, half-relieved to finally let the pain out. The last time she'd cried in her mother's arms like this, it had been about her boyfriend slapping her. And now, a dozen years later, she was crying over the emotional slap she'd endured from Matt's mother.

When the tears began to taper, her mother asked again what was wrong. Lena shook her head, unable to look into her mother's eyes. "I'm in love. I was in love. Everything is wrong," she whispered in Spanish. This wasn't a conversation for English.

Ana left her side and moved to the stove. She began shutting off burners and turned to her husband. "Go watch television. Lena and I are going to talk."

"It's okay, Mamacita. I'm fine. I'm sorry."

"You aren't fine. Come with me now."

Sliding off the stool, Lena followed her mother upstairs. They went to the room Ana had turned into her own sanctuary. Bookshelves lined the walls and photographs of family and landscapes hung on every inch of available wall space. There was a rocking chair with her knitting basket beside it and a double-wide lounge chair for reading.

The two women curled up on the lounge chair. "Tell me what's going on. Is this about Matt?"

Lena rested her cheek against her mother's shoulder, feeling six years old again. It was nice. To let go of the weight of responsibility. Being a grown-up wasn't nearly as great as kids thought it was. "It's over."

"Did you want it to be over?"

Not trusting her voice, Lena shook her head.

"I'm sorry."

"No," Lena said. "You were right."

Ana leaned back a little and Lena felt her stare. She peeked up. Her mother looked puzzled. "About what?"

"You and Papa want me to marry a Hispanic man."

Ana sighed. "Lena. We want you to be with someone who loves you. Who you love. Yes, we think that being with someone who shares a culture with you might make things easier. Marriage is the hardest work you'll ever do. But the most important thing is to be with someone who accepts you for you. One hundred percent."

"Then what was with all that Hispanic Bachelor fixing up y'all were pushing on me?"

"We were just trying to give you choices."

Choices. "I have a choice to make now, Momma. An important one. And I don't know what's right."

"Dígame."

Lena told her. Told her everything. Toward the end, she got up to pace while the angry words flowed out of her. "So this is where I am," she finished, sitting on the edge of the lounge chair. "I love him. He's amazing and talented and kind and smart and everything I'd ever looked for in a man. But…"

Ana sat forward and took her hand. "But his family isn't."

Lena shrugged. "I don't know. I liked his father. He seemed like a nice guy. It was his mother, pulling that vileness out of nowhere. I love Matt, but I want kids and the thought of my children's grandmother…" She rubbed the backs of her arms.

"Tell me what you're thinking right now."

"That part of me wants to say it doesn't matter. I love him so much that I want to pretend that his family stuff will work out. But I know it's going to always be there. His mother planted a poisonous seed in our relationship that will grow and strangle out any love we have." Ana stood and took both Lena's hands in hers. Lena looked bleakly into her mother's eyes. "There is no way to go on from here," she whispered.

"There's always a way," Ana said. "Sometimes it's a very difficult way, but there is always a way."

"How, Momma?" Lena's voice broke on the words. "How?"

"Talk to him. Be honest. Brutally honest. Tell him exactly what you just told me. That poisonous seed metaphor is perfect. Use that."

Dropping her mother's hands, Lena turned away. "Have you been talking to Sadie? That's all she says. *Talk to him.*"

"It's good advice."

Lena turned back, surprised by the anger in her voice. "I don't want to talk to him," she said.

Ana pointed a finger at her. "Don't let your pride keep you from love, Magdalena."

"What is love if I don't have my pride?"

"Pride isn't the same thing as dignity. It's your choice now, Lena. You can keep watering that seed she planted and let it grow. Or you and Matt can work together and make it wither and die.

"But for now, come back to the kitchen. We've got about a thousand tamales to roll. Hannah is picking up Jules and bringing her and the kids for dinner. Lucia is bringing her kids too."

"I'll be down in a minute," Lena said, throwing herself down in the rocking chair. She needed a minute. Her mother's words stung. *Like this was her fault. This wasn't her mess to clean up. That was on Matt and his starchy mother. And he had wanted her to stay there after she'd been disre-*

spected! He hadn't even *called* her. Hadn't tried to talk to her. Nothing. *It's only been a day.* Standing, she scowled at her own thought. *Shut up. It's done. Over. You've walked away from men for the stupidest of reasons. This is an actual, real reason to walk away.*

She crossed the hall to the bathroom and splashed cold water on her face. Trying to hide the evidence of her tears. Drying her face, she met her own eyes in the mirror. Lifted her chin. *You are Lena Reyes. You are the most sought-after financial guru in this town. You bow to no one. You certainly won't bow to that stuck-up, evil, mean bitch. Mrs. Charles Beaumont Matthews the Fourth. Who is she to judge you?*

Squeezing her hands into tight fists and shaking them loose, she took another deep breath. Matt's mother wasn't even worth the energy of her anger.

A loud ruckus arose from downstairs. Hannah and Lucia had arrived. With at least eight kids in tow by the sound. Lena let it wash over her. The happy, loving noise. A single voice rose above the others. Jules.

"Is Auntie Lena here?"

She took the joy in that sweet little voice and rubbed it like a balm over her bruised heart. If all she was ever going to be was an auntie, then she was going to be the best damned aunt on the planet. Let Mrs. Stick-Up-Her-Butt Matthews go back to her cold, silent mansion. Lena would stay right here with her messy, loud, loving family.

MONDAY MORNING, LENA was deep into her office routine. She kicked her shoes off under the desk and powered up her computer. Mose's report of the weekend activities in the worldwide market was on her desk. She thumbed through it, making notes between sips of coffee. It looked to have been a relatively uneventful weekend so no major reevaluation of assets needed to be attended to immediately.

She set the report aside and focused on her daily schedule. She loved this. The game of numbers. Move this here, sell that there. Watching her clients meet their financial goals. It filled her with pride. Making rich people richer was only the means to the end. Because of them, she could take someone like Josh Sanders, Sadie's first hire from paycheck-to-paycheck poverty to having financial security. That's where her real love of the game came was. Helping others.

Speaking of which. She switched from her work calendar to her personal one. She had a lunch date with several women key in her outreach project for the teens at St. Toribio's. She had a team. The series of talks was starting to come together. The phone on her desk buzzed.

"Yes?" she asked Chloe as she picked up.

"Mr. Matthews is here."

She froze. Matt. She was aware of the time stretching out, of Chloe patiently waiting for a response but she had nothing. Thoughts tried to form but scattered before she could grab one. Her fingers clenched around the receiver. When she found her voice, the words fell out in a stuttering staccato. "No. Meeting. Busy. Make up something. Anything."

She couldn't do this. Not here. Not now. No. If they were going to talk about this, it was going to be on her terms. He didn't get to just show up here out of the blue and...

"Lena."

She looked up and blinked. He stood in the doorway of her office holding a package. Chloe peeked over his shoulder. "He walked past me, Lena. I'm sorry."

"It's okay, Chloe," she said through numb lips. Sliding her hands off the desk to hide their trembling in her lap, she forced herself to look into Matt's eyes. He looked terrible, and that both pleased her and made her heart ache. She looked back at Chloe. "Go on—it's okay."

Matt stepped through the door and Chloe lifted her hands in apology. Lena gave her a slight shrug.

"Close the door," she said. Her voice surprised her. Calm. Her heart was about to beat out of her chest. Matt reached out and gently closed the door.

"I have something for you," he said quietly.

"I was going to give it to you last night, but you weren't home."

Lena looked at the brown-paper-wrapped package in his hands. A painting, maybe. "Matt, what are you doing?"

"I made this for you. I just didn't have time to give it to you before."

"I don't want it."

He smiled that bad boy smile. Yeah, she was going to miss that. Her chest filled with pain. "Too bad," he said. "Because it's yours now." He set it down, leaning it against the wall just inside the office door and turned back to her. "I want to tell you something."

No. That she couldn't do. Her heart hurt too badly. It wanted him too badly. She couldn't listen to him. She'd make stupid decisions. "No," she said, shaking her head. "Just go, Matt. There's nothing left to be said."

The look on his face surprised her. His eyes narrowed and he took the few steps to stand in front of her desk. Looking up at him, she realized he was angry. That stoked her own anger. He had no right to be angry with her.

"I listened to you, Lena." His voice calm but the words wrapped in steely determination. "Give me the same respect."

She leaned back in her chair, pressing her lips together against the angry words that wanted to fly out. Words she wanted to hurt him with. She lifted a hand. *Well?*

He sank down in the chair across from her. "I'm sorry about what happened. I'm sorry my mother used you to hurt me. I'm sorry I didn't realize how hurtful it was to you when I tried to make you stay. If I'd had any idea that she hadn't accepted my apology, if I hadn't believed that she was sincere when she said we would try to become a family again, I would have never put you in that position. I love you, Lena. I love *you.* I can't take back what my mother did or explain it away or do anything about it. But that kind of behavior is the reason I left home when I was eighteen. That whole world they live in, of living for other people's expectations of you rather than living a life you love? I couldn't do that."

Lena crossed her arms against her chest. *White boy whining. This was rich.*

Matt stood and paced around the small office. "I envy you, Lena. You had what I wanted."

"You wanted to grow up in a trailer park? You wanted to shop at the Goodwill for your clothes? Buy used shoes? Attend schools that were falling down around your ears? You wanted to be called names because of your skin color?"

Damn it. She hadn't meant to say anything. She was going to sit here, pretend to listen to whatever excuses he had to make and send him on his way.

He stopped pacing and turned back to her with a frown. "I'm sorry, Lena. No one should have to go through those things. Your family loved you. That's what I'm fumbling around trying to say. You felt loved because you were loved. When I was twelve, I won an award for a painting I did. My father told me art was for, quote, pansies, end quote, and I needed to concentrate on getting better grades so I could get into Harvard or Yale."

He lifted his hands, palms up. "Did you win an award in school, Lena? Bet you did. Bet you had at least a dozen family members there, cheering and embarrassing you. That's what I envy. That's part of why I love you. You did this." He made a sweeping gesture, encompassing her office. "You did all of this for your family. They were with you for every step. They never once told you your dreams weren't worthy."

Lena resisted a smile. At least a dozen. More like a couple of dozen. Yeah, they'd embarrassed her more than once with their support.

"You were right. My parents? My mother? They've done nothing. My father was handed the keys to the law firm. But, you. You, Magdalena Reyes. Wow. You fought your way to the top with your family cheering you on the entire way. You like to tease me about being a rich trust-fund kid, but let me tell you something, all that money means nothing. Nothing without the love of family."

Matt came back and sat down, pulling the chair closer so he was leaning over the desk, his eyes intent on her. "I love you. I want to be part of your life. The woman I see in front of me now. That amazing, strong, passionate woman. I've never known anyone like you. I want to paint you for the rest of my life, and even then, I don't think I could capture all the emotion I see in your eyes."

Lena swallowed down the lump in her throat. *Don't get sucked into this. It's not going to be this easy.* "Matt," she said, her voice cracking. She cleared her throat. "You can't fix this."

"You're right," he said. "I can't. But can *we*?"

Her mother's words echoed in her mind. She shook her head. Confused. She didn't know what to do. What to say. Matt slowly stood.

"Think about it, Lena. You love me. I know you do. I felt it." He motioned at the package. "That's for you. I hope you like it. I hope I hear from you soon."

She nodded, indicating that she'd heard his words. A bone-deep sense of loss filled her, making her limbs feel heavy as she watched him move to the door. He paused and held eye contact for a long beat. Then he was gone. She crossed her arms on the desk and lowered her head.

"Lena? Are you okay?" Chloe asked tentatively.

She rocked her head on her arms. "Sure," she said, her words muffled. "Fine."

"What's going on?" Mose asked from the doorway.

"Matt was here," Chloe said.

"And?"

"I think he just broke Lena's heart."

"Should I go find him? Beat him up or something?"

Lena lifted her head to find them both standing in the doorway, staring at her as if they weren't quite sure what to do or expect. "Don't you two have jobs to do?"

Chloe crossed to the desk. "Taking care of you is part of my job. Are you okay?"

"No, not really. But I will be."

"Do you want me to reschedule your meetings this afternoon?"

"No. Why would you do that?"

Mose perched on the edge of the desk. "So you can go home, eat ice cream straight from the carton, watch chick flicks and cry like a normal person after a breakup?"

Lena scowled at them. "And at what point in our acquaintance have you ever found me to be this mythical normal person? Mose, when you and Anna Marie broke up, you went to the gym and beat up a body bag until your knuckles were so swollen you had to go to the doctor. And

Chloe, I'm pretty sure the last guy who dumped you had four flat tires the next morning."

Chloe raised her hands in the air. "That was not me! That was an impossibly incriminating coincidence."

Lena rolled her eyes. The teasing eased the mind-numbing pain. "In other words, the perfect crime. Both of y'all get back to work. I'm fine. Work is what I need right now."

Shooing them out, she woke up her sleeping computer. She hadn't lied. Work had always been a place to hide. She'd hidden in it all her life. Teasing at school? Hide in a book. Culture shock of college? Hide in the library with a stack of books. Being the best. Being the fastest. Being the first. Doing anything and everything she had to do to outrun all her doubts, outrun her past. That was her comfort. Her safe place. As long as she was working, she was going to be okay. Nothing else mattered.

Except now. Matt mattered. More than she thought. As if she hadn't realized how much she loved him until the moment she'd lost him.

But you didn't lose him. You walked away from him.

She shook her head firmly from side to side. "For a very good reason. Let it go now," she said out loud.

CHAPTER TWENTY-EIGHT

SHE ALMOST LEFT the package there, leaning against her office wall. Some vague idea about texting Chloe and telling her to get rid of it in the morning before she went in to work drifted around her mind. But in the end, she brought it home with her.

It currently was serving as Sass's throne. Probably not the best treatment of a Matt Matthews original painting, considering the current market value of his work, but right now she didn't care. She'd set it down on the coffee table and left it there. After washing her face and changing into yoga pants and her College of Charleston sweatshirt, she glanced at it as she went to the kitchen.

"Get off there, Sass," she said.

Sass ignored her.

Dropping the tamales her mother had sent home with her onto a baking sheet, she slid them into the oven to warm. She opened a can of cat food. That got Sass off the package. "What do you say, Sass? Get it over with?"

Sass didn't care. She had her two-dollar can of rabbit-flavored cat food. Pouring a glass of wine,

Lena realized her hand was trembling. She set the bottle down slowly, deliberately and took stock of herself. Shaky hands. Fluttery stomach. Heart galloping away in her chest. She was scared. Nervous. Shaking her head, she scooped up the wineglass and took a sip. Walked to the living room and looked down at the carefully wrapped package.

He'd painted something for her. She couldn't ignore her curiosity. He knew she preferred his landscapes over the abstract art that was selling like crazy right now. Was it one of those? She sat at the edge of the couch and reached out to touch the brown paper. She imagined him picking one out for her. There had been one he had been working on the night she'd gone to him. That first night. Her body flushed with heat as she remembered. Oh, she remembered every second of that. But what had been in the painting? Was it a marsh scene? Waterfront Park?

The delicious scent of warmed tamales made her stomach growl. She hadn't had much at lunch. It had taken too much energy to be "on" for the women she was meeting with. Her heartbreak could wait. The kids at St. Toribio's could not. She had smiled and talked, been upbeat and used every last damned leadership skill she could remember. What she had not done was eat more than a bite or two of her meal. But she'd sealed the deal. Two more enthusiastic speakers lined up.

"After dinner," she said out loud as she reached down to tap the package.

She forced herself to sit at the dining room table. To eat her dinner from a real plate using real silverware. Sass sat on the chair at the opposite end to keep her company. "What do you think about all this, Sass?"

An ear twitch.

"Yeah, I know. He's awesome. But I feel like he's ready to give up on his family. When just a few weeks ago, reconciling with them was the most important thing in his life."

She stopped and took a sip of wine. That was the core of it right there. She didn't want to be the reason he walked away from his family. The very thought of it made her feel sick. Sass put her front paws on the tabletop. Lena pointed at her.

"Don't even think about it." She stood and picked up her plate. "Come on, Sassafras. Let's do this."

She cleaned up the kitchen, refilled her wineglass and sat down on the couch. Sass jumped up beside her and sat down, her warm purring body pressed against Lena's thigh. Lena reached over to scratch at an ear. "I'm pretty sure it's a marsh scene." Lifting the end of the package to her knees, she began to work at the tape on the bottom and back. "I can't keep this, of course. If Matt won't take it back, I'll sell it and donate the money to St. Toribio's or somewhere."

She pulled the paper away and tossed it over the back of the couch. Sass followed it but the sounds of cat claws murdering innocent paper never reached Lena's ears. She sat, paralyzed, at the edge of the couch. Mouth falling open, she hitched in a quick, shocked breath. *Dear God.* It was her. A portrait of her. That night. That night she'd gone to him, seduced him. He'd painted her. The streaks of paint across her cheeks, the stripe down her forehead to her heart. Was that how she'd looked? The eyes of the woman in the painting glowed with a fierce heat.

She set it down quickly, as if it were hot. Her heart was pounding. Her thoughts skittered through her mind. Bringing her hands to her mouth, she continued to stare. Her eyes fell on a single word written on the left bottom corner. *Fighter.* That's what he'd said that night. She was a fighter. Strong. Loyal. Compassionate. A blink sent tears streaming down her cheeks. God help her, she loved him. Loved that man who looked at her and saw this. Saw nothing but her soul. She shifted her gaze to the bottom right. *Matt5.* His signature mark. Wiping the tears from her face, she stood.

"I have to go, Sass. I'll be back."

She grabbed up her purse and slipped into her running shoes before she could think about what she was doing. Ran to the parking garage. Kept the image of the painting fresh in her mind's eye as she navigated the narrow, tangled mess of one-way streets that made up downtown Charleston.

"I LOVE YOU," she said when he opened the door.

And burst into tears.

Then his arms were around her, pulling her close, pulling her inside, shutting the door against the cold October night. Rocking her. "Shh, shh," he murmured. "Don't cry, Lena."

She pushed back and wiped angrily at her face. "I don't want to cry. I don't know what to do, Matt."

She looked up into his eyes. Those blue eyes. Reaching up, she pushed her fingers through his hair. Her heart hurt so badly, surely it couldn't take anymore. "I love you," she said again. "But we need to figure all this out."

He cupped her face and kissed her gently on the lips. "We will. We'll figure it out." Taking her hand, he led her to the armchair in the living room area. She sat down, clenching her arms tight around herself, trying to hold herself together. Matt pulled the other chair around so he was facing her. Knee to knee. "Talk to me."

"I... It's all jumbled. I said something to my mother. About what your mother did. I told her it was like a poisonous seed she'd planted in our relationship."

Matt put his hands on her knees and nodded. "What did your mother say?"

"That I could keep watering it and let it grow or the two of us could work together to make it wither and die."

"I don't know about you, but I'm going to go with the 'make it wither and die' option."

She let go of herself and put her hands on his. "Matt. What your mother did, that's easy for us to unite against. I see that now. But before this happened, you were reaching out to your family. You wanted to mend fences. You wanted to be a part of their lives again. You wanted me to be a part of not only your life, but your family's life. How is that going to work now?"

He was shaking his head. "No. That ended it for me. That showed me that what I hoped for in a family would never happen."

"But it can't be like that," she pleaded. "If you quit on your family to be with me, that's going to be something more poisonous than what your mother did. Because we can't unite against that, Matt. If any tiny part of you still wants to make amends, then you will end up resenting me. You'll end up blaming me."

"But I won't."

"How do you know?"

He turned his hands up so he was holding hers. "There was this guy I knew. Nice guy. He and I were roommates when I first left home. I was eighteen. Got my first job scrubbing dishes in a restaurant. Was trying to save up money to go to college. But he was a party guy. Wanted to hang out, get drunk, chase women."

"What does this have to do with us?" Lena asked.

"I'm getting to that. Like I said, he was a nice guy. I considered him a friend. But I had to walk away from him. He was a toxic person. I think you understand this, Lena. If you have a goal, a plan for your life, you know you have to move away from toxic people."

"Yes. But this is your family, Matt."

"And my father and I have made our peace. My grandfather? We're good. My older sister and I are good. We've always been best friends. I have the family I need. I wish my mother and my other sister could be a part of my…our life, but until they stop being toxic, they won't. My decision has nothing to do with you, Lena. I'm doing it for me. For my peace of mind."

Lena stared at him. She did understand that. She'd left behind so many people. So many friends who'd given up. Joined gangs. Used drugs. She'd given up the sorority that she'd joined after the first four months because it was a toxic mean-girl environment.

"Okay," she whispered. "We can work with this."

He tugged on her hands and pulled her onto his lap. She looped her arms around his shoulders and smiled up at him. "We can definitely work with this. I love you."

She snuggled down into his arms, pressing her cheek against his chest. "We'll test out your Viking warrior skills next weekend when you meet the entire family."

The sound of his laughter rang in her ears and vibrated against her cheek. She felt everything in her relax into the sound of it. Everything was going to be okay.

* * * * *

Be sure to check out the other stories in Janet Lee Nye's
THE CLEANING CREW *miniseries!*

SPYING ON THE BOSS
BOSS ON NOTICE

Both available now from
Harlequin Superromance.

And look for a new Cleaning Crew book from Janet Lee Nye, coming soon!

Get 2 Free Books,
Plus 2 Free Gifts—
just for trying the Reader Service!

Get 2 Free Books,
Plus 2 Free Gifts—
just for trying the Reader Service!

HP17R

Get 2 Free Books,
Plus 2 Free Gifts—
just for trying the Reader Service!

Get 2 Free Books,
Plus <u>2 Free Gifts</u> —
just for trying the Reader Service!